ELIZABETH ELIOT
ALICE

Lady Germaine Elizabeth Olive Eliot was born in London on 13 April 1911, the daughter of Montague Charles Eliot, the 8th Earl of St Germans, and Helen Agnes Post.

She twice married—first to Major Thomas James in 1932, then to Captain Hon. Kenneth George Kinnaird, the 12th Baron Kinnaird, in 1950. Both marriages ended in divorce. She apparently applied for American citizenship in 1971. She published five novels, the first of which, *Alice* (1949), was a Book Society Choice. Her non-fiction *Heiresses and Coronets* (1960, aka *They All Married Well*), about prominent marriages between wealthy Americans and titled Europeans in the late Victorian and Edwardian period, was a success on both sides of the Atlantic.

Elizabeth Eliot died in New York in 1991.

WORKS BY ELIZABETH ELIOT

Fiction

Alice (1949)*
Henry (1950)*
Mrs Martell (1953)*
Starter's Orders (1955)
Cecil (1962)*

Non-fiction

Portrait of a Sport: A History of Steeplechasing (1957)
Heiresses and Coronets (1960, aka *They All Married Well*)

available from Furrowed Middlebrow/Dean Street Press

ELIZABETH ELIOT

ALICE

With an introduction by
Elizabeth Crawford

DEAN STREET PRESS

A Furrowed Middlebrow Book
FM26

Published by Dean Street Press 2019

Copyright © 1949 Elizabeth Eliot

Introduction © 2019 Elizabeth Crawford

All Rights Reserved

Published by licence, issued under the UK Orphan Works
Licensing Scheme.

First published in 1949 by Cassell & Co.

Cover by DSP
Cover illustration shows detail from *A Girl in a Yellow Dress on a Sofa
with a Dog (unfinished)* (c.1937-1940) by Rex Whistler

ISBN 978 1 912574 59 9

www.deanstreetpress.co.uk

To

FAITH COMPTON MACKENZIE

with gratitude

INTRODUCTION

REVIEWING Elizabeth Eliot's debut novel, *Alice*, for the *Sunday Times*, C.P. Snow noted in the author 'an astringent sympathy, a knowledge from bitter experience that life is not easy' while the *Times Literary Supplement* review of her second novel, *Henry*, mentioned her 'light-heartedness, delicious wit and humanity lurking beneath the surface'. Comparisons were drawn with the work of Nancy Mitford and Elizabeth von Arnim, although Snow observed that 'Alice was set in the world of the high aristocracy, loftier, though less smart, than the world of Miss Mitford's "Hons"'. This 'high aristocracy' was, indeed, the world into which, on 13 April 1911, Germaine Elizabeth Olive Eliot was born, her birth registered only as 'Female Eliot'. Time was obviously required to select her full complement of names, but by the time she was christened decisions had been made. 'Germaine' does not appear to have been a family name, although it echoes that of the earldom – St Germans – of which, at that time, her great uncle, Henry Cornwallis Eliot, the 5th earl, was the holder. 'Elizabeth' was the name of her maternal grandmother, Elizabeth Wadsworth, whose grandfather, General James Wadsworth, had been military governor of Washington during the American Civil War. Transatlantic connections were to prove important to this 'Female Eliot'. No hint of an 'Olive' appears in either her paternal or maternal line, so that may have been a mere parental indulgence. Of these three forenames 'Elizabeth' was the one by which the future author was known.

At the time of Elizabeth's birth her parents were living in Marylebone, London, the census, taken just ten days previously, giving us a glimpse into the household. At its head was her 40-year-old father, Montague Charles Eliot, who, with a script replete with flourishes, completed the form, listing also her 26-year-old American mother, Helen Agnes; a butler; a lady's maid; a cook; two housemaids; and a hall boy. Doubtless a few days later a nursemaid would have taken up her position in the nursery. Montague (1870-1960) and Helen (c.1885-1962) had married the previous June. Helen (or 'Nellie' as she was known), although American-born and of American parentage, had, in fact, spent most of her life in the United Kingdom. Her father had died when she was four-years-old and her mother had then married Arthur Smith-Barry, later Baron Barrymore of Fota House, near Cork, Ireland. As Elizabeth Eliot's novels reveal a knowledge of Irish estates and relations, she probably had on occasion visited Fota.

In the newspaper reports of his marriage no mention was made of Montague Eliot's connection to the St Germans earldom, so far was he at that time from inheriting. However, tragedy has long hovered around the St Germans family and in 1922 the death in a riding accident of the 6th Earl meant the title and estate passed to Montague Eliot's elder, unmarried and childless brother. On his death in 1942 Montague Eliot became the 8th Earl of St Germans and his daughter Elizabeth acquired the title of 'Lady'. Montague Eliot had joined King Edward VII's household in 1901 and at the time of Elizabeth's birth was Gentleman Usher to George V, later becoming Groom of the Robes. He held the latter unpaid position until 1936 and from 1952 until his death was Extra Groom-in-Waiting to Elizabeth II.

The 8th Earl's heir was Elizabeth's brother, Nicholas (1914-88) and the family was completed after a long interval with the birth of another son, Montague Robert Vere Eliot (1923-94). Around this time Elizabeth and her family moved to 111 Gloucester Place, a tall house, one of a long terrace on a canyon of a road that runs north-south through Marylebone.

While it is on record that her brothers were sent to Eton, we know nothing of Elizabeth's education. Was she taught at home by a governess; or did she attend a London day school, or an establishment such as 'Groom Place', where we first meet the two young women in *Alice*, or 'Mrs Martell's 'inexpensive but good school on the south coast of England'? Elizabeth's mother, certainly, had had a governess, 70-year-old Miss Dinah Thoreau, who took rat poison in December 1934 and killed herself in her room in Paddington. Lack of money was not a problem for the Eliots, unlike the Pallisers, whose daughter, Anne, narrator of *Henry*, remarks that her family had been 'too poor for my sister or me to be properly educated (although Henry, of course, had been sent to Harrow)'. Naturally boys had to go to school in order 'to have a good answer when people asked where they had been at school. That was why Henry had been sent to Harrow.' The fact that the young women in her novels invariably received an education inferior to their brothers may indicate that Elizabeth did indeed feel that she had not been 'properly educated'. Whatever the reality, a review of the US edition of *Alice* revealed that Elizabeth 'Like many authors, has been writing since she was 10'.

Nor do we know anything of Elizabeth's relationship with her parents. What is one to make of the fact she dedicated *Cecil*, the story of a loathsome, manipulative mother, to her own mother? What is one to make of the tantalising information contained in the publisher's blurb for *Cecil* that the book is 'based on fact'? Which strand of *Cecil*'s plot might have been developed from a factual base? For the novel, quite apart from placing a 'veritable ogress' of a mother centre stage, also deals with drug-taking, murder, and impotency. *Cecil* was published in November 1962, a couple of months after Nellie Eliot, Dowager Countess of St Germans, committed suicide in a hotel room in Gibraltar, having arrived the day before from Tangier where she had been visiting her son Vere. Whatever their real-life relationship it is fair to say that in Elizabeth Eliot's novels mothers tend to be seen in a somewhat negative light, while fathers are noticeable by their absence.

In 1922 the elevation to the earldom of St Germans of her unmarried uncle brought significant changes to Elizabeth Eliot and her family, with visits to Port Eliot becoming more frequent. In 1926 Elizabeth had the honour of opening the St Germans parish fête, held in the grounds of Port Eliot, and made, according to the *Western Morning News*, 'an effective and amusing speech'. Port Eliot, an ancient house, shaped and reshaped over the centuries, is so extensive that, its guidebook confesses, not once in living memory has the roof been completely watertight. If not so ancient, similarly large houses, often in the west-country and sometimes decaying, certainly play their part in Elizabeth Eliot's novels. When Margaret, the narrator of *Alice*, visits 'Platon', Alice's Devonshire family home, she sat in 'one of the drawing rooms. There was no fire, it was bitterly cold, and everything in the room, including the chairs and sofa on which we sat, was covered with dust sheets.' 'Trelynt', the west-country home of Anne Palliser is, post-Second World War, similarly large, damp, and servantless.

Naturally Elizabeth Eliot's position in society meant that in due course she 'did the Season' as a debutante, her presence recorded at hunt and charity balls and even in a photograph on the front of *Tatler*. In *Alice*, Margaret admits that 'The basic idea was rational enough. When a girl reached marriageable age, she was introduced by her parents into adult society, where it was hoped she would meet her future husband. There are many examples of such practices in *The Golden Bough*. Only somehow by the nineteen-thirties it had all got rather silly.' Margaret is presented at court, her Uncle Henry, like Montague Eliot, being a member of the royal household, and observes that this connection 'meant that we had seats in the Throne Room, which was fun, as there was always the chance that someone would fall down. Not that one would wish it for them, but should it happen, it would be nice to see it.'

Elizabeth's 'Season' produced the desired result and in January 1932 her engagement to Thomas James (1906-76) was announced in the press on both sides of the Atlantic. The wedding took place barely two months later in St George's Hanover Square. Thomas James' father, a former MP for Bromley, was dead and his mother too ill to attend. The bishop of Norwich gave a particularly didactic address, much reproduced in press reports, stressing the seriousness of marriage. Were the words of the cleric tailored specifically for this flighty young couple?

After a honeymoon in Rio and Madeira in early 1933, delayed perhaps until after the death of Thomas James' mother, the young couple settled down to married life. Tended by five servants, they occupied the whole of 4 Montague Square, a five-storey house, five minutes' walk from the Eliot family home. In the years after the Second World War Thomas James was employed by BP, but it is not clear what his occupation was during the years he was married to Elizabeth. On the ship's manifest for their 1933 trip he is described as a 'Representative'. Was fiction imitating life when, in *Alice*, Alice and her new husband Cassius sailed to Rio where he was 'to represent a firm of motor-car engineers'? Despite both Elizabeth and dashing, Eton-educated Thomas James having family money, rumour has it that during their marriage they ran up considerable gambling debts, a contributory factor to their divorce in 1940.

On the outbreak of war in 1939 Lady Elizabeth James, now living alone in a flat in St John's Wood, was registered as an ambulance driver with the London County Council. However, nothing is known of her life during and immediately after the war until the publication of *Alice* in 1949. A few months later, in March 1950, she married the Hon. George Kinnaird at Brighton registry office. When asked by the *Daily Mail* why they had married 'in strict secrecy', Kinnaird replied 'We are both too engrossed in our work'. The *Daily Mail* then explained that 'Lady Elizabeth is authoress of Book Society choice *Alice*. Mr Kinnaird is a literary adviser.' Kinnaird was at this time attached in some capacity to the publishing firm of John Murray. This marriage ended in divorce in 1962.

For some years in the 1950s Elizabeth Eliot lived in Lambourn in Berkshire, a town renowned for its association with horse racing. This was clearly a sport close to her heart for during this period, apart from *Henry* (1950) and *Mrs. Martell* (1953), she produced two books devoted to horse racing, one, *Starter's Orders*, fiction, and the other, *Portrait of a Sport*, non-fiction. In *Henry* the narrator's much-loved but feckless brother, the eponymous Henry, is a haunter of the race track. As he observes, 'I can always reckon to make quite a bit racing, and then there's backgammon. Backgammon can be terribly paying if you go the right way about it.' Of Elizabeth's brother, thrice-married Nicholas, *The Times*'s obituarist wrote, with some circumspection, that he was 'a supporter of the Turf in his day, as owner, trainer and bookmaker'. On inheriting the title and estate on the death of his father in 1960, Nicholas Eliot, 9th Earl of St Germans, made the estate over to his young son and went into tax exile.

After her second divorce Elizabeth seems to have spent a good deal of time in New York, mingling in literary circles, and in June 1971, while living in Greenwich Village, at 290 Sixth Avenue, applied for US citizenship. Thereafter she disappears from sight until *The Times* carried a notice of her death in New York on 3 November 1991. For whatever reason, detailed facts of Elizabeth Eliot's life have become so obfuscated that even members of her own extended family have been unable to supply information. Fortunately for us, her mordant wit and powers of social observation survive, amply revealed in the four novels now reissued by Dean Street Press.

Elizabeth Crawford

ONE

THE TABLE was covered with a green baize cloth, and was littered with discarded candy wrappers. It was Sunday morning and six or seven of us were in the classroom writing the more or less obligatory letters to our parents. They were dull letters, or at least mine were.

Despondently I looked across at Alice. Alice was my best friend; one had to have one, and she was the only person in the school who wasn't horrible. Alice sat writing busily. She wore a black silk dress which was too old for her and which had probably belonged to her sister. As Alice leant over her letter a shaft of sunlight fell on the top of her fair head.

I went back to my letter: 'Darling Mummy, Nothing very much has happened this week, and can I have some more money?' Except to ask for money it was difficult to find anything to say. I used to ask my mother for money every Sunday, and then I discovered that one could get it from the school secretary and have it put down on the bill like the Norwegians. I was all right for money after that. My mother was careless about that sort of thing and she never noticed. 'Please remember me to Miss Partridge and with lots of love from Margaret.' My letters always ended like that, except when I added: 'PS. I'm sorry that there doesn't seem to be any news this week.' The postscript was meant to imply that if only my mother would be a little patient she would soon receive a letter containing the news of a fire, a murder or a robbery. I should have welcomed any of these. They would have been something to put in my letters.

I helped myself to another toffee and wished that I was Alice. It would have been so much less dull than being me. Alice was amusing; she had a brother and sister and in the holidays she hunted. She had even been abroad. Everybody but me had been abroad; even the Norwegians. Though they were being it here in Berkshire, which of course made it less interesting for them.

Alice finished her letter and smiled at me. 'Do you want to read it?' She stretched across the table and gave me an envelope which had not yet been sealed.

I began to read Alice's letter.

DARLING MUMMY,

Nothing very much has happened this week. Except that one of the Norwegians lost her temper on the golf course and threw her clubs about. We have got a new visiting drawing master. As he is a master, Miss Dent has to sit in the room during his lessons.

Isn't it silly when there are always at least eight of us? We are learning book illustration. It is great fun. Perhaps I might do it when I leave school. A sister of one of the girls here is on the stage and they are very nice, you know, not common, and Esther, that's the girl, thinks that her mother used to know you.

And the letter went on for another page and a half.

Alice asked if she might read *my* letter and I gave it to her.

'Who's Miss Partridge?' Alice asked.

'I've told you,' I said. 'She's my mother's companion and she chooses my clothes.'

It was one of the supposed advantages of Groom Place that we did not wear a uniform. Our personalities were thus given full scope to express themselves through the medium of our clothes. At least that was what it said in the prospectus, and more or less what my mother had said when she sent me to the school. But, as far as I was concerned, it didn't work out like that. My clothes expressed nothing but Miss Partridge's distaste for shopping and our mutual antagonism to each other. I longed for the stuffy anonymous blue serge and black stockings of my High School. There, there had been no nonsense about personality. But there was nothing I could do about it except pretend that I *wasn't* wearing an apple-green stockinette dress. I didn't like green and I didn't like stockinette. It was hard to have to endure them both in one garment.

Alice asked if I had learnt the extra verses which Miss Dent was going to 'hear' after church.

I replied that I supposed I had, and hoped that none of the others were listening.

'Extra verses?' Pauline Crane, a fat reliable girl who had been at Cheltenham Ladies' College, looked at me enquiringly.

'They're for Miss Dent,' I said uncomfortably. 'I told her in geography that Panama was in Italy.'

'It isn't.' Pauline was looking at me with evident distaste.

'Isn't it? Well, it used to be when I was at my last school. I told Miss Dent that too.'

'How could it be?' Pauline asked.

'It could be if it was,' I said stiffly, 'and I remember about it particularly because it's where our summer hats used to come from.'

'Miss Dent is a fool.' Marie Carrington's dark eyes glistened. Marie was reputed amongst us to be an adopted child and illegitimate *and* Italian. We were very envious of her. 'I don't know why Madame ever engaged Miss Dent,' Marie said—Madame Dubois was the woman who kept the school.

'I suppose she would be quite *cheap*,' Alice said thoughtfully. 'She hasn't got any degrees or anything, has she?'

'None of them have,' Marie said. 'That's why it's such a rotten school.'

'Margaret, Madame wants to see you at once.'

I looked round resentfully. Beryl Lawes, the head girl, stood in the doorway. She was fat and smug and had her hair done in plaited 'earphones.' All things I disliked.

'At *once*!' Beryl repeated loudly. Like many people who are unsure of themselves, she took refuge in the midst of noise. The gramophone in her room always played at full blast. In the absence of any mechanical aid she shouted.

'What does she want?' I asked, playing for time. 'I haven't exactly finished my letter home yet, and my mother will be most annoyed if I miss it again this week.'

'She didn't tell me what she wanted.' Beryl sounded regretful and censorious. 'But I think she's very annoyed.'

'She's always annoyed,' I agreed.

'Only because you're so tiresome,' Beryl said.

Alice said that she didn't think Monsieur Dubois was very kind to Madame and that was what made her so cross. Marie Carrington started a long story about how she had overheard them quarrelling in their room.

I should have liked to have stayed and listened to it, but Beryl, looking like a stand-in for an avenging angel, waited for me with marked impatience.

'Margaret,' Madame began. I was alone with her in her sitting-room, Miss Wilson, her secretary, having left it ostentatiously—too ostentatiously for my peace of mind—when I came in. The desk occupied by Monsieur, when he was not in the garage, was empty. Monsieur, strangely enough, lived almost entirely in the garage. It was where Madame kept him, as I did my white mice when I was at home; and he even had his meals there. I thought it was rather unkind of his wife, but perhaps he preferred it. He had, however, this desk in Madame's sitting-room, and his own lavatory on the ground floor, and in the evenings he and his dog could be heard coming into the house, and going up to the bedroom which they shared with Madame. Marie collectively flattered us by saying that he couldn't be trusted, and that he had once been caught holding somebody or other's hand; but as the somebody or other—even according to Marie—had left years before, it wasn't possible to check up on the story. Myself I didn't believe it, and besides he was very old.

'Margaret,' Madame was saying, 'I have written to your mother.'

I gave her a smile which was meant to imply, 'How extremely kind, but really you shouldn't have given yourself the trouble.' Madame didn't look at me and went on, 'I have asked her to take you away from here, and given her the addresses of some schools that might be suitable for you.'

I felt my knees go weak and hoped—vainly—that they weren't going to start trembling. At every crisis in my life it has been like that, but at fourteen I still thought that I might grow out of it.

'I'm afraid my mother won't find that very convenient,' I said. 'She doesn't like looking for schools for me, and anyhow she's in the South of France.'

'But you are naughty, naughty all the time,' Madame objected. 'It is not right that you should be here. In another school where there is more discipline you will learn more. Here we trust our girls; *you* it is not possible to trust.'

I asked her what I had done now. The accent was too markedly on the 'now' for politeness. Madame made one of her despairing gestures. She was a frail little woman always looking worried. I think that the school can't have been paying, and we should have felt sorry for her.

'It is everything that you do wrong, always I have complaints of you, and now with Miss Dent . . . before Miss Dent has always been defending you.'

I was ashamed that I needed so much defending, surprised that Miss Dent had been the one to do it, and hoped that her complaint against me was not connected with Panama. I was tired of Panama.

'In her class yesterday she had to send you out of the room.' Madame was still talking. 'That was a great disgrace; you should be old enough for that not to be necessary. She said that by your behaviour you were disturbing the others.'

'I wasn't,' I said. 'Really I wasn't, but Miss Dent suddenly got cross.'

'I refuse to discuss the matter. I have written to your mother, and when I receive her reply you will leave immediately.' Madame's unwonted firmness sounded rather desperate.

'But I can't go to another school in the middle of the term,' I said, 'and I don't think it was very nice of Miss Dent to say I was making a disturbance, when I wasn't doing anything.'

It was here that Madame's inherent weakness betrayed her. Instead of repeating that the matter was finished and dismissing me, she permitted a discussion. I was able to tell her that my fault lay in sticking two small pieces of paper on to the lens of my glasses. I admitted that there was no particular point in it, but said that I could not see that it was a matter for expulsion.

It was more like a nervous trick, such as scratching, or clicking one's plate. I often did that too I said, and would hardly know I had done it. Yes, it had made some of the others laugh, but some people would laugh at anything, wouldn't they? Personally, I had seen nothing particularly funny in it. If I had wanted to be amusing I would have done something else. I went on and on. Madame became flustered. I dwelt on my mother's ill health. Finally Madame covered her face with her small white fingers.

'What am I to do with you, *what* am I to do?' She sounded in despair. I took the opportunity to apologise for any inconvenience I might have caused her. The scene ended with her in tears, throwing the letter to my mother dramatically into the fire. She was having a nervous breakdown, of course. I left the room feeling rather shaken—she had spoiled my triumph. I wondered if it was because the bit about my mother's ill health wasn't true. All the same my mother would have been very angry with me had she received that letter. I was relieved.

I went back to the classroom. Everyone but Alice had removed themselves and their attaché-cases—though they had left the candy wrappers.

'What did she want?' Alice asked.

'She expelled me.' I felt light-headed and boastful. It seemed an anti-climax when I had to add, 'But she let me off after I had talked to her.' Then I told Alice about Madame's crying, but she wasn't as impressed as I had expected.

'She always does that when she expels us.'

'Has she ever expelled *you*?'

'Oh, yes,' Alice said carelessly. 'In the Easter term before you came. As a matter of fact I cried too, so then she said she would forgive me "this time," and I had tea in her sitting-room and Miss Dent came and poured out and pretended not to notice how red our eyes were. Of course,' Alice said, 'I was younger then, about the same age as you are now. If she expelled me this term, I don't expect I should mind.'

Rather crestfallen, I described the scene that had just taken place between Madame and me.

Alice said that she thought my glasses would have been an awfully dull thing to be expelled for. 'She expelled *me* after we'd had a midnight feast on the roof and I left a pickle jar where it blocked up one of the drains so that the roof leaked.'

Groom Place was the sort of fourth-rate school which went in for midnight feasts. This term we were having quite a little season of them. Their organisation had become a fairly heavy social responsibility. 'What shall we have to eat?' 'How shall we get it?' 'Who shall we ask?' 'Well, everyone we like, and then Joan and Daphne.' 'Must we have them?' 'Of course. They asked us to theirs.' 'I thought at the time it was a great pity we accepted.' No hard-working dowagers with marriageable daughters could have taken greater trouble over their dinner-parties and dances and I really believe it was only the necessity of concealing these entertainments from Madame Dubois and her assistants that prevented us from hiring a band. Invitations were issued on the same principle as those for the Royal Enclosure at Ascot; that is, you couldn't go without being invited, but you still had to pay—though with us you didn't have to pay so much—about half a crown usually. Once a Norwegian had, unasked, offered a half-crown to the organiser of a feast. A lot of people told each other how awkward this had been. But the Norwegian did not go to the feast. Midnight came and went and she remained in her bed.

'Have the others gone to get ready for church?' I asked Alice.
'Yes, you'll be late if you don't hurry up.'
'Don't you have to go?'
'My sister's coming down to take me out. She'll probably be early, so Madame has excused me church.'
I said I'd forgotten and how lucky she was, and then I went gloomily up to the bedroom Alice and I shared and put on my hat and coat. They were hideous, of course.
Miss Dent and I walked to church together. As Alice wasn't there I had no friend to walk with, and by the time I had de-scended to the hall, even the inevitable 'odd men out' had got

coupled up with each other. Miss Dent and Matron used to escort us to church on alternate Sundays.

Miss Dent and I were both rather embarrassed at having to walk together, as we gloomily started to follow the others towards the church. At least I know *I* was embarrassed, and I think she must have been also. Her manner was uneasy, and after all, conversation wasn't going to be too easy. I had, within the last half-hour, been nearly expelled on her recommendation, as it were, and there were still the verses which I was supposed to be going to repeat to her when church was over. I reflected in passing that if I had allowed Madame to expel me it wouldn't have mattered about not having learnt the verses. I looked sideways at Miss Dent. Her drab bobbed hair appeared untidily beneath the brim of her saxe blue hat. She clutched her fur coat around her. Miss Dent, strangely it seemed to us, was engaged to be married to someone called 'My Fiancé.' He was a tea-planter or a sailor, I forget which now, but anyhow he was abroad, and Miss Dent would carry his letters with the foreign stamps on them into class. I don't believe that we ever got beyond the first five minutes of any of her lessons. It was too easy to distract her attention by asking her about 'My Fiancé.' Considering how often we asked, and how many times she told us, it seems strange that I can remember so little about him. Miss Dent's other and perhaps even more easily exploitable subject of conversation was 'The Prince of Wales,' for whom, although she had never met him, she had a great affection. Once I had enquired if, in the event of 'The Prince of Wales' proposing to her, she would break off her engagement to 'My Fiancé.' I think it is to Miss Dent's credit that she admitted that her choice would be 'The Prince of Wales,' but Alice thought it was very disloyal of her. It was from Miss Dent that I first heard the name of Karl Marx, but she cannot have thought much of him, for I can remember that a girl called Beatrice something or other, exclaimed, 'Bad luck for Jess.' Jessie Marks was Beatrice's best friend, and Miss Dent hastened to assure her that the spelling was quite different and that there could be no possible connection between the two.

Nevertheless, we couldn't feel the same towards Jessie for quite several days.

Miss Dent ended up, I am sorry to say, by going mad at supper. She went on piling meat on to the plate of one of the Norwegians. We looked at her aghast, then she fell back in her chair, turned a horrid colour, and was dragged from the room by excited members of the staff. I don't remember that we saw her again.

But all that was later. This morning she was quite sane, and on the way to church, as we turned from the high road into the fields, I forgave her for reporting me to Madame, and broke our hitherto uneasy silence by asking a pleasant question about 'The Prince of Wales' (she must at the same time have decided to forgive me for muddling up Panama with Leghorn), for she answered civilly, and we carried on an amiable if pointless conversation about his hunting until the church porch was reached. Miss Dent held two conflicting theories as to why His Royal Highness fell off his horse so many times. One was that this showed that he was much braver than any of the other people who hunted with him, and the second was that the others fell off just as frequently, but that not being 'Royalty' the papers did not consider it worth while to print photographs of them doing it. This, Miss Dent said, was 'victimisation,' and she may have been right. Personally I always thought of him as a younger un-whiskered version of the White Knight, and too young anyhow to marry Miss Dent. Here I was probably wrong, for I had no idea in which year either of them had been born.

As we sat in the red-brick church I thought about Alice, who was still presumably writing her letters in the deserted classroom, while she waited for her sister.

Alice, I felt, was different from anyone else. I don't mean by that that she was 'not quite like other girls' in the way Hyde Park Nannies used euphemistically to describe the idiot children of the aristocracy. 'Backward,' by the way, was reserved for children of the same class who were only half mad.

Alice was gayer and much more sure of herself than most of her contemporaries. She could at fifteen return happily to nursery games. 'You be the Wreek of the Wrekin and I'll be Mrs. Smellie of Loch Smellie, who's come to take your house that hasn't any drains, only you mustn't tell me about the drains, because I'm very particular about them.' Later the same afternoon she might try to explain Dunne's *Experiment with Time* to me. 'But Margaret, it's quite easy, you can see by the diagrams, and it's true, isn't it, that if time's going to move, it's got to have another time to move in, and then the other time outside the first one has got to have another time for *it* to move in, and it would go on and on like that and get so complicated that it just isn't likely, so it's much more probable that it's the other way round, and that we're moving through time, and then there'd only have to be one of it.' And Alice would look anxiously at me, hoping I'd understood, and flush slightly with the effort of attempting to make it clear to me, and her fair hair would fall across her cheek as she bent over the book. Beryl Lawes said of Alice that she tried to show off, but she was quite wrong. It was a pity though, from Alice's point of view, that Groom Place offered its pupils no education whatsoever.

When we got back from church Alice had gone. Her sister had come down from London to take her out to luncheon. How I envied Alice having a sister. On week-days when we were supposed to talk only in French she was able to speak of *'ma sœur,'* which sounded very glamorous to me who had neither sisters nor brothers. Sonia, that was Alice's sister, had been at school at Groom Place and had left behind her an enviable reputation for charm and bad behaviour. It was rumoured that Sonia had been expelled and sent away—not forgiven, with tears and tea, in Madame's sitting-room. One gathered that it was for something more exciting than sticking paper on her glasses. Besides, Sonia wouldn't have worn glasses. She was six years older than Alice, and at this time was twenty-one. Old, but not too old still to enjoy life. To have a sister six years your senior was very nice. Any more and it would have been sad. I remember a girl at my High School. 'Poor Iris, she has a sister fifteen years older than she is, isn't it sad?' And I can recall the genuine sorrow I felt as I agreed. I was twelve.

Alice came back from lunching with Sonia in a subdued mood. They had been to a large hotel in Maidenhead; the food had been very good, Alice said. It was so good in fact that she didn't want the usual half-pound slab of milk chocolate which we were each in the habit of eating every Sunday to fill in the gap between tea and supper.

'. . . and I had a cocktail,' Alice said.

I was impressed, and asked her if she had enjoyed it.

'Well, truthfully, not very much,' Alice admitted. 'But we shall have to get used to them, you know.'

We both agreed about drinking being one of the things you had to do when you were grown up. Fortunately we already enjoyed smoking, so we wouldn't have to bother about that. It wasn't until after we were in bed, and Matron had been in and turned off the light, that Alice told me. I heard her voice, an urgent whisper carrying across the room.

'Margaret, are you asleep?'

I said that I wasn't, and after asking me politely whether I was sure, Alice went on.

'You promise that you'll never tell anyone?'

'Cross my heart.'

There was a long pause. 'It's something rather awful.'

There was another pause and I waited, hardly daring to breathe for fear that Alice wouldn't tell me after all. Then she started, in a whisper that didn't sound like Alice's whisper but like somebody I didn't know. I wondered whether I should like the somebody, decided that perhaps I shouldn't, and remembered that it wasn't a somebody but Alice. It seemed that Sonia had run away from home and was living in London. It wasn't just an ordinary going up to London; Sonia often did that. This was different. Sonia was never going back to Platon again, and there had been a terrible row with Mummy and Daddy, and Sonia's allowance was going to be stopped, and so she hadn't got any money.

'Though she'll have to go back if we have any funerals, won't she?' Alice asked. 'Not that that will make it any better though, because of course we don't want to have one, but it seems so awful never going to a place again, especially when it's your home where you've lived all your life.'

I agreed that it was awful, and Alice explained that Sonia had got a job in an interior-decorating shop belonging to a friend of hers, and that she was going to be paid thirty shillings a week, and was going to live on it. I said that it didn't sound very much and Alice agreed that it wasn't. I asked how Sonia had managed to pay for luncheon at Maidenhead, and Alice said Sonia had borrowed the money from her.

'She promised to pay it back, but I don't know what out of. She won't be able to save up out of thirty shillings, at least not very much, will she?'

I said that I supposed not, and asked how much the luncheon had cost.

'Well, just under two pounds, and with the tip just over, and then Sonia said that she was my sister and that I couldn't leave her to starve in London, and she sort of persuaded me to give her the money I had left, so now I shan't have anything until the end of the term, and it's going to be very awkward.'

I agreed again. There was nothing else I could do, for I knew that Mrs. Norton, unlike my own mother, had a way of checking her daughter's school bills, and that therefore it wouldn't be any good for Alice to pretend she was a Norwegian like I did, and get advances of money from Madame's secretary. She couldn't sell any of her clothes either, because the Nanny who still lived with the Nortons knew exactly how many she had.

'If Sonia sold her car, perhaps she could pay you back then.'

Alice told me not to be silly, Sonia would never do that, she used it all the time. Anyhow, it had only cost twenty-five pounds when Mummy and Daddy had given it to her on her twenty-first birthday three months before—instead of pearls because of Sonia thinking it would be more useful, and she had run into one or two things since then. So it wouldn't be worth so much now. I said, 'Bad luck,' and offered to get some money by my own methods and lend it to Alice. She refused angrily and a few minutes later I heard muffled sobbing. I was appalled. We were too old to cry. At first I pretended not to notice. Then as time went on and Alice continued to cry, I got out of bed and stood hesitantly in the middle of the room in my white cotton nightgown. The nightgown reached half-way down my calves and was another of my grievances against Miss Partridge. 'Everyone Else' wore pyjamas. My feet clung uncomfortably to the cold linoleum.

'Alice,' I said, 'it isn't as bad as all that.'

The sobbing stopped. Encouraged, I went over and stood beside her bed. It was nice to be standing on a mat instead of linoleum.

'Shut up,' Alice said fiercely. The crying was resumed.

I had no idea what to do next. Then she started to speak again.

'You're too young to understand, but it isn't the money I mind about. I don't mind not having any really; at least—not much. It's Sonia having taken it away from me. It wasn't fair, and she's *always* been fair. Nanny said last holidays that there'd never been anyone as honourable as Sonia, and that Anthony and I ought to try and be more like her, and I always have tried.'

'I'm sure you have.' I sat down on the floor beside Alice's bed. I had a vague idea that I was being helpful. Alice told me again that I was too young to understand anything about it. I could just see her face by the light of the moon which came round the edge of the cretonne curtains. Alice remarked that I would catch my death of cold if I stayed there, and turned her back on me, lying with her face to the wall. She wasn't crying any more. I began to shiver, and in the end I went back to bed. I was so cold that it was a long time before I went to sleep. How long Alice remained awake I don't know. We never referred to the incident again.

TWO

MOST OF THAT Christmas holidays I spent with Alice at Platon. My mother and Miss Partridge were still abroad. My grandmother had come over from Ireland and was living in her London house, where I remained with her for a week. She did not allow me to go out alone in London and her maid was unwilling to accompany me. If I stayed indoors it was known as 'hanging about the house,' and was considered to be bad for me. Of course I could read, but my grandmother then worried as to what books were suitable; and I was too old to play with the lift.

I travelled down to Devonshire at the end of December and was met at the station by Alice, her younger brother Anthony, and Nanny, who had been with the family since Sonia was born. Colonel and Mrs. Norton were away, having left as soon as Christmas was over. The object of their visit was pheasant shooting, the only reason for which Colonel Norton ever left home.

Platon was a gigantic house, which had been built by a Norton in the middle of the eighteenth century. When it was new, I suppose, the Nortons had had twenty or thirty servants and the house was possibly comfortable. Now it was very uncomfortable and there were six servants who had disappeared in it, as ferrets do in over-large rabbit warrens. One was apt not to notice that they were there at all.

Mrs. Norton, in common with other mistresses of enormous houses, had an idea that the barring up of a certain number of doors would somehow make the house smaller, and only two outside doors were ever used at Platon. One led into the kitchen passage, where the kitchen-maid kept her bicycle, and the other was a side door opening into a lobby. It may of course have been economical to use this instead of the front door; it was certainly very inconvenient. There was no drive up to it, and in rainy weather the family and their guests could get very wet walking round to it. Guests who had not previously been to the house got much wetter than anyone else, because they spent time in finding the door. If they started round the house the wrong way, it meant a very long walk indeed.

In the afternoon of the day after my arrival, Alice, Anthony and I were reading in one of the drawing-rooms. There was no fire, it was bitterly cold, and everything in the room, including the chairs and sofa on which we sat, was covered with dust-sheets. The fire-irons were done up in newspaper. Alice had apologised to me for the room and had said that they were mostly like that. This was the warmest because it faced south, or very nearly south, and had the additional advantage of being over the stoke-hole. If it hadn't been for Nanny we could have sat in the nursery, which at least had a fire. Alice, I remember, was reading a book about child psychology and she and Anthony were discussing whether or not they were leading a sheltered childhood. A sheltered childhood, according to the book, was almost invariably a great disadvantage in later life.

'You see,' Alice was very earnest, 'if we'd lived in the slums and our mother had had fifteen children, and our father had got drunk and knocked us about, we should have been brought up against "real life."'

'Daddy does drink—a *bit*.' Anthony was hopeful. 'It's what makes him do card tricks after dinner.'

'I don't think the book would count that.'

'Anyhow'—Anthony was not to be deterred—'we know a lot about real life, we knew about Kathleen getting herself into trouble almost as soon as it happened. Though of course it mayn't *be* a trouble to her. I went down to the kitchen this morning, and she was peeling the potatoes and seemed perfectly happy.'

'I don't think this book would count that either.'

'Oh, what a pity.' Anthony was disappointed. Almost immediately he had a more cheerful thought. 'Anyhow, I don't expect the people in that book hunt, so they can't be faced with sudden death nearly so often as we are, and then there's "courage in the face of danger" that Mummy's so keen on. I don't expect they get much of that either.'

'But we aren't always brave, quite honestly, *are* we?' Alice said. 'But I do see what you mean, and death's much more real than life.'

'Oh, *much* more,' Anthony agreed. 'And far rarer. Are you looking forward to going out tomorrow?'

The last part of his remark was addressed to me. I told him that I was. I had never hunted before, but I had wanted to for as long as I could remember. One of my favourite daydreams was of myself, very small, mounted on a very large horse leading an enthusiastic field of foxhunting ladies and gentlemen. I never put in the fox and quite often forgot the hounds. Frequently I broke my arm, when my gallant horse fell and rolled on me, through no fault of his own, or indeed of mine, but due to circumstances outside our mutual control. Of course I never just fell off. Now I was going to take part in the real thing and I realised with relief that it was bound to be less spectacular. For one thing I was going to ride Sonia's horse, which Alice assured me was very quiet and rather slow. 'I'd lend you Starlight,' Alice had said, 'only she isn't used to a side-saddle, and Tubby has often carried one.'

I wished that I could ride astride, but it had taken many years to persuade my grandmother to allow me to ride at all, and when she relented she had made the stipulation that I was to ride side-saddle. It was the only possible way for ladies and could look very elegant when well done. I gathered that in her youth my grandmother had done it very well indeed. Anthony was looking enquiringly at Alice.

'If she has Tubby, does that mean that I'll have to have Nebuchadnezzar from the riding school?'

'Yes, you don't mind, do you?'

'You know perfectly well I *hate* Nebuchadnezzar.' Anthony was sulky. 'And anyhow,' he went on, 'Mummy said that Margaret wasn't to hunt at all, because her grandmother had written to say so.'

'Anthony!' Alice was furious with him. 'You promised not to say anything about that—you're an absolute beast.'

Anthony said that he didn't care. I was horrified. They were going to quarrel, and it was all my fault. If I hadn't been there, Anthony could have ridden Tubby, which was evidently what he wanted, and how dared my grandmother write to Mrs. Norton behind my back. I wished I was someone quite different who had arrived with their own hunters. The door opened behind us, and turning I saw Sonia for the first time. She was very beautiful.

'Sonia!' Alice shouted. 'Have you come home?'

'Obviously.' Sonia sank into one of the chairs; the springs were evidently broken. 'Is this really the most comfortable room you can find to sit in?'

'It's not very uncomfortable,' Alice said. 'Only rather cold, and anyhow we're wearing our golf mittens like we do at school,' She held out her hands; the ends of her fingers protruding from the mittens were purple.

'God!' Sonia said. 'I'm not surprised you get those awful chilblains.'

'Perhaps I'll grow out of them,' Alice said. 'Oh, I forgot, you haven't met before—this is Margaret, she's my friend at school.'

Sonia accepted the introduction with a mortifying lack of interest.

'Does Mummy know you've come back?' Alice went on.

'No, I only decided to this morning.' Sonia seemed disinclined to discuss the situation. She started instead to talk about hunting, and it soon became clear that she, like Anthony, wasn't at all pleased that I should have Tubby. This led to a lot of confusion, with Alice and me competing with each other over being unselfish. In the end it was decided that Alice should stay at home, an arrangement which suited neither of us. As I had counted on Alice to show me what to do, the prospect of the next day was almost spoilt for me. My suggestion that another horse should be hired was turned down immediately, it being certain that the riding school would have nothing to spare for any meet during the Christmas holidays.

'It was only by the greatest luck that we even got Nebuchadnezzar, and Anthony's the only one who is light enough to ride him,' Alice explained.

This reminded me that I must offer to pay for the hire of Nebuchadnezzar. I decided to leave it until Alice and I were alone.

'How did you get from the station?' Anthony asked Sonia.

'I hired a taxi—what do you think?'

'I hadn't thought,' Anthony admitted. 'As a matter of fact, I was only making conversation.'

'That's very kind of you.'

'It's all right,' Anthony said. 'I do it more or less naturally now.'

That evening we had supper in the nursery. Nanny was annoyed with Mrs. Palmer, the cook, and also with the butler, for not giving Sonia dinner in the dining-room. 'With Mummy and Daddy away, those servants have nothing at all to do, except tittle-tattle between themselves. They're not like me whose work goes on all the time. You should ring the bell and order your dinner.'

Sonia remained indifferent to the suggestion, although Nanny made it intermittently in different forms until the under-housemaid arrived in the nursery with the supper tray. The supper was cold meat, about enough potatoes for two people, and stewed apples. Nanny wondered loudly and angrily what Mrs. Palmer found to do all day. Anthony suggested that perhaps she mended her underclothes, and Nanny said that if Mrs. Palmer saw the washing and mending that *she* had to do for the lot of them, it would give Mrs. Palmer something to think about. 'And as for the way you brought your things home from school'—she turned to Alice—'I don't know what you can have been doing with them.'

'Just wearing them,' Alice said, refusing potatoes. Nanny remarked that *that* matron ought to be ashamed of herself.

'But we do our own mending, don't you remember?'

It appeared that Nanny only remembered that Sonia's clothes had never got 'like that,' and anyhow she couldn't see any point in Alice having silk chemises at her age, because they only went into holes. Running through it all was criticism of Alice. I felt that I shouldn't be listening.

I tried to think about something else.

Tomorrow and the hunting were going to be awful. For the first time I faced it squarely. I didn't ride well enough to hunt, and if Sonia's rearrangement of the horses meant that I was going to have to ride astride, I was done for. And my grandmother had written to Mrs. Norton and told her I wasn't to hunt at all. How right my grandmother was and how angry she was going to be; but I should be dead, so it wouldn't matter. It was sad to die so young. It would have been sadder still if I had been even younger. 'A child's funeral with white plumes instead of black.' Perhaps fourteen counted as a child for funerals, although it didn't on trains or buses. I could have white horses and a coffin covered with the Union Jack. No, that was for soldiers. Perhaps they would lay my new hunting-crop on the coffin, together with a simple bunch of primroses. It would be very moving and my mother would be there, sent for by cable, and she would wish that she hadn't spent these holidays in the South of France. I wondered who else would be at the funeral and whether anyone would say: 'Neither child nor woman, but somehow more beautiful than either.'

It was a pity in a way that I wasn't going to die during the term, for then the whole school, carrying lighted candles, could have followed me to my last resting-place. And there would have been a lot more people to be sorry for the unkind things they had said to me. I was brought back from this charming scene of general remorse to find that Nanny, Anthony and the supper-tray were about to leave the nursery. They—that is, Nanny and Anthony—were going down to the basement to play whist with Mrs. Palmer and the butler.

'For money,' Anthony told us, 'but not much of it.'

Nanny said he was not to talk like that, or Mummy and Daddy would think they really *did* play for money. Anthony argued that he didn't think they'd mind, as they did it themselves, only at bridge. Nanny said that was quite a different thing and, still squabbling, they left us.

Without Nanny the room became instantly more cheerful and also, a little later, warmer, for Sonia at once put a great deal more coal on the fire—even as long ago as that Nanny was practising fuel economy. We all imperceptibly relaxed. Alice took Nanny's chair by the fire; Sonia told me to sit on the sofa, but herself remained at the table. The hard light fell on her face, which she supported between her hands. I noticed how tired she was looking. She asked Alice whether her father and mother had missed her when she was away: 'Or perhaps they didn't even notice I wasn't in the house?'

'I think Nanny missed you most,' Alice said. 'She kept on saying how sad it was we weren't all together for Christmas, and wondering how you'd feel without having a stocking, and she asked Mummy if she couldn't send you some things for it in a parcel. Not that it would be the same if you had to fill it yourself. And she kept on remembering what lovely Christmases you used to have, when there was only you in the nursery, and Anthony and I hadn't been born.'

'Well, we weren't all together then.' Sonia's voice sounded rough. I thought that she must be annoyed with Alice.

'But that was different,' Alice objected. 'It doesn't matter not being together when you haven't been born, because nobody knows you're not there. Did you have a nice Christmas, by the way? I do think you might have told Nanny something about it when she asked, because I think you've hurt her feelings, and that's why she was so cross at supper.'

'Christmas was bloody actually, but it always is anyhow.'

Alice said, 'Was it?' and added that she didn't know what it would be like in London, as she'd never spent it there.

'I wasn't in London, I was in Paris.'

'Were you *really*, how simply *thrilling*.' Alice turned her head, and looked at Sonia over the back of Nanny's chair. 'Or did you just go to that family you were with before you came out?'

'No, of course I didn't, I went to a hotel.'

'How thrilling,' Alice repeated doubtfully. It was evident that she longed to ask Sonia more, but did not like to. Alice believed that you should never ask people questions that they mightn't want to answer. It had to do with human dignity, she explained to me, and it saved them from telling lies.

'As a matter of fact, I went with a man called Paddy, and you can tell Mummy and Daddy about it if you want to.'

'I don't think I particularly want to,' Alice said bleakly.

She wasn't looking at Sonia any more, but into the fire. I couldn't see her face, only the top of her head and an arm which hung over the side of the chair and her knees in their woollen stockings. The light reflected brightly on her wrist-watch; its leather strap was rather shabby.

'I suppose you're shocked, and your little friend too?' Sonia turned to me and I felt embarrassed. If I left the room she might think it was because I *was* shocked. I didn't want to be shocked; it was a horrid thing to be, besides I wasn't, only I didn't know how Alice was feeling about it.

'No, I'm not.' Alice was speaking slowly. 'People must lead their own lives.'

Sonia didn't seem particularly pleased by that. There was a long silence, and somehow I knew that Alice's disillusionment in Sonia was now complete and that Alice minded terribly. Eventually Sonia went and sat on the floor beside the bookshelf. When we went to bed she was reading *Stumps*.

On the way to our rooms I asked Alice if she really couldn't hunt the next day, as I would have no idea what to do by myself, and I again suggested that I should be the one to stay at home. Alice said that of course I was to go, and that perhaps Sonia would change her mind about going out, but that in any case I would find it quite easy, because one just did what everyone else did. 'Only rather behind them,' Alice advised, 'so that you can hear them saying, "'Ware wire" and "'Ware crops."'

'And what do I do when they say it?'

We had stopped in the passage, and I can remember staring unhappily at a stuffed squirrel in a glass case. The squirrel had a nut in its mouth, and it was sad to think that it would never eat one again. I felt as if I was cramming for an examination.

'Well, if it's wire, you say it too and don't jump it, and if it's crops you don't ride over them, but keep to the side of the field. And it's better not to say "'Ware crops" yourself, because if they're not it sounds rather silly.'

I nodded miserably. It was only too likely that I should do something silly, and then there were gates. I understood that those who didn't jump them opened them for each other with their hunting-crops, an almost impossible feat, as far as I was concerned.

The meet was a success. I speak for myself, for from the point of view of the Master or the Huntsmen I suppose that it is not possible for a meet to be a failure. It was held in a village about two miles from Platon. Sonia, Anthony and I hacked to it and Alice came with us on her bicycle. It was a comfort to have her there to talk to while we waited for hounds to arrive, and again after their arrival while the Master conferred with local farmers. Many of the field seemed to know the hounds personally. It must have been very gratifying for them, like knowing a member of the Jockey Club when at a race meeting, or the names of the waiters at a large hotel. My mother, I knew from the rare occasions when she had taken me to luncheon at Claridge's, was very well up in the waiters' names, but I doubted whether she knew a single hound in England. I looked round for one with whom I might start an acquaintanceship.

It was too late; the Master was preparing to move off. The hounds were being collected into a pack. They looked like the picture of one which had adorned a jigsaw puzzle I had had when I was six years old. I hadn't expected them to look like that in real life. I gave a despairing look at Alice and moved off in the wake of the field. Sonia was way ahead, talking to one of the beautiful young men from the barracks. How I wished I could know somebody like that! Anthony was with some schoolboy friend of his own.

A few days later I was proud to read in the paper that: 'A fox from Riffa ran by Tavy to Hessenford and over Perrotts Moor to Blue Coat Wood and was killed after an excellent hunt of just over an hour.' That 'Another fox from Furze Park Wood ran by North Righton round Tavy down to Hessenford and right-handed through Bailey's Whin almost to Stanton Moor.' That 'He went back to Tavy past North Righton over the main road and railway straight to Newport Wood, and that there a dead beaten fox was left.' That 'This was a splendid hunt of seventy-five minutes with a five-mile point and fourteen miles as hounds ran,' and that 'it was one of the best days spent for many years.'

I kept that cutting for ages and ages in a China box, which had been bought by my mother in Dresden, but the sport had not been for me. After all, I was riding astride, and Sonia having taken Tubby, I was riding Starlight. She and I jumped one very small fence together in our pursuit of the first fox. The next fence was large and terrifying; we were going too fast, and I could do nothing to slow us down. I shut my eyes; this was the end of the world, anyhow I wasn't breathing any more. We rose to the fence, then an extraordinary thing happened—Starlight remained poised in mid-air, and wriggled. If she was supported at all it must have been by invisible wires like the fairies in the pantomime. Below us was a beautiful ploughed field. I fell into it, and remembered the reason for wearing a bowler. Starlight went on; all the other horses went on, no one else fell off. I was alone in a beautiful ploughed field; there were lots of little bits of flint, and I wasn't riding a horse, and I wasn't dead, it was delightful. But it wasn't to last. One field ahead someone was catching Starlight, and worst of all, leading her back to me. It was Anthony. He found a gate, and as I stood up, he was beside me. I realised he was being unselfish and tried to thank him; he said it was all right and asked if I could get up alone. I said I could, and then of course Starlight and I walked round and round each other, she leaning heavily on my right arm. A foot follower joined us and helped me to remount. It was all humiliating.

Anthony and I rode for miles looking for hounds. When you are looking for hounds you are allowed to use gates; you are not expected to jump anything, you are saving your horse. More than willingly I saved Starlight. When we came up with them they were drawing Furze Park Wood. Waiting in a lane with some farmers I saw a fox break covert; he looked both ways and ran down the side of the hedge, then he crossed the road only a very little in front of us. For what seemed a long time no hound was to be seen; oh, where were they? If they didn't hurry up, they would never catch the fox. I couldn't bear it; someone had shouted from the inside of the wood, there was the sound of the horn. Please, *please* be quick, everything was going to be spoilt, and just because the hounds were so stupid. Then the first one emerged from the covert and cast first in the direction which the fox had not taken. Now he was casting the other way, two or three other hounds scrambled out of the wood; they were on to the line, they crossed the road at the same point as the fox; that fox which must be literally miles away by now. There was the cracking of whips, the rest of the pack were being encouraged to follow the leaders, but of what use was it now? I hated the hounds passionately; they were masquerading as foxhounds, they should have been somewhere else chasing rabbits. The master followed his forlorn hope of a pack. I looked at the farmers; weren't we all going to follow? Some of them galloped away in a quite different direction. I had noticed one old man with a beard; he must be too old to do any unnecessary jumping. I decided to follow him. He went through a gate. There were several of us and we followed one another along a kind of track; we could see hounds running in the valley below us. Far ahead of them I thought I could distinguish the fox. The fox that I longed to kill. The longing, very properly, was not to be gratified. In the first place the fox was left dead beaten after a magnificent hunt with a point of five miles, and fourteen miles as hounds ran, and in the second, Starlight and I ran for only about a mile. The track along which we had been following the bearded farmer came to an end in a lane. To get into the field on the other side of the lane it was necessary to jump a very small post and rails—the sort that is made up of old twigs. The farmer jumped it, but another farmer turned right-handed up the lane which evidently led to the open moor. Perhaps he thought that hounds would be going that way later, or perhaps he didn't like jumping either; anyhow I followed him, and that was the last I saw of the hunt. Presently he disappeared, and Starlight and I were left to mountaineer over boulders by ourselves.

Horses in that part of the country are very good at mountaineering, and after the first surprise that they should be able to do it, it is not unduly frightening for the rider, but the boulders over which we climbed were larger and rougher than any I should have attempted if I had been on foot and wearing my sandshoes. After a while it seemed obvious that there was little point in staying out. I was horribly tired, it was beginning to rain, and not by the greatest stretch of the imagination could it be said that I was still hunting. I decided to try and find my way back to Platon. This took a long time and many enquiries. Once

I tried to force Starlight into a bog, which I had failed to recognise as such. Fortunately she refused to go into it, showing her distaste by sweating all over and trembling, and once we were lost in a mist. In the end, though, we rode into the stable-yard at Platon at ten minutes to two. The Nortons' groom-gardener, who had been sitting in the harness-room, came forward to help me dismount and appeared surprised at my early return.

'Didn't she go well for you then?' He patted Starlight on the withers, and there was regret in his voice. 'Most generally she likes a good day's hunting.'

I felt that I was guilty of having ruined poor Starlight's day. I explained that she had gone very well, excellently in fact, but that we had got lost. He looked unbelieving, and went on to ask for details of the day. I was unable to give them to him, and he led Starlight away. I went into the house hating him.

Then I remembered again that I wasn't dead. I had fallen off, I had been made to look foolish in the eyes of a great many people, and at the end of it I wasn't even going to have a funeral. As well as hating the groom I hated myself.

I found Alice in the same drawing-room we had sat in yesterday.

As I came in she looked up.

'I've been spending the day sticking pins into Sonia. Into a model of her. I made it in plasticine as soon as I got back from the meet.'

'Do you think it will kill her?' I asked, sitting down.

'It might if one really believed in it,' Alice said. 'But I didn't put one through her heart just in case it *is* true you know. But she ought to have very bad rheumatism after what I've done. I'm sure she was beastly to that man she went to Paris with. Actually,' Alice went on, 'I don't particularly mind missing a day's hunting because I've always got a lot of other things to do. But it was so mean of her to prevent me going out with you on your first day, when you obviously needed somebody to look after you.'

'It didn't matter,' I said. 'Can I see the model of Sonia?'

'It's buried,' Alice said carelessly. 'You're supposed to bury them after you've finished with them.'

*

The next day Alice showed me over the house. We walked for miles up and down staircases and through deserted rooms. We paused in the front hall with its pillars and its white marble floor. Alice opened the shutters of one of the windows.

'It's lucky we don't use this as a hall now, isn't it?' she asked. 'Imagine if it had to be scrubbed every day. It would take *hours*. Nanny says that when she was a young girl, housemaids used to get up at four in the morning. It's not surprising when one thinks what they had to do.'

We contemplated the floor, thinking with sympathy of the Victorian housemaids who had scrubbed it.

'Though perhaps it was the odd man,' Alice said more brightly, and for the sake of the housemaids we were glad.

A large picture hung over the fireplace. It was of a woman dressed as a harlequin. She had the baton and the mask, but she wore a full skirt which ended above her ankles.

'She was an actress,' Alice said.

'Like Mrs. Bracegirdle?' I asked.

'Not so famous and a bit later. Her name was Mrs. Ashdown. She had an illegitimate daughter, who married the man who built this house, so that makes her an ancestress.'

'She's not very like you,' I said, looking from Alice to the small wooden face of Mrs. Ashdown.

'Of course, it's not a very good picture, or it wouldn't still be here. The valuable ones have mostly been sold.'

I went closer to the picture. You could see the patches of bloom on the canvas; it was exactly the same as that on black grapes. Beneath the bloom stood Mrs. Ashdown. One square-toed shoe pointing outwards, her baton held over her head.

'I wonder if I'd like to go on the stage,' Alice said, also coming and standing before the picture. 'Or perhaps I shall be an artist. I think I shall ask if I can start learning to paint in oils next term. The only thing is that I like the tubes of paint so much better than the pictures, especially meridian green.'

*

I left Platon before the end of the holidays. On my last evening Sonia came back from a long conversation on the telephone and said that she would be travelling to London with me. I was rather sorry, as I still looked upon a journey alone as an adventure, an idea fostered by my grandmother who, by her insistence on compartments for Ladies Only, not speaking to anyone, not going to the restaurant car, and being placed in the care of the guard, who had to be tipped five shillings, contrived to make the shortest journey undertaken in a first-class carriage in England seem as dangerous, and very nearly as interesting, as the traipsings of Miss Rosita Forbes into the interiors of black continents.

Alice and Nanny saw us off at the station. I could not see a Ladies Only, and in any case I felt that Sonia would have despised one. She chose a smoking compartment in which we found ourselves alone. As soon as the train started she offered me a cigarette, which I modestly refused. At fourteen it is conventional to smoke behind haystacks, or at the end of the garden at school, but *not* in railway trains, and I was very conventional. Sonia leant back in her seat and seemed to regard me with a slight air of amusement. She looked very grown up, I thought, much more so than she had at Platon, where it had been possible to think of her as being only a little older than myself and Alice. Again I wished I was travelling alone, or even with Ellen, my grandmother's head housemaid. When I was younger Ellen and I had made a lot of journeys together and we still did when any changes of train were involved. She had all the cosiness of a traditional Nanny, with very little of her authority.

'Will you be seeing your mother before you go back to school?' Sonia asked.

I was surprised that she had taken enough interest in me to find out that I had a mother, but then when speaking to children people often surmised parents where none existed. I told her that I thought my mother would remain in France during the whole of the Christmas holidays.

'It must be marvellous having a mother like yours.'

This time I was so surprised that I couldn't think of anything to say. I had never considered my mother as being in any way an asset.

'I suppose most holidays you go and stay with her abroad?'

'No,' I said regretfully. 'As a matter of fact I don't, but she's generally in England during the summer holidays, and sometimes at Easter. I live with my grandmother really.'

'Oh, do you?' I could see that Sonia was losing interest.

'My father and mother are divorced,' I said in the hope of pleasing her.

'Everybody knows that.'

'Do they?' I asked. 'I didn't for ages.'

'I suppose it *is* true that your mother is going to marry the Marchese Buonagrazia; everybody's talking about it?'

'No,' I said firmly. 'As a matter of fact she's engaged to a very rich *English* millionaire.'

I was astonished. Why English, why a millionaire, and why had I invented such a thing and so suddenly?

'He's very devoted to her,' I went on, 'but I'm not allowed to say what his name is—yet.'

'It oughtn't to be difficult to guess.' Sonia was looking superior. 'But do tell me some more about your famous mother.'

I longed to ask Sonia what she was famous *for*. For a dazzling moment I thought that perhaps she might have written a lot of books that they hadn't told me about, or perhaps she was a lion-tamer, or danced the can-can before audiences composed of enthralled French Dukes and Italian Marcheses. But how to ask about it?

'I don't think she's so *very* famous,' I said tentatively.

'Of course she is.' Sonia seemed quite cross. 'Everybody knows the beautiful Mrs. Boswell; she's an international figure.'

'Is she?' I felt more and more doubtful. Could it be that my mother went in for all-in wrestling matches or boxing tournaments. 'On my left the beautiful Mrs. Boswell from England, on my right Miss Something from Czechoslovakia.' No, it wasn't likely. Nice, but *not* likely. Sonia was waiting for me to say something. Regretfully I tore myself away from the boxing ring just as my mother was throwing the Czechoslovakian lady clean over the ropes. Ropes which must surely have been specially blancoed, so dazzling was their whiteness.

What could I tell her about my mother?

'She gets temperatures very easily,' I said, fully aware of the dullness of the information. 'But they go down again awfully quickly.' I hurried on, trying to make up by quantity for what was clearly lacking in quality. 'She can have a temperature of a hundred and two one day, and the next be quite well and able to go out to luncheon.'

'And she's very beautiful?' Sonia was trying to help me.

'Oh, yes,' I said eagerly, though I had never thought so, and had more than once overheard my grandmother say that Hermione spoilt what looks she had by using too much make-up. I wondered, should I tell Sonia about my mother spoiling her looks, but decided 'no.' Instead Sonia told me the names of the artists who had painted my mother. I agreed that they had done so and added the names of two she had forgotten. The conversation dwindled into nothingness. Sonia asked me about myself and expressed surprise that I should be such a great friend of Alice's.

'Don't you find her rather limited after meeting such interesting people at home?'

'They're not as interesting as Alice,' I said. 'And anyhow, they don't talk to me much, except to ask me questions and laugh at the answers.'

'And Alice doesn't ask you questions?'

'Not that kind; we just talk.'

'And you don't find her dull at all?'

'Oh, *no,* if you do I expect it's just because she's your sister. Brothers and sisters quite often don't like each other, do they? So perhaps in some ways it's a good thing I haven't got any.'

Sonia said it depended on who you had for a sister. By the time we reached Reading, she had told me all about Paddy. I was flattered that she should think me old enough to confide in, and I was glad to hear they had made up their quarrel. Sonia said that we must all meet in London, and I said that would be lovely, and wondered how it could be arranged without telling my grandmother anything about it. From what Sonia had told me, Paddy was not the sort of young man of whom my grandmother would approve.

At Paddington I was met by Ellen. Sonia had disappeared into the crowd, so I had no chance of seeing Paddy.

'Oh, Ellen, I'm so glad it's you and not Miss White.'

Miss White was my grandmother's maid and Ellen didn't care for her either.

'Would you like us to have a quick cup of tea in the buffet before we go home? If anything was said, we could say that the train was late—as a matter of fact, it is too.'

There was a convention between us that tea in the refreshment room was a treat for *me,* so I agreed, with what I hoped were signs of delighted gratitude, and Ellen settled down to a prolonged tea-drinking, and to telling me the news of the house. 'Annie's left, I don't suppose you know?'

'Oh, I am sorry.' Annie was the second housemaid.

'Can't say I am, she was turning into a proper young madam. Walter was paying too much attention to her, that was the trouble there.'

'Yes, I suppose it was.'

'And your mother arrived back in England last night. No one was expecting her; she came in to see Mrs. Boswell after dinner. She's got her hair done red again.'

I supposed then that Sonia was right about the Marchese; with my mother red hair usually meant that she was engaged to a foreigner. I wondered if Mrs. Norton ever changed the colour of her hair. Somehow I thought not. I wondered what Alice was doing, and whether Nanny was being horrid to her, and as Ellen talked on I thought how very disagreeable Sonia had been about Alice.

THREE

I DO NOT THINK there was any time in my life when my mother had actually disliked me. Unfortunately, though, I bored her. Had I been a boy I think it would have been different. When she divorced my father the court gave her my custody. She didn't want it and gradually I came to live most of the time with my father's mother. It wasn't a bad arrangement; my grandmother had two large houses in either of which I could, when necessary, be kept out of the way. I wasn't unhappy. She had sympathetic servants, with the exception of Miss White, and she herself was fond of me. She was a widow and had been an American. She had two sons—Uncle Henry, who was the eldest, and George. George was my father. After the divorce my father had gone to America, settled there and married an American wife. My grandmother considered this to be a retrograde step. America even in her day had been inferior to Europe, and in the last forty years it had certainly not improved. People had married people one didn't know; nice people no doubt in their way, but one wouldn't want to live amongst them. Certainly her money came from America, but that could be no reason why she or any of her family should go there. Who ever heard of a coal owner who lived down a coal-mine? So she wasn't pleased with my father, and when he brought his new wife to England on a visit, my grandmother deplored her provincialism.

My mother, although she had in a great part shifted the responsibility for me, tried all the same quite hard to do her duty by me. She would from time to time take me on visits to such of her friends as happened also to be afflicted with children. She paid my school bills out of the money awarded her by the court for the purpose. Through the agency of Miss Partridge, she provided me with clothes and had my teeth attended to by a reputable dentist. She improved my mind by taking me to art exhibitions and luncheon at Claridge's.

When Ellen and I got back to Hill Street, my grandmother greeted me affectionately and told me that I was to spend the last few days before going back to school at my mother's flat. I was agreeably surprised. I thought the flat very romantic. It occupied the two top floors of a house in South Audley Street. The important room in it was the studio, which was furnished simply with two square divans covered in red serge, and a grand piano. The lamp-shades were made out of cartridge paper held in place with drawing pins. If there was any other furniture in the room I don't remember it.

The studio seemed always to be full of people. In Hill Street, too, there were visitors. They came to meals, and at the proper times after the meals were over they went away again. One saw them as a background for the furniture, which was larger and more important and more permanent than they were. In South Audley Street it was the people who were in the foreground.

On the last day of the Christmas holidays Alice came to the studio. I can see her now, sitting carefully on the edge of one of the divans, her lips parted in a polite smile, while she listened to a young man playing Bach on the piano. Alice hated music. No one else was listening to the young man, but Alice had been taught that when people played the piano other people were supposed to listen, so Alice listened.

My mother on the other divan talked alternately into the telephone and to a professor with a bald head and a badly cut suit. She nearly always had a professor around; I think she found them useful to offset the Marcheses and the artists. Every time the telephone rang my mother expressed annoyance, but she did not fail to answer it. When the professors were really interesting she left the receiver off.

Hemmed into a corner near Alice's divan, I listened to a lady who looked like an aged Dresden shepherdess telling a Labour peer of the lamentable way the opera was run in England.

A young man with lapis-lazuli cuff-links went and sat beside Alice. He crossed one cloth-topped boot over the other and asked her if she was enjoying 'all this.' With a beautiful gesture of his hand he indicated the room. Alice, relieved of the necessity of listening to the music, looked at him gratefully and said that she thought it was wonderful.

'You're Hermione's daughter?'

'Oh, no,' Alice said, 'she's that.'

The young man looked at me and quickly looked back at Alice.

'You were saying,' he said, 'what it was you found so wonderful about this party?'

'Me being at it,' Alice said simply and smiled divinely at the young man.

The Labour peer had managed to escape from the Dresden shepherdess. She gazed after him with hurt childish eyes, and then turned to me. If she was to be publicly humiliated, she would conceal it by being kind to Hermione's child.

When I could again turn my attention to Alice she was deep in conversation with the young man.

Time wore on, people drifted away. Alice looked up, seemed surprised to find that the room was nearly empty, thanked my mother for having invited her to tea, told me that she would look out for me on the school train to-morrow and left.

The young man, whose name was Geoffrey Newman, remained behind to tell us what a delightful child Alice was.

'She's a friend of yours?' he said.

I admitted that Alice and I were friends.

'Splendid,' Geoffrey said. 'I shall come down and see you both at school. What shall I bring, chocolates or a bottle of gin?' He turned to my mother. 'We'll both go, Hermione. We'll have luncheon at the Ritz and then we'll fill our pockets with praline chocolates and go down to Berkshire.' With a flash of unusual perception, I realised that Geoffrey must really be quite young to be taking such palpable pleasure in placing himself in a different generation from ours. Probably he was only nineteen or twenty. I smiled at him and said that it would be nice to see him if he came to Groom Place.

Later that evening, when my mother came to tuck me up in bed—I suppose somebody must have told her that that was the right thing for mothers to do—she asked me what Alice was like.

'Very nice,' I said.

My mother told me rather sharply that that wasn't an answer, and that it was time that I tried to co-ordinate my ideas. 'When I ask you what a person is like you must try and give me some idea of them, some little picture.'

'Well, she's nice,' I said, 'and she lives in Devonshire.'

My mother said that I mustn't get into the habit of thinking that just because people lived in the country they were necessarily dull.

I said no, and that I didn't and that anyhow the Empress Eugénie had lived at Twickenham and that that was practically the country in her day, wasn't it? My mother sighed deeply and left the room.

The next term was the diseases term and Alice bit Matron. She was having measles in the sick-room at the time and Matron was looking after her before the arrival of a nurse from the local hospital. Matron was very angry about it and told Miss Dent, who told a great many other people. Alice, shut up in the sick-room, was unable to tell anyone until later. The school opinion about the incident was divided. There were those who blamed Alice and said she must be mad, those who said she was quite right, but that Matron must have tasted nasty, and those who sought to be reasonable and so talked of delirium.

The hospital nurse proved to be very nice. No one bit her. Matron had of course warned her about Alice. But the nurse didn't seem to take the warning very seriously and she and Alice got on well together. By the time I joined them in the sick-room, Alice appeared to know everything about life in Voluntary and Cottage hospitals, and was thinking of taking up nursing.

'Not, I suppose, that I'd ever be allowed to,' she said. 'But it might be quite fun, though I still think I'd sooner be your mother.'

'But you can't *be* somebody else,' I objected.

Alice said you could be very like them if you did all the same things and would I please tell her some more about my mother.

I did my best, but the conversation was rather like the one I had had with Sonia in the train.

'I don't suppose I'll ever be able to do anything I want, Alice said. 'They'll always be able to stop me, because, you see, I'm frightened of them.'

'But you weren't frightened of Matron or you wouldn't have bitten her.'

'That was different. I was pretending I was a bear. But I think perhaps my temperature must have been rather high, because of course bears don't bite.'

Here the nurse came in with my baked custard and the news that Beryl Lawes had now definitely got measles and would be coming into the sick-room after lunch.

'That won't be much fun for us, will it?' Alice said, and I ate my custard and thought about fear.

After we were through with the measles, the young man with the lapis-lazuli cuff-links, whom Alice had met at my mother's, kept his promise and came down to visit us.

Alice and I had just come in from riding one afternoon, when a red two-seater car drove into the stable-yard. We turned to watch it, and as it stopped Geoffrey Newman jumped out of it and came towards us. He looked very nice and clean with his well-brushed mouse-coloured hair and his highly polished brown shoes which, I was sorry to see, were getting so muddy.

He was followed by another and really beautiful young man, over six feet tall and a natural platinum blond. Geoffrey introduced him as Cassius.

'We've come to take you out,' Geoffrey said. 'But first you must show us your school.'

'Geoffrey,' Cassius said, 'is morbidly interested in girls' schools. Angela Brazil is his favourite author.' And Cassius turned his head away and stared into the distance, looking exquisitely bored.

'We thought,' Geoffrey said, 'that you might like to have dinner in Maidenhead.'

I said that I didn't suppose we should be allowed to go as they weren't relations, and Alice said that four o'clock was rather early for dinner.

Geoffrey said we would say they were our cousins—he would be mine and Cassius could be Alice's. It was an idea and we started to walk up to the house. Cassius spoke very little. Geoffrey asked us if we had midnight feasts; we said we did. He seemed pleased, and wanted to know if there was a madcap of the fourth and whether he could meet her. We explained that it was really a finishing school and that there wasn't a fourth. He asked us if people had crushes on other people and whether the bath water was always hot. We began to feel antagonistic towards him and said that the bath water was always boiling, which wasn't true. We forbore to tell him about Miss Dent and the Prince of Wales, or about poor Molly Hodgson and her overwhelming and public passion for Marie Carrington.

'Perhaps,' Alice suggested when we got to the front door, 'you had better wait out here, while we go in and explain about you to Madame. I'm afraid it seems rather rude, but you know what schools are.'

Geoffrey and Cassius agreed to wait. Alice and I went straight to Madame's sitting-room; we explained, in French, that our cousins who at this moment were outside the front door had come to take us out to dinner. 'A very early dinner,' Alice said. 'Plus comme un high tea, nous serons rentrèes de bonne heure, mème avant lights out peut-être.'

Madame, as usual, was nervous. To gain time perhaps, and to fulfil the exigencies of politeness, she told us to bring our cousins in. Perhaps she thought it would be a change to see two young men after so many girls. The young men were brought in and introduced.

'Ceci,' said Alice, 'est mon cousin Cassius Skeffington, at ceci est le cousin de Margaret, Mr. Geoffrey Newman. sont amis, c'est drôle, n'est ce pas, une coincidence vraiment extraordinaire?'

I thought how well Alice was managing it, and wondered what I would be expected to wear for dinner; as I thought of my clothes they seemed even more horrid than usual. It was with something of relief, therefore, that I heard Madame refusing to let us go. Instead she offered us to give tea to our cousins in the salon. She and Geoffrey wrangled over it; he would not dream of putting the school to so much trouble; she on her side was sure that he must readily understand the rules of the establishment. Dinner at Maidenhead was out of the question. Even if Geoffrey had been our mother she would have hesitated to permit it. Cassius, who hadn't appeared to be listening, suddenly remarked that the rewards of motherhood were indeed few.

We found ourselves conducting our 'cousins' across the hall and into *le petit salon*. Madame said that tea would be brought to us there. In *le petit salon* a constraint fell upon us. Madame had said that we must have a great deal to tell each other. If Cassius and Geoffrey *had* been our cousins that might have been true. As they weren't, and as we hardly knew them, we could have nothing to tell them.

Le petit salon was a little-used room. Looking back on it, I suppose it must have been furnished to give a 'home atmosphere.' Parents visiting their daughters were put to wait in it. They were told that we often sat here in the evenings. We didn't. There were sofas. One has those in a home of course, and there were bowls in which Matron from time to time placed flowers. There were occasional chairs and on the mantelpiece a clock which didn't work. There was a carpet and there were curtains. It may well be that there *are* homes like that.

Cassius took out a cigarette-case.

'Are we allowed to smoke?' We told him 'yes'; he looked round for somewhere to put his used match, there was no ashtray.

Cousins imply aunts. If Cassius had been my cousin I could have said, 'And how is Aunt Maude, Cousin Cassius.' No, it was Geoffrey who was supposed to be *my* cousin, 'And how is Aunt Eileen, Cousin Geoffrey?' We all sat down. Perhaps if Aunt Eileen had existed she would have been my favourite aunt. It would be nice to have a favourite aunt, and another aunt whom everybody hated, and could talk about. ('Isn't it extraordinary, in the spring she goes broody and makes birds' nests? She puts them in trees and robins have been known to lay their eggs in them.' 'That must be very bad for them; it encourages them to be lazy.' 'She doesn't make very many nests so it only encourages a few of them, not enough for it to be a problem.' 'There are so many problems connected with charity, but flannel petticoats are "all right"—but rather old-fashioned—old-fashioned things are never a problem.')

The tea was brought in by Winnie. She was pink-faced and giggling. 'Men are much easier to talk to.' How very untrue, but Alice was managing to talk. I listened, waiting for a pause in the conversation so as to join in. Cassius had unbent. He was pouring out; he was pretending to be Matron. It was strange that never having seen her, his imitation was so good. They were making a great deal of noise. I hoped that people passing across the hall would hear us and be envious. After tea they became quieter. They talked about psycho-analysis. Alice had read a book about it while she was having measles. I had read the beginning of the same book and hadn't understood it. Nobody seemed to think that that was very interesting. I didn't myself.

Geoffrey told us that he had been to a psycho-analyst.

As a patient? We felt awkward and impressed; perhaps he was a lunatic, or perhaps he suffered in some of the same ways as the people in the case histories at the back of the book. We looked at him speculatively but didn't like to ask.

'You are wasting your time going to an analyst.' Cassius said to Geoffrey. 'One's behaviour is quite unimportant; it is the fear with which each one of us lives which is so terrible and so pathetic.'

There it was again, 'fear.' I looked at Cassius. He was standing with his back to the mantelpiece and the clock which didn't work. He didn't look at all frightened. His head was thrown back; he would have done nicely for the model of a statue called 'Valour,' or 'The Young Warrior.' I imagined that the King of the Belgians had looked like that when defying the whole of the German army. The German army must have been frightened, not then perhaps, but at the end of the war when they had been beaten by the English. Children were afraid of the dark and Italian peasants of the eruptions of volcanoes. The Japanese were frightened of earthquakes, or they ought to be, considering they were always being killed by them.

'Of course you can't eradicate fear,' Geoffrey was saying. 'The analyst's problem is to find the best way of dealing with it. To begin with it shouldn't be concealed.'

'I absolutely disagree with you,' Cassius said. 'It should be modestly hidden away with the other emotions.'

'Why?' Alice asked.

'Because if people didn't conceal things we should know how horrid they really were and we would never be able to bear it.'

'But some people may be nice,' I said.

'One can only judge from oneself.' Cassius turned away.

The tea-party was brought to an end by the entrance of Madame, who regretted the lateness of the hour—it was six o'clock—and regretted the impossibility of asking Geoffrey and Cassius to stay to supper.

Alice and I saw them off at the front door. We would have liked to walk down to the stables and watch them get into their car, but Madame said that we had already missed quite enough of 'preparation,' and we weren't even changed yet.

We went upstairs to take off our riding things. Alice was worrying as to who she should say Geoffrey and Cassius were if Madame ever said anything about them to Mrs. Norton.

'The only cousin I've got is still at school, you see, so Mummy would know it couldn't have been him.'

I advised her, if the question was ever raised, to tell Mrs. Norton that Madame was mad, and that anyway they were both *my* cousins. Alice said that she supposed that would have to *do*.

We had left the door of our room open and Beryl Lawes, on the way to her bath, appeared and asked us why we were not talking in French. As head girl she was permitted, even required, to ask such questions. But, considering we had all had measles together, I thought it was rather mean of her. She was wearing a shiny art silk peacock green kimono, with hanging sleeves. We weren't talking French simply because we didn't know enough of it, but this was not a valid excuse, so we said that there had only been a few words of English and left it at that. Beryl sat down on Alice's bed, her kimono parted to show the top of her bright pink cami-knickers, elaborately worked with insertions of false coffee-coloured lace. Beryl made them for herself in *la coupe*, which was apparently the French for sewing lessons. These took place in an attic called *l'atelier*. I found them absolute torture and it wasn't only the sewing. It was being ordered to try on whatever it was one was making. When that happened I was exposed to the whole class in my white cotton round-necked bodice edged with white cotton lace. My desperate suggestions that I should try on a crêpe de Chine petticoat over a jersey and a tweed skirt met with neither understanding nor sympathy. That petticoat, getting grubbier and grubbier, was my task for two terms, and in the end the Mademoiselle, who presided over the class, finished it herself.

Beryl (perhaps, after all, she had remembered the measles) became more friendly, and although we didn't like her we were flattered. She wanted to know all about our visitors; with her we kept up the fiction that they were our cousins. Alice and I went on changing our clothes more and more slowly. We gossiped with Beryl, we told her what Madame had said, what Geoffrey and Cassius had said. In deference to Beryl we placed at least one French word in every sentence. If you did that, custom allowed you to answer, 'Quelques mots,' when your name was called at the little ceremony which took place every evening after supper. If you had spoken English all day you said, 'Quelques phrases'; if you had spoken only French you said, 'Non,' which was a most unusual and a generally unprincipled reply.

Because it was one way of wasting time, and we preferred doing that to going down to 'preparation,' we told Beryl what Geoffrey and Cassius had said about fear.

Beryl said she saw what they meant, but that surely it was only weak characters who gave way to fear.

'Oh, do you think so?' Alice looked thoughtfully at Beryl. Then she turned to me, 'Ne pensez-vous pas que Geoffrey was rather silly when he said that I was afraid of Sonia?'

I said that I hadn't heard him say that.

'But he did,' Alice insisted, 'and I thought it was very silly. Ce n'est pas even as if he knew her—being votre cousin,' she added hastily for Beryl's benefit. 'And as for spoiling my life, that's absolument ridiculous.'

'Well, she did spoil the hunting,' I said.

I didn't say anything about her borrowing the money; it was too painful a memory.

Beryl said that she imagined that Sonia could be very selfish. Beryl, who was now eighteen, had been at Groom Place for one term with Sonia.

'She was a very bad influence when she was here,' she said censoriously.

Alice said that that was better than being a good influence.

Beryl hesitated. It was evident that she thought Alice was 'getting' at her.

'Good people are so terribly dull,' Alice went on, and I am certain that her thoughts were miles away. Probably she was still thinking about Cassius or about Sonia.

'Marie Carrington saw Sonia at a night club during the holidays and she was drunk,' Beryl said.

Alice, in her underclothes, stood quite still. A blush covered her neck and shoulders; her face was scarlet, her right hand holding her hairbrush was suspended half-way to her head.

'I think it's awful for women to drink,' Beryl went on. 'I wouldn't have told you, but I thought somebody in her family ought to know. It ought to be stopped. Doesn't your mother ..."

Alice swung round. The next moment she was attacking Beryl with the hairbrush. She hit her over the head, she hit her arms. Beryl, cowering on the bed, seemed unable to defend herself; she uttered refined little shrieks. Alice had dropped the hairbrush and was using her fists. For a moment I watched them fascinated. I was unable to move. I knew I *ought* to move, I ought to do something. I *must* do something. With an effort Beryl threw Alice off. I caught Alice by the arm and held her. Beryl got off the bed. She clutched her kimono round her. It made her look fatter than ever. She told Alice that she was amazed at her behaviour. She must have been *really* amazed too. She said the whole sentence in English. She said that really she ought to report the whole matter to Madame. I was relieved. 'Really she ought'—that meant she wasn't going to.

I said that I was sure Alice was sorry. Beryl swept out of the room. Alice, with her back to me, picked up the hairbrush and went on brushing her hair. As the door shut she said that she expected Sonia *had* been drunk. She said it looking steadily into the glass.

Beryl didn't go to Madame, but the story of the attack was circulated widely. Those who after the assault on Matron had spoken of delirium now talked of dementia. And as before there were those who applauded. Beryl, they said, was like Matron, and could do with a beating up, but they added that they were quite glad it was me and not them who shared a room with Alice. 'Perhaps she'll go mad in the middle of the night and murder you.'

The next evening I heard Pauline Crane, the reliable girl from Cheltenham, and Marie Carrington discussing the whole thing. I was sitting behind an embossed leather screen, which shut off part of the hall below the stairs. The retreat thus formed had a window and was sometimes used as an extra classroom. I, as usual, was learning an extra collect as a punishment (probably for not learning some other collect).

Pauline and Marie were sitting at the round oak table in the middle of the hall. Between them lay *The Times*, the only newspaper we were allowed to read.

'I should never be a bit surprised if that kid went clean off her rocker,' Pauline was saying. Pauline was one of the older ones. 'Not that Beryl didn't probably ask for it; she's altogether too superior with the kids. Now at *Cheltenham*,' she went on, 'the prefects always . . .' and there followed a long disquisition on the excellence of the Cheltenham prefects.

At the end of it, Marie remarked that Alice was a pretty child.

'Is it true,' Pauline asked, 'that you really did see the sister drunk in London?'

'Yes, but she wasn't all that bad,' Marie said. 'She hadn't passed out or anything. She was just having a hell of a good party. You know how it is.'

Then Marie began talking about a young man who had promised, she said, to take her to a different night club every night of the Easter holidays. I hadn't known there were such a lot of night clubs, and began to calculate how many that would make. It was difficult as I didn't know whether to count in Sundays and Good Friday.

My own Easter holidays were dull. I went to the dentist again, and my grandmother and I spent some time at Scarborough, where she did a cure. We saw Anne Brontë's grave, which was very sad, and of course interesting, but it hardly filled the holidays. I wondered how Marie was getting on, and wished again that I was illegitimate and Italian. My grandmother said that I must try to be a more animated companion, and we went and looked at the Bronte tombstone again.

Alice and I wrote to each other. She said that she was reading Smith's *Wealth of Nations* and that she had had a postcard from Geoffrey and Cassius. She asked me if I knew that Louis XVII had become an American clergyman instead of being guillotined like everybody else.

When we returned to Groom Place for the summer term, we had a new English mistress. Her name was Miss Frost, and she taught us about the stars. Apparently there were even more of them than one had supposed. Just as we got used to the stars the lesson changed to single life cells appearing out of the mud. To illustrate it all, Miss Frost produced a shiny magazine with photographs taken always either through telescopes or microscopes, and although her magazine didn't mention it, Miss Frost assured us that the stars and the life cells both proved the existence of a creator.

That summer was very hot, and we had a great many classes out of doors under the trees. Midnight feasts were held in the garden, and came to include raids on the strawberry beds and strolls on the public highroad which ran beside the school grounds.

One night when Alice and I couldn't sleep we climbed out on to the balcony over the front porch. In the unlikely event of Matron finding us, we had arranged to say that we were studying the stars, as Miss Frost had told us to do. We were well aware that Matron and Miss Frost were on bad terms. To practice a little for the intended deception, I pointed out a planet to Alice and told her it was Venus. She said it wasn't. She then directed my attention to the Plough and the North Star, and I agreed that they were the Plough and the North Star. After the heat of our room the night air was beautifully cool. Enjoying it we fell silent. A silence which I broke by saying how very far away the Milky Way looked, and how small it all made one feel. I regret to say that I thought the remark was original.

Alice said wasn't it extraordinary to think that the whole of the solar system might quite likely be nothing but an atom amid millions of other atoms, which together formed a small ring worn by a giant?

I thought how terrible it would be if the giant lost us. But somehow having all those other solar systems all round us made it feel safer.

'If it's true,' Alice said, 'anything that happened to us personally would be too small to matter.'

'Things *seem* as if they matter,' I said. 'Suppose something *really* awful was to happen, I don't think the universe being so big would make one not mind.'

'But it wouldn't *really* be important.' Alice's face, still raised to the stars, was sad. 'It wouldn't matter about Sonia and it wouldn't matter about us all being afraid of each other.'

'I don't believe it's Sonia you're afraid of,' I said, and as I said it I was surprised. The words seemed no longer to have any meaning.

'What am I afraid of then?'

'I don't know,' I said. 'I thought I knew, just for a minute, but now I've forgotten.'

Alice stood up and stretched her arms above her head. 'It doesn't matter anyhow, because nothing does.'

'But *some* things must matter,' I said desperately. 'One ought to go on being kind and all that, oughtn't one?'

'Are you kind?' Alice asked coldly.

'Well, *trying* to be kind,' I amended and thought guiltily of Miss Dent.

*

The next day Alice ran away from school.

She ran away in the most unspectacular way possible, leaving a letter for Madame. I never saw that letter, but I believe that in it Alice merely said that she was not happy and was returning home.

She timed her departure so that she would not be missed until after she had been gone some hours. Everybody was very cross. My sincere protests that I knew nothing about it were received with furious disbelief. At tea-time Madame retired into her study suffering from nervous prostration. Late that evening a telephone call was received from Devonshire.

Alice had arrived home. Mrs. Norton would let Madame know later what she intended should be done about it.

What Mrs. Norton actually did was to forget that Alice was fifteen and, with the assistance of Nanny, give her a good beating. Alice was then put to bed for three days on a light diet.

During those three days Mrs. Norton found out quite a lot about Groom Place and at the end of them she wrote to Madame saying that she was afraid that the tone of the school was no longer all that it should be and that she was therefore obliged to make other arrangements for her daughter. Would Madame please have Alice's clothes packed and forwarded immediately to Platon?

Alice then spent several terms in being compulsorily domesticated by a school of Domestic Science. She didn't like it, but it was at least better than Groom Place.

She and I then went to a finishing school in Paris. With it we inspected the Castles of the Loire, the battlefields and Chartres cathedral. Alice had been instructed by her mother and I by my grandmother to make friends with our fellow scholars. Conscientiously we did our best. By careful questioning during the holidays, it was usually found that we had managed to make friends with the wrong people. The right people, of course, were those whose parents were going to give dances for them when they came out. We would be redespatched to school with orders to try again. It was all rather discouraging. On the side we managed to learn a little French, and I discovered that I wasn't musical and hated the opera.

During our first term in Paris we had noticed that it was the fashion for the girls to receive letters from young men. As it is disagreeable to be out of the fashion, Alice and I spent our first holidays from France in trying to get to know some young men who would write to us during the term.

It was the summer and there were lawn tennis parties. Alice and I both disliked lawn tennis, but going to these parties was a way of getting to know people.

It was at a lawn tennis party that Alice met David Mason. When we got back to school Alice told me about him. He was a few months older than Alice and he was at Harrow. His family, who appeared to be very rich, had taken a house for the summer at Torhole. (Torhole was a seaside resort a few miles from Platon. It consisted almost entirely of large hotels and expensive villas.)

David, unlike Alice and me, played tennis rather well. He was a nice-looking boy, and probably his grandmother was a Jewess. He and Alice enjoyed discussing books. Mrs. Norton discouraged the friendship from the first. She said that the Masons were 'common.' When Alice protested, she changed 'common' to 'anyhow very ordinary.'

When we went back to school David and Alice started a correspondence. His letters were all about Harrow and his father's factory. Alice's contained descriptions of the Castles of the Loire and the battlefields.

Somehow we got through that disagreeable time when more than ever a girl is neither child nor woman.

FOUR

WHEN ALICE WAS eighteen and I was seventeen and a half we 'came out.' Alice's family took a furnished house in Cadogan Gardens from which Mrs. Norton and Alice were to operate. Our campaign was conducted from Hill Street.

Looking back on it, the whole business was an incredible performance. The basic idea was rational enough. When a girl reached marriageable age, she was introduced by her parents into adult society, where it was hoped she would meet her future husband. There are many examples of such practices in *The Golden Bough*. Only somehow by the nineteen-thirties it had all got rather silly.

It was one day in March when we were having luncheon together in Marshall and Snelgrove's that Alice asked my opinion on the propriety of our going to night clubs.

I told her that I thought night clubs were 'all right' provided they could be 'managed.' Which meant if one could escape from one's mother. In one's first year as a debutante a night club was as exciting as a midnight feast at school. I did *not* tell Alice that I had never been to one, except Ciro's, which didn't count. You never knew; she might be sorry for me. It was not a subject on which pity was welcome.

'Is your mother very strict?' I asked. It was the natural development of the night-club theme.

'She is when she remembers, because of Sonia you know, but she hates late nights, and she gets headaches.'

I didn't like to say, 'How lovely for you,' but I quite saw that Mrs. Norton's headaches must have their advantages.

'Mummy adores late nights,' I said, 'and when it isn't her it's Grandmamma.'

'What are you doing this afternoon?' Alice asked.

I said I wasn't doing anything, and Alice said in that case would I come to Selfridge's and have my photograph taken thirty-six times by a machine.

'What's the point?'

Alice said it could be quite funny, because you could make faces, which you weren't allowed to do at a real photographer's. We broke off to compare how many real photographers had invited us to sittings free of charge.

'Though it isn't really free,' I said, 'because you always have to buy some of the photographs afterwards.'

'And anyhow I'd sooner pay half a crown and make faces,' Alice said.

'But who wants a photograph of you making a face?' I asked, reasonably enough, I thought. 'And how can you think of thirty-six different ones?'

'I pretend to be different people and I make faces to go with them. Anyhow, they're not very big. You can get them all into one photograph frame. If you like one of them especially, you can have it enlarged.'

The waitress interrupted us by presenting the bill, which we halved.

We went to Selfridge's and had our photographs taken, and spent a little time in going up and down in one of the lifts and learning to intone: 'Going up, cutlery, turnery and ladies' corsets, third floor.'

'It's important to get it just right,' Alice whispered to me.

'Important for what?'

'For making conversation to those awful silent young men one's always sitting next to at dinner. You know, the ones who don't hunt, and aren't interested in art.'

I said I knew only too well. But asked what happened if one did the imitation and they still didn't say anything.

'Usually they do,' Alice assured me. 'At the very least they'll tell you about some of the lifts *they've* been in.'

'It doesn't sound very interesting.'

'*Conversation* never is,' Alice said. 'Talking to people is different. But Mummy gave me such awful warnings about what I wasn't to say that quite often I'm struck dumb.'

'Isn't it dreadful?' I said. 'Grandmamma told me to keep smiling as if it was a war or something and my mother said I wasn't to be self-conscious. What shall we do now?' I asked.

'Let's go on talking,' Alice said.

I agreed and suggested that we should go back to Hill Street.

'But I thought your grandmother was having a luncheon-party.'

'She is, but we can dodge them.' We started off, and having agreed to talk were for some time silent.

'I'm going to tea "on guard" at St. James's Palace,' Alice said at last. I asked who with, but I knew perfectly well that it was Martin Yorke. Alice and Martin had met at a Hunt Ball in December, and so had known each other for three months. A long while, as we reckoned time in those days.

He was tall and handsome; he was rich. When he came of age, he would inherit a place in Leicestershire. I had sat next to him once at a dinner-party; it had been unnecessary to do any imitations for him, as he talked about hunting.

We dodged the luncheon-party successfully, and got up to my bedroom. Alice fiddled with the things on my dressing table. She said that she and Martin were going to Sandown Park on Saturday. He had given her the gold cigarette-case she was using.

'How lovely!'

'Yes, isn't it?' Alice said, and added primly that it was 'very kind' of him and that Mummy said that it must have cost a lot of money. I agreed that it probably had. Money meant very little to us. We supposed that all young men were rich and that most of them were lords. Perhaps it would have been a help if somebody had explained to us.

Alice left to have tea at St. James's Palace. I had nothing to do before getting ready for the evening's dinner-party, so I rang up my mother and asked if I might go to tea with her. She said 'Yes,' and I walked round to South Audley Street. When I arrived, my mother was lying on one of the divans and seemed bored. She asked me about a young man who had recently shown signs of attaching himself to me at dances. I said that he was very nice and my mother advised me not to waste too much time on him. I said I wouldn't.

Presently Geoffrey Newman came in. I had only seen him once since he had visited us at school and was surprised that he should still look so young. I had forgotten that it was less than three years ago. He asked after my 'triumphal progress' in the world. I said it was all right, thank you, and wished I wasn't so boring, and he and my mother joined in mocking at the young.

'It seems that your friend Alice is getting on very "nicely,"' Geoffrey said. 'Do you approve of this young Yorke?'

I said that I hardly knew him, but that he seemed very nice. 'That was my impression. Perhaps a thought too attractive, though?'

'Nobody can be too attractive.' I was sure of this.

'It doesn't always make them faithful.'

'Oh?' I saw Alice abandoned and in floods of tears, going into a decline, like a Victorian heroine, "the bright roses fading from her cheeks."

'I've warned her, of course,' Geoffrey continued. 'Yesterday she had tea with me at Gunter's and we *bared* our souls to each other.'

I thought Geoffrey was being presumptuous. Who was he to warn people, and anyhow, how did they bare their souls, and at Gunter's, too?

'Did she show you the rather charming cigarette-case Martin gave her?' Geoffrey asked. 'It's all so delightful at that age.' He turned to my mother. 'Such beautiful presents, and quite innocent, you know.'

'Does anybody give *you* cigarette-cases?' my mother asked me.

I had to confess that they didn't.

'What's happened to Cassius?' I asked Geoffrey. 'I haven't seen him since you brought him down to school that time.'

'He's gone to China.'

'Does he like it?'

'He finds it interesting and he enjoys the opium.'

Captain Parsons was announced. He was the father of one of my fellow debutantes, 'poor Jennifer.' He was better-looking than his daughter and my mother seemed pleased to see him.

It was the morning after my dance. Ellen, having set down the breakfast-tray, lingered at the foot of the bed. She now looked after me and my clothes, in addition to being a housemaid. There had been a small domestic storm over this arrangement, and there had been suggestions of a young maid to train under Miss White, of an extra housemaid to be trained by Ellen. Either way, I gathered, they were to practise on me.

I was glad that neither materialised and I was left in peace with Ellen, although my grandmother remained firm in saying that Ellen could *never* be spared to go away with me. Somehow it was explained to her that young ladies were no longer expected to travel with their maids.

Miss White thought it a pity that my poor grandmother should have to be bothered by having me to live in the house. She was understood to say that my coming out should be my mother's affair, as was the case in other families. 'Poor madam was not strong, nobody *thought,* and everybody expected her to do everything.' At first I was genuinely worried by these remarks and the head-shakings that accompanied them. How terrible if I was to be the cause of my grandmother's death! I thought about it a lot; eventually I decided that as my grandmother was only sixty-three, as strong as a horse and extremely fond of parties, she would probably survive— which she did.

Ellen and I discussed the dance, as we had variously seen it from the ladies' cloakroom and the ballroom.

'Aren't you tired, Ellen?'

But Ellen, as I might have known, didn't 'believe' in being tired, and anyhow it wasn't as if it happened every day, and some of the dresses were really lovely, but not *all,* she added darkly. We became a little gloomy contemplating some of the unlovely dresses of the night before. Ellen rallied and remarked that she thought they'd all enjoyed themselves. I said I hoped so, but that it was difficult to tell if five hundred people had had a pleasant evening.

'Well, most of them must have, to have kept it up so late, though there were a few who spent more time upstairs than they did down.'

'Oh, Ellen, how awful!'

'Poor little things. You couldn't help being sorry for them; they kept coming back and back to powder their noses. I suppose they didn't like to be seen standing about, with nobody dancing with them. I hope that doesn't happen to you in other people's houses?'

She said this jokingly, but all the same she looked at me anxiously. I hastened to assure her that I was usually 'all right.' She went on to tell me of the difficulty she and Miss White had had with the cloakroom tickets. 'You see, there were two lots, one started with six hundred and one, and the other with seven hundred and one, and when we got busy we were using them both, so some of the numbers were the same.'

'How awful!'

'Well, it would have been if one book hadn't been yellow and the other pink. Even so, it was awkward.'

'It must have been.'

'I tell you,' said Ellen reflectively, 'who's turned out better looking than I ever thought she would, and that's Miss Norton.'

'Oh, but she was always lovely.'

'Too boney! Of course she's still thin, but that's what they admire nowadays, isn't it?'

Ellen turned her head to look at her own reflection in the glass. She was certainly not 'boney,' but she had a small waist and neat feet and ankles.

'Was that her mother Miss Norton came with?' she asked.

'Yes,' I said. 'Large. Black dress with pink printed flowers.'

'She's not a bit like her daughter, is she? I'd say she was the domineering type too.'

Miss White came in to say that it was some time since the under-housemaid had swept under my grandmother's bed. Miss White would be glad if Ellen would see to it. If any of the ladies had happened to look there last night Miss White would have been quite ashamed. They wrangled on about it. I tried to decide what kind of a guest it would be who would elect to spend the evening under my grandmother's bed. 'Poor Jennifer' perhaps; she so seldom had any partners, and to judge by her appearance, she had no objection to dust.

'We were discussing the dance,' Ellen was saying placatingly. 'They sent us up a lovely supper, didn't they, Miss White?—with champagne.'

Ellen beamed at me, knowing I would share her pleasure. Miss White pursed her lips, as if to say that champagne never crossed them.

'Fancy, five o'clock this morning, before it was all over, and Miss Margaret's been telling me what a lovely time she had, and her dress was pretty too, wasn't it?'

We both turned to Miss White. Surely she would say something pleasant? But she only remarked that as it was my own party people had to dance with me. She was, of course, perfectly right.

Alice and I were both presented at one of the March courts.

My grandmother had arranged that my presentation should be attended to by Aunt Maude, the wife of Uncle Henry who was her eldest son. Uncle Henry was a member of the Household, and so Aunt Maude had the entree, which meant, briefly, that she was relieved from queueing. It also meant that we had seats in the Throne Room, which was fun, as there was always the chance that someone would fall down. Not that one would wish it for them, but should it happen, it would be nice to see it. Aunt Maude and I got through our curtsies without incident. I noticed Uncle Henry standing at some distance from the throne. He was looking very handsome in lots of gold braid. Seeing him gave me the same sort of impression that might be expected were one to recognise a small angel in a large stained-glass window during a religious service, and, as it would have been with the angel, one forbore to wave. For his part, Uncle Henry did not appear to recognise either his wife or his niece.

Towards the end of what for some time had seemed an endless procession of feathered curtsying women, I saw Alice and Mrs. Norton. In a whisper I drew Aunt Maude's attention to them. Co-operatively she whispered back, 'Very nice—*pretty!*' But as from where we were we had only a back view of the curtsies the remark must have been more a tribute to friendship than an expression of opinion.

*

The Nortons had a house-party that Easter. Colonel Norton was very put out by it, and spent most of the time locked in his sitting-room. If on coming into any of the other rooms he found them occupied, he would heave a deep sigh and go back to his sitting-room. He was a discouraging man to be the guest of.

The party was small, consisting only of Alice, Martin Yorke, Geoffrey Newman and myself. Both Sonia and Anthony were away.

Mrs. Norton proved to be an energetic hostess of young people. That is she was determined that *we* were to be energetic. She sent us to point-to-points, to a local dance and on to the lawn tennis court. If she came upon any of us sitting down she sent us to find the others.

Alice and Martin were obviously having a wonderful time, completely absorbed in each other's company. How beastly it had been of Geoffrey to say that Martin might not be very faithful!

'I suppose,' Geoffrey said, 'people do come to point-to-points to enjoy themselves?' It was Easter Saturday and, shivering with cold, we sat in a hedge beside one of the jumps. It was a bigger jump than some of the others and it had been recommended to us as being the one at which the riders most usually fell off. I don't think that either Geoffrey or I particularly wanted to see anyone hurt themselves, but obediently we sat in the hedge. The casualties so far had been of an unspectacular nature: one or two horses had fallen over and got up again; their riders had done the same. Several horses had decided, wisely one thought, that the jump was altogether too big, and had refused to have anything to do with it.

Before the start of the second race we were joined by Martin and Alice. They had made money on the first race. It seemed they had a big bet on this one. Martin stood with his field-glasses to his eyes. He told us what the horses were doing at the start, and what they were doing as they went out into the country. Personally I was almost too cold to care and I think Geoffrey was too. Alice crouched beside us, looking admiringly at Martin, and he did look very handsome, and so convincing somehow with the coloured vouchers dangling from the case of his glasses, his bowler hat set at a becoming angle on his head. Compared with him, Geoffrey's soft hat and crumpled raincoat looked unutterably dreary. Although he was so elegant in London, Geoffrey never did look right in the country.

'Here they come,' said Martin informatively. As he had not taken his glasses down since the start of the race, I suppose that he was unaware that the horses were now within a few feet of us, blowing in our faces practically, so that even we poor things were able to see them quite fairly plainly.

'Which is ours?' Geoffrey asked me, becoming momentarily less detached from his surroundings.

'The pale blue quartered,' I said.

'It seems to be rather behind the others,' he said regretfully.

'There's another time round yet.'

'Is there?' said Geoffrey. 'How awful for them!'

The leading horse came at the fence. He cleared it beautifully. Judging from the noise Martin was making, this was the horse he had backed.

'They've a long way to go yet.'

Geoffrey sounded suddenly quite professional. There were several more horses and then our blue quartered. It looked rather a sad little horse now that one saw it close-to. Somehow it clambered over the fence, and Geoffrey cheered it. The race went on and on, with the horses going slower and slower, that being one of the differences between a point-to-point and, say, the Grand National, where the horses start slowly and go quicker towards the end.

Even at this distance of time I am glad to think that the race was won by the pale blue quartered, who Martin had said had cheated through getting in front of his horse at one of the more distant jumps.

We scrambled down from the hedge and made our way towards the cars. As unostentatiously as possible Geoffrey and I detached ourselves from the others and slunk off to collect our winnings. We received, with much pleasure, seventeen shillings and sixpence each. On the way back we passed the rider of the winner, now wearing an overcoat over his blue quarterings; he was talking to some grey-haired ladies who we supposed must be his aunts. We skirted the paddock, passed the man who was selling gold watches for almost nothing at all, and stopped to stare at the provincial Houdini who lay writhing upon a rug. We agreed that as there was still a bottle of cherry brandy left in the luncheon basket, we might as well go and help to finish it.

'After all,' Geoffrey said plaintively, 'cherry brandy is *supposed* to keep the cold out.'

We found Martin's grey Bentley. As we came up to it it seemed to be full of people. With a little shock of surprise I recognised Sonia, who sat beside Martin in the front seat. With her fur-lined overcoat flung back over her shoulders, she looked like a *Vogue* illustration of a lady at a point-to-point. 'Never be self-conscious, it puts people off.' My mother had said that. Sonia was obviously completely unpreoccupied with her own perfection, but then Sonia was twenty-four. It would be easy not to be self-conscious at that age. Geoffrey opened the door of the car. Sonia, stopping in the middle of a sentence, drew her coat more closely round her; he had let in a blast of cold air; standing behind him, I could see the glance in which she summed him up. 'No good. Yes, perhaps for some things.' She smiled. Alice introduced them. I smiled too, a welcoming grin on my cold purple face. Sonia, saying something to Geoffrey, did not appear to have seen me. Geoffrey and I levered ourselves into the back of the car, where Alice sat with a man of about thirty-five, whom she introduced as Major Wordsworth and herself addressed as Felix.

There seemed to be very little room, mostly because Major Wordsworth took up so much of it, and Geoffrey wriggled on to the floor and sat on our feet.

'Been having a good day, what?' Major Wordsworth asked.

We said smugly that we hadn't done too badly.

Felix Wordsworth looked rather nice. He had a neat cavalry moustache and nice blue eyes. The skin under his eyes was softer than the rest of his face. He reached over and offered me the bottle of brandy; it was almost empty so I passed it on to Geoffrey. Sonia turned round to say that there must be an awful squash in the back there. It became obvious that she was not going to bother to recognise me. I could see Alice wondering whether she ought to reintroduce us.

'So I suddenly remembered it was one's own point-to-point,' Sonia was saying, 'and I explained to the people I was staying with, and left at the crack of dawn this morning. Of course I was too late to get anywhere near the winning-post, so I left the car outside, and came to look for all of you. I remembered Mummy wrote to me that you were having some sort of party for Easter.'

Alice smiled nervously. Geoffrey asked Sonia if she had left her luggage in the car park too, as if so, it would almost certainly be stolen.

'Not in Devonshire,' Sonia told him. 'Besides, the man in charge is an old friend of mine; I used to know his ferrets.'

'Jolly little things, ferrets,' Martin said. 'I had one when I was a boy that I made a tremendous pet of.'

Major Wordsworth said that he had a tame badger at the moment. Perhaps Martin would like to come over and see it. Perhaps we all would if we hadn't arranged to do anything on Sunday.

The horses passed in front of us on their way to the start of the third race. No one suggested that we should go and look at them. With the coming of Sonia our interest in racing seemed for the time being to have mysteriously vanished. Sonia borrowed Martin's race card, remarked that a horse called Othello was absolutely certain to win the race, and would there be time to get the bet on?

Martin said that there would if one ran.

Sonia said, 'Two pounds each way if the price is right, otherwise a fiver to win.'

Martin jumped out of the car and started towards the bookies. He didn't wait to ask anyone else if they wanted anything.

Major Wordsworth said, 'Othello, what?' and looked knowing.

Geoffrey and I, after consultation, decided not to risk it. We were not the kind of backers to place our bets in a hurry. As it happened Othello was placed second.

Martin was delighted and carried Sonia off to drink whisky with a friend of his, whose car, according to Martin, was 'absolutely crammed with bottles.' I supposed he would have asked

Alice to go with them, only unfortunately at that exact moment she was being persuaded by Felix to go with him and have a drink in his car which was parked farther down the course. He told Geoffrey and me that we had better come along too.

'We haven't got a party for the point-to-point this year,' Felix said to Alice. 'As a matter of fact, my wife's up in London.'

'How very sensible of her,' Geoffrey said.

'Very lucky I ran into you,' said Major Wordsworth, still talking to Alice as he opened the door of his Buick. 'I tried to ring you up this morning to find out if you were coming, but I couldn't get any answer.'

'One often can't,' Alice said, and got into the car.

Martin and Sonia did not rejoin us until after the last race. I caught glimpses of them from time to time, wandering about, talking to friends who had dismounted and other friends who were just about to mount, or sitting in other people's cars and exchanging drinks with them. They seemed to be quite unaffected by the cold.

Geoffrey and I stayed together and Geoffrey continued to 'follow his fancy' and so lost four shillings on each of the next three races. He became cross and said he was never going to leave London again. He had my sympathy and it was getting colder and colder.

'Dr. Johnson felt just as I do,' Geoffrey said as the wind blew his raincoat almost over his head, 'and he was perfectly right.'

'Still, he did go to Scotland.'

'But he didn't enjoy it. And anyhow I think Scotland is warmer than Devonshire.'

I said that was probably because of the Gulf Stream.

Eventually our misery came to an end. We met the others at the car. Felix was still hanging about and I heard Sonia whisper to Alice that she ought to ask him to dinner so that we should be even numbers at the dance we were going to that evening.

'But Mummy . . .' Alice objected in a whisper.

Sonia said, "Nonsense," very loudly and invited Felix to dinner herself. He accepted at once.

Dinner at Platon that evening was more than usually difficult. Mrs. Norton was clearly upset by Sonia's presence, and frankly annoyed by Felix's.

Colonel Norton seemed to be even more deaf than on the previous evening. Sitting on his right side I had a hard time of it, and Sonia on his other side didn't even play fair. In the end she withdrew altogether and talked to Felix. With a feeling of panic I realised I was being left quite alone with Colonel Norton. After much agonised thought, I told him that we had driven twenty miles to the races. He said, 'Oh, no,' it was only fifteen. In a tone of delighted surprise I said, was it *really*, and he didn't answer. After a long pause, he asked me whether I lived in London. He had asked me the same question on Friday night, when I had said, 'Yes,' and it hadn't led us anywhere. So this time I said, 'And in Ireland,' but that didn't help us either. Out of the comer of my eye I looked to see if I might talk to Geoffrey, but no, he was having an animated conversation with Mrs. Norton. Drearily I returned to the attack and asked Colonel Norton how far it was to Exeter, and he said, 'What?' I thought how lovely it would be to be in Exeter. One wouldn't have to talk to Colonel Norton. One could have wandered through the streets and spoken to nobody at all. One could have sat in the cathedral. In church people are not *allowed* to talk. I was recalled by Colonel Norton saying, 'What?' very loudly indeed. I pulled myself together and asked him how far it was to Exeter. I looked across the table at Alice and Martin; their conversation too appeared to be flagging. Perhaps we were all overtired.

After dinner we went to the dance. Mrs. Norton came with us. Colonel Norton, to no one's surprise, remained at home. In the ladies' cloakroom there was a young woman reporter from the local paper. She asked us our names and what we were wearing. We emerged into the ballroom. Mrs. Norton installed herself amongst some palms with other mothers and their middle-aged escorts. Geoffrey asked me to dance. He was being very nice. I told him about the lady reporter, and he said she sounded fascinating, and regretted that there had not been her counterpart in the gentlemen's cloakroom.

I met some young men who I knew in London and they danced with me so I felt a success and enjoyed myself. I was at that happy stage when as long as somebody danced with me I didn't very much mind who it was.

Towards the end of the evening I was sitting in the almost deserted supper-room with Geoffrey. We were watching our blue quartered hero of the afternoon, who was drinking with several cronies. Seen close-to and in a ballroom, he was rather disappointing. I had noticed that he danced badly and that his pink coat didn't fit him properly. Sonia came in with Martin. They paused beside the young man, whom she greeted as Jimmy, and congratulated him on winning his race. Jimmy said that she was a game little mare, wasn't she? But that honestly, the first time round, he hadn't thought they had a chance.

'Oh, *we* did,' Geoffrey said suddenly. 'We always thought you were going to win, and such a charming horse too.'

Jimmy stared at him without saying anything. Sonia laughed. Martin went to fetch her a drink. As she waited for him, I studied her. She wore a closely fitting grey dress, and the sort of diamonds that might well have been left her by a great-aunt. I was struck again by her quality of perfection. She stood completely apart from the provincial background of the callow young men and the girls in green net. But Martin coming towards her, holding two glasses of champagne, was not a background figure either. Nor, I remembered, was Alice. I wondered where Alice was. Probably dancing with Felix.

'You notice what's happening?' Geoffrey jerked his head in the direction of Martin and Sonia.

I thought I knew what he meant, but I hesitated.

'About young Yorke,' Geoffrey went on. 'It seems to me, don't you agree, that he's being very faithless indeed?'

'I don't know,' I said uncomfortably. 'I think perhaps . . . it's . . . just the way things have happened.'

'You know perfectly well,' Geoffrey said crossly. 'He's changed over. He's dropping Alice and taking up with Sonia.'

'Of course he's not.' My own unacknowledged anger against Sonia and Martin, which had been mounting all the evening, rose higher as I listened to Geoffrey. But perhaps it wasn't true; let it not be true. This was just an accident, a set of circumstances which had combined to give a wrong impression. It was Alice who Martin truly loved and when he was twenty-one he was going to marry her. Not that he was nearly good enough to marry Alice.

'Sonia,' Geoffrey was saying, 'is a bitch.' This from Geoffrey who disapproved of vehemence on principle! 'And Martin, I suppose, is any young girl's dream?'

I didn't answer.

'And who's this extraordinary man Alice has picked up?' Geoffrey asked.

'He's a neighbour. I think he's rather nice.'

'Oh, is he?' Geoffrey said. 'You may be right, dear. But I didn't think Mrs. Norton seemed very keen on him.'

'That's because he's married,' I said, 'and doesn't get on with his wife. Alice says that she's very neurotic.'

I saw Alice and Felix coming towards us. Major Wordsworth was holding Alice's elbow in rather a proprietary way, I thought. As they sat down, he said that this had been a perfectly splendid dance, what!

The dance came to an end. Mrs. Norton shepherded us into the two cars in which we had arrived. In arranging who should go in which, she managed to separate everyone from the person they would have most liked to be with. When we arrived home she made us go immediately to our rooms. On the way upstairs I lingered. Would Alice want to talk to me, would anything be said about Martin? As we reached the door of Alice's room I hesitated, but Alice went straight in and shut the door behind her.

The next day was Easter Sunday; it was cold and wet. Having refused Mrs. Norton's invitation to go to church, we wandered round the house in the bleak hope of finding some congenial occupation. Sonia had wisely remained in bed. Without much enthusiasm we started to play billiard fives. Presently Colonel Norton came in and glared at us and we felt compelled to stop. He said that he'd supposed we had gone to church. Geoffrey and I began to wish that we had. I wondered if one might read one's

book, but the atmosphere was wrong for it. Alice and Martin settled down to play backgammon in the drawing-room. Geoffrey
disappeared altogether.

I went upstairs to look for Nanny. I had only seen her for a
brief moment since my arrival and thought perhaps she would
be glad to renew our acquaintance. I found her in the nursery
surrounded by piles of mending.

'Hullo, Nanny.'

Nanny looked up; her glance was scarcely welcoming.
'Well, *you* haven't changed much.' Her tone implied that it
would have been better had I done so.

I smiled, hoping to ingratiate myself with her.

'You're much fatter than Alice.' She considered me. 'But then
you always were.'

I smiled again. This time it was a real effort and I prepared
to leave the room.

'This'—Nanny indicated the mending—'is what I get nowadays.'

'Oh, well,' I said, 'it does mount up, doesn't it?'

'Alice is still hard on her clothes. I thought as she got older
she'd grow out of that, but she hasn't. Now Sonia was always
quite different.'

I tried to strike a brighter note.

'Didn't Sonia look lovely last night?'

'No more than on other nights.' Nanny was uncompromis-
ing. It was as if one had tried to get up a conversation on the
good looks on one *particular* day of the Taj Mahal. Sonia came
in in her nightdress, her dark hair unbrushed. She perched on
the fender.

'Good gracious unto me, child!' Nanny said. 'Haven't you got
a dressing-gown?'

'I suppose so, but I'm not in the mood for it.'

'You know perfectly well you've got one.' Nanny got up.

Sonia lit a cigarette, and turned to me. 'What are they all
doing, being perfectly appalling?'

'They're not doing anything very much.'

'I suppose you started to play billiard fives, and I suppose Daddy stopped you.'

'Well, not exactly.'

Sonia looked out of the window.

'This is a ridiculous house for any of us to try and give a party in. For one thing there aren't enough servants, and it's bloody uncomfortable.'

I started to remonstrate, but obviously Sonia wasn't listening, so I stopped. Nanny came back with the dressing-gown which she helped Sonia into.

'Well,' she said pleasantly, 'and who have you left this time?'

'I don't know what you mean?' Sonia was indifferent.

'Well, you never come back to see us unless you've had a row with somebody, do you, now?'

Sonia smoked on without speaking and Nanny continued.

'Of course I don't blame you not coming down here. There's no life in the place. I don't know why I stay myself now you're all grown up. Sometimes I think I'll leave and take another baby.'

'Nonsense,' Sonia said. 'How could you leave after twenty-four years?'

'Well, it's a good long reference anyhow; not that they want references these days, I suppose. If only you'd get a bigger flat, I'd come and look after you.'

'It's an idea,' Sonia said.

My thoughts went back to the night Alice had cried so at Groom Hall after Sonia had taken away all her money for the term. Was Sonia still trying to live on thirty shillings a week? Somehow I thought not. Probably, the Nortons had long ago restored her allowance and probably too, if she was still working, she had a better job. It was reasonable to suppose that after three years she had worked her way up.

But Sonia didn't look as if she had to work. Could it be that she was being 'kept' by one of the people with whom she had the rows?

I regarded her for a moment with interest and respect. But of course it wasn't true. I was making it up. I was horrified at myself.

I had a lurid imagination, like those dreary girls who always thought that men were in love with them when they weren't.

But Sonia was beastly enough for anything. Look how she had behaved about Martin yesterday! She was a bitch. I no longer cared to be in the same room with her. I got up and went downstairs again.

I started to wander aimlessly about the house. Human nature was horrible, people altogether were horrible. I couldn't be bothered with them. I was disenchanted with the world.

I put on my mackintosh and walked slowly down to the river. The path descended sharply. It was damp and unweeded and overhung by laurels which had run to seed and all this would have been described as a pleasure garden.

I rounded a bend and came suddenly on Geoffrey sitting on a bench which had once been painted green.

'Hullo,' I said, startled.

'Come and sit down,' Geoffrey said, and stared gloomily at the encroaching undergrowth. 'You know, I'm quite worried about Alice. I'm sure I was right last night when I said that Martin was dropping her and taking up with Sonia.'

'But he couldn't do that,' I said. 'It would be so awful.'

Geoffrey turned to me quickly. 'That's what I mean; in this case it *would* be awful. Most girls, I suppose, fall in and out of love dozens of times and it doesn't matter, but Alice takes any kind of disillusionment too . . . well, too seriously.'

'She minds things so much,' I said. 'She minded terribly when she first found out, years ago now, that Sonia wasn't as honourable as she had always thought her.'

'I know,' Geoffrey said. 'Alice does mind things too much and it makes one afraid for her.'

FIVE

WELL, WHEN Easter was over, we all went back to London, and it turned out that Geoffrey had been absolutely right about Martin Yorke, and for the next few weeks he and Sonia were seen together at race meetings and restaurants, and Martin hardly ever appeared at debutante dances.

Obviously, Alice was miserable about it. But she never discussed it with me or, as far as I know, with Geoffrey.

At the beginning of May it happened that Geoffrey and I were sitting together on two small gilt chairs in the hall of a house in Belgrave Square. It was two o'clock in the morning. From the floor above came the sound of the band playing *The Blue Danube*. There were flowers everywhere, in tubs, in hanging baskets and even tied to the banisters.

Alice came down the stairs with a young man. The young man was talking earnestly. Alice smiled at us as she passed, but somehow she did not look happy.

'You know, she still can't bring herself to speak about Martin,' Geoffrey said.

I nodded.

'She comes to tea with me at Gunter's, just as usual, but our conversations are impersonal. Only she told me the other day that she was afraid the world would stop floating.'

'That's Miss White,' I said. 'She's my grandmother's maid. When she used to cross the Atlantic she was always afraid that the liner would stop floating and sink to the bottom. Not because anything had gone wrong with it, you know, but because the rules about what *could* float and what *couldn't* had suddenly altered.'

'How very morbid,' Geoffrey said with a shudder.

'I suppose it is,' I said. 'I used to think it was funny; that's why I told Alice about it.'

'I think it's terrible,' Geoffrey said, 'and after all, what guarantee have we that natural laws will remain for ever unchanged. So many of them seem only to be conventions in any case. Sleep, I think, is the prettiest of the conventions, don't you?'

I said that I supposed so, and couldn't we do anything about Alice being unhappy.

'I shouldn't think so,' Geoffrey said. 'I don't think anything could make her happy except a sense of security. Of all the people we know, Alice seems to me to be the one who most needs to feel herself absolutely secure and safe.'

'I suppose you can feel safe without getting what you want?' I said.

'Fortunately, yes,' Geoffrey said decisively.

And I remembered that Geoffrey, who had wanted to be a composer, now worked in a museum cataloguing books. And I wondered what emotions and conflicts lay under his suave exterior. I was incapable of judging. I saw him only as he chose to present himself.

The season wore on and we moved in our droves from dinner-party to dinner-party, and from dance to dance. Some of us went to the Opera and most of us went to Ascot. We learnt that our allowances could be supplemented by pawning our jewellery. There was the Aldershot Tattoo and the Eton and Harrow match. There were the Commemoration balls at Oxford and Cambridge.

Alice told me that David Mason, the boy to whom she had written letters when we were in Paris, had asked her to go down to Cambridge, where he was now an undergraduate, but that Mrs. Norton had refused to let her go.

'Because the Masons are "Ordinary"?' I asked.

And Alice nodded and we had deplored the snobbishness of our parents.

There was talk of Goodwood and of Cowes and of Scotland. The end was in sight.

Engagements were announced, in good time for autumn weddings. Marriages took place.

The engagement which interested me the most, and which particularly surprised me, was that of my mother to Captain Parsons.

Captain Parsons was the father, it will be remembered, of 'poor Jennifer.' My mother told me about it casually one afternoon when we were sitting alone in the studio. I was stupefied. This wasn't at all the sort of thing I had expected from my mother. 'Darling, you're not pleased?'

I said that I was, very pleased indeed, only rather surprised, and I reflected with distaste that 'poor Jennifer' would now be my sister.

I asked my mother if she was going to have Jennifer to live with her.

'Not for the moment; she is very happy with an aunt in Sussex. I understand they do raffia work together.'

Captain Parsons arrived, and I practised a little calling him Charles. (My mother had said that I must call him Charles.) He was nice. It seemed that as well as living in Regent's Park, he had a house in Devonshire which was quite near to Platon. A fortnight later they were married. The wedding, which took place at Caxton Hall, was rather funny. Charles unexpectedly produced a company of female relations wearing wigs and tartan skirts. There was one who was better-looking than the others and wore a black toque, but she turned out to have been 'poor Jennifer's' governess. A few of my mother's professors turned up and were audibly rude without being funny about the wigs.

When I got home, I went up to the top floor. Ellen would want to know about the wedding. I called her softly; I had not rung in case she should be lying down. She answered me at once, and I went into her room. She was sitting sewing at the table. Ellen's room was so ugly that I could not believe that my grandmother had ever seen it, and yet furniture didn't get into a house by itself. There must have been a time when my grandmother had gone into a shop and chosen that terrible chest of drawers, and the pitch-pine washstand with the inset water-lily tiles, and the black hanging cupboard and the iron bedstead. Had she said to the salesman, 'That's *exactly* what I've been looking for for my housemaid's bedroom'? I would have liked to ask Ellen if she minded her room being so hideous. Probably she did, but had long ago decided to ignore it. Probably she didn't see it any more. For her sake I hoped that was the case. She had certainly added nothing to it in the way of photographs or small ornaments such as abounded in Miss White's room.

'Well,' Ellen asked, 'and did you enjoy yourself at the wedding?'
I said that I hadn't been expecting to exactly.

'Well, it wouldn't be the same as if it had been in a church of course, but I expect it was very nice. What was she wearing?'

'Grey.'

'That's right,' Ellen approved. 'They usually do for second weddings. Do you think there'll be pictures in the papers?'

'There were a lot of photographers when we came out.'

'Then I expect it will be all right.' Ellen liked us to have our photographs in the papers.

'You know,' she went on, 'it's better than if she had married one of those Counts or Marcheses we used to hear such a lot about. I don't hold with people getting married to foreigners.'

'Don't you?' I asked. 'Why on earth not?'

'They're not always very nice,' Ellen looked mysterious, 'And besides, how can you ever be sure that there won't be a war against them? A cousin of my sister-in-law's married a German (he'd lived over here for years, and it's a long time ago now of course), but then the war came, and it was ever so awkward for her, and just as much so for her little boy, and not very nice for my sister-in-law.'

'Well, Captain Parsons is English,' I said, 'so we won't have to worry about that.'

'That's what I mean,' Ellen said. 'And from all that Miss White's been able to hear, he's very well off. They're cotton people. I suppose you know that.'

'He's very nice,' I said irrelevantly.

'That's a good thing then,' Ellen said comfortably. 'And it's nice to have one wedding to finish up with. Not that it's *our* wedding exactly.' She paused for reflection, and then asked what had been happening to Alice.

'Happening? Why, nothing.'

'Oh!' Ellen was unconvinced. 'It seems to me I heard that *she* was thinking of getting married a little while ago, but that it's all off again.'

Did Ellen really know about Martin, I wondered. It didn't seem very likely, but then Ellen and Miss White had a terrifying way of getting to know things.

'I thought her looks had gone off, when you brought her upstairs the other day,' Ellen said. 'She hadn't got that same bright smile, and I said to myself that probably something had happened. Not that she isn't probably well out of it. Mr. Yorke wasn't the right one for *her,* I shouldn't have said.'

'Ellen!' I said accusingly. 'You've been gossiping.'

'That I certainly haven't, it's not a thing that I do,' Ellen defended herself, 'but you can't help people telling you things, can you?'

I said I supposed one couldn't, and she said that she'd been over to Cadogan Gardens. They had a housemaid living with them who was a friend of hers, and as it happened, they'd had tea upstairs with Nanny.

'I don't think Nanny ought to have talked to you about all that.'

'Neither do I,' Ellen agreed frankly. 'But then of course, she's all for the other one, isn't she, Miss Norton's sister.'

'Yes, I suppose she is.'

'And that's another thing I don't hold with,' Ellen said, 'making a lot of one at the expense of the other, and being so unkind about it. Now if *I'd* brought that child up, I'd be sorry to have her looking the way she does.'

'I don't think she's changed as much as all that.' I felt that I owed it to Alice to go on insisting that she hadn't changed. All the same Ellen was right up to a point. Alice had changed.

Eventually the season came to an end, and my grandmother and I went to Ireland, and 'poor Jennifer,' one supposes, went to her aunt in Sussex, and Alice went back to Platon.

My mother and Charles, after only a few weeks abroad, went down to Devonshire. I had asked my mother if there was a lot to be done to the house, Tor Cross, and she had said, oh no, it was in *terribly* good taste throughout and absolutely filled with art treasures.

'But do you like it?' I had asked.

My mother said that anyhow there were a lot of bathrooms.

'You must come and see it very soon, darling. I'd have invited you this August, but if you came there would be no good
reason for not having poor Jennifer, would there?'

So I went to Ireland, which was where my grandmother had
her other house. It was in County Cork, a large square white
house, built at the beginning of the nineteenth century.

Owing to the war, and the recurring troubles, I had spent little
of my childhood in Ireland, and it had remained for me a land of
mystery and imagination, where Scottish housekeepers held off,
single-handed, hordes of marauding Irish, where grooms always
lived to be a hundred years old and leprechaun's shoes were very
nearly a commonplace. Moreover, Ireland wasn't joined to England, and hens lived in the same rooms as their owners. It was
very nearly abroad, and I was glad to be there.

Then one morning I read in *The Times* that Alice had been
married quietly in London to Cassius. I was very surprised because that wasn't the way we got married, and for another thing
Geoffrey had said that Cassius was in China. I went to find Ellen,
who as a great treat had been allowed to come over to Ireland
with us. A strange caretaker had been left in Hill Street, which
was rather a worry to my grandmother, as she was afraid the
London burglars would find out about it not being Ellen there,
and then there would be a burglary.

'Hmm,' Ellen said when she had read the notice. 'Quietly—
that means a coat and skirt, not very *nice* for a young girl.'

'I can't understand it,' I said. 'She never wrote to me, and
there hasn't been an engagement, and we were always going to
be each other's bridesmaids.'

'And who's this Mr. Skeffington?' Ellen went on. 'It's not a
name that *I* know.'

'Oh, he's all right,' I said, 'except that he's supposed to
be in China. He came down to see us at school. Mr. Newman
brought him.'

'Well,' Ellen said, 'if it was some people, one would know
what *that* sort of a sudden wedding meant.'

'You mean,' I asked, 'that they *had* to?' It was nice being worldly-wise with Ellen. She nodded portentously.

'But Alice isn't *like* that,' I said. 'I'm absolutely sure that *that* isn't the reason.'

'So am I,' Ellen agreed. 'I only said what one would think with *some* people. All the same it *is* funny, and I must say, she might have written you a note or something, seeing how long you've known each other, and what friends you were. A postcard would have been better than nothing.'

'Perhaps she'll send me a postcard when she's on her honeymoon,' I said hopefully. For no reason at all I imagined it would be in sepia and of the Giants' Causeway.

'As she's under age,' Ellen said, 'she can't have married without the permission of her parents. But what surprises me is them permitting it like that.'

'It does me too,' I said.

'Did you say Mr. Skeffington lived in China?'

'Well, he did,' I said, 'but he seems to have come back from it.'

'Perhaps he's just on a short holiday, and that's why they had to be married so quickly.'

'But I shouldn't think he'd be taking Alice to live there.' Ellen asked why not, but I didn't think I ought to tell her that—anyhow, according to Geoffrey—Cassius, when in China, had 'gone native,' and that surely one didn't take one's wife to a country which one had gone native in? It would, I felt, be lacking in feeling.

A week later Alice rang me up.

'You're wanted on the telephone Miss—a Mrs. Skeffington.'

My grandmother and I were in the garden. It was one of those 'soft' Irish days, when one feels one *ought* to sit in the garden, because this is as good as the weather is going to get. We wore overcoats, and my grandmother had a rug over her knees.

'Mrs. Skeffington?' Then I remembered: 'Alice.' I jumped up and ran into the house. Alice was telephoning from Dublin. Would my grandmother like her and Cassius to come and stay tomorrow, only for a night or two?

'No,' I said, 'I'm afraid she wouldn't. She likes visits to be arranged a long time beforehand, but I'll see what I can do.'

'Oh, do!' Alice said urgently. 'I want to see you, I want you to meet Cassius. Do you remember him? Were you surprised when you saw about our wedding? I can't tell you how happy I am.'

I said I was so glad and that I did remember Cassius. I said I longed to see them both. I asked where they were staying in Dublin. It was the Shelbourne, of course. I promised I would start persuading my grandmother right away, and would let Alice know as soon as possible.

I hung up the receiver. Persuading my grandmother turned out not to be so difficult as I had feared, for there were no other guests in the house and Uncle Henry and Aunt Maude were due to arrive the following day. My grandmother had a nervous fear of being left alone with them. They would advise her to lie down after luncheon and Uncle Henry would warn her not to smoke so much. Smoking, according to Uncle Henry, was injurious to the health at *any* age. It was the *any* which must have been so irritating. So my grandmother thought it would be nice to have the young Skeffingtons for 'just a night or two.' She took the precaution of looking over the Skeffingtons in *Who's Who* and found a Judge, who was quite probably Cassius' father. She agreed to their being invited. 'Though it's a pity they should come such a long way for such a short visit. If he's nice, we might ask them to stay on. They'll do to amuse Henry and Maude.'

The next evening Alice and Cassius arrived. He was just as exquisite as ever. My grandmother asked him at once about the Judge, and it was all right.

Uncle Henry said he believed he had once seen the Judge at a levee and asked Cassius if he too was at the Bar.

'No,' said Cassius. 'No, I do nothing at all.'

'Nothing?' Uncle Henry, who had done nothing during the whole of his life, sounded shocked.

'Nothing,' Cassius repeated. He implied that it was enough that he should exist.

'Cassius has just come back from China,' Alice said quickly, and Uncle Henry said, 'Ah,' which brought the conversation to an end.

As we went upstairs to change, my grandmother drew me aside. 'You must find out why they got married so quickly,' she said, and I loved her for her curiosity.

After dinner she and Cassius played chess. Aunt Maude worked at her *gros-point*. Alice and I were told to walk on the terrace, from which the view across the estuary would, my grandmother said, be beautiful at this hour. When Uncle Henry showed signs of accompanying us, she reminded him that he was tired from his journey.

It was almost dark. Alice and I walked quickly up and down the terrace. We wore coats over our evening dresses. At first Alice made no attempt at conversation. 'I suppose you want to know all about it?' she asked presently.

'Not unless you want to tell me,' I said. 'I think Cassius is most terribly good-looking.'

'He's not bad,' Alice said, and there was adoration in her voice. 'They let me marry him like that, because he saved me from drowning myself.'

I stood still, horrified. Then:

'What were you drowning yourself *in*?' I asked carefully. I had an idea that suicide and violence generally should be treated in as matter-of-fact a way as possible. I imagined myself as a nurse in stiff white cuffs.

'In the sea,' Alice answered. 'It seemed the best place.'

'Bigger,' I agreed. 'And Cassius stopped you?'

'He said he came all the way from China especially for that.'

'Oh!' I said. 'How lucky he found you; I mean, you might so easily have missed each other.' I was getting confused.

'Geoffrey and he were staying down at Torhole, in a pub, and they rang me up at Platon, and Nanny answered the telephone, and told them that I had gone over there that afternoon to bathe. So they went down to the beach to look for me, although it was quite late by then. Well, they didn't find me, but Cassius said that as they were on the beach, he thought he would go for a swim anyway, and he swam straight out to sea, and then he found me and I was drowning.'

'What was Geoffrey doing?'

'Sitting on Cassius' clothes.'

'But Alice, were you really . . . you know, what you said?'

'Committing suicide? I suppose so. I had some stones round my neck in a string shopping-bag. I'd walked out with them as far as I could, and then put the thing round my neck, just as I began to be out of my depth. But I think I must have changed my mind, because I was trying to get it off, so probably even if Cassius hadn't turned up nothing would have happened, and I would have got rid of the stones, and nobody would have known anything about it, and I should have caught the last bus back to Platon. But it was *awful*.'

We had resumed our walk, and she turned towards me. 'I had already been down twice, or perhaps oftener; one can't tell, you know, and I couldn't get the beastly thing off my neck, and it was quite quite horrible.'

'But why?' I asked, and stopped myself. I *knew* why.

'It wasn't really Sonia's fault,' Alice said. 'If she hadn't collected him someone else would have.' She looked out across the estuary and one felt as she spoke of Martin that she thought of an infinitely remote past.

'Go on,' I said, 'about you and Cassius.'

'Well,' Alice said, 'he helped me back to the beach, and I was being horrible, and coughing up all that revolting sea water, and we got to where Geoffrey was sitting on Cassius' clothes. He was wearing a panama hat and looking rather sweet.'

'Wasn't he surprised to see you?'

'No, I thought that was so charming of him, and I told him I had been committing suicide, and that Cassius had stopped me.'

'And he still wasn't surprised?'

'No, he just said, "How beastly for you," and offered me a cigarette.'

'What happened then?'

'Well, Cassius put on his clothes, and we went to find mine, and they looked so pathetic lying there with a stone on top of them, and I thought how sad it would have been if I'd really got drowned and never seen them again. And I wondered why I'd been so careful and made sure that they wouldn't be blown away, when I thought I shouldn't be needing them again. So I dressed, and we walked up to Geoffrey and Cassius' pub to have a drink, and while we were having it, Cassius said to Geoffrey, "I think I'd better marry Alice, don't you?" and Geoffrey said that he thought it would be an excellent idea, so Cassius asked me if I would.'

'Oh, Alice, what did you say then?'

'I said I thought that would be very nice if Cassius was sure that he wanted to. But that I was afraid that what had just happened showed that I wasn't a very reliable sort of person, and Cassius said that was all right, because he wasn't reliable either.

'Geoffrey said that Cassius would have to ask my parents' permission, and Cassius said what a nuisance, and should we get in the car and go and get it over?'

'And you did?'

'No, we had dinner first, and then we all went back to Platon together, and Cassius asked Daddy, and then of course there was a row. Daddy wanted to know how long we had known each other, and it only came to four hours, counting that time when Cassius came down to school. So that was awkward, and then there was all the sordid business of what did Cassius *do*, and how much money had he got, and how much he could put into a marriage settlement, and it went on and on, and I cried. Then Geoffrey lost his temper and said that if Mummy and Daddy went on like that they'd have me committing suicide again, and how would they feel then? So naturally there was another row, especially as Daddy had been saying from the beginning that he couldn't think *why* Geoffrey was there at all. But it did the trick, and Daddy agreed to our being married a week later by special licence. And just as that was settled Cassius said that he couldn't *possibly* be married in a church, feeling as he does about Confucius, you know. Daddy said that no daughter of his was going to be married by Confucius, and what was Cassius anyhow, a Chinaman? But in the end, it was all right, and we went to a Registry Office, and Daddy was quite pleased, because he'd found out by then that it's the bride's family who pays for all the expensive part of a church wedding.'

'Still, you must have missed getting all the presents you would have had if there had been a proper wedding.'

Alice said that it didn't matter, because soon they were going to buy a yacht and sail round the world, so most of the things that got given as wedding presents would not be of much use to them. 'What could you possibly do with all those lamps and things on a yacht?'

'Still, there are other things which might have been useful, ash-trays for instance?'

'Cassius says we can buy jade ones as soon as we get to China.'

'Is Cassius rich?' I asked. I was thinking that jade ash-trays and yachts sounded expensive.

'Medium,' Alice said. 'His mother's dead and his father always talks about "Cassius, of course, having all his mother's money." Cassius says that he lives on his wits. Really he's got about fifteen hundred a year.'

'And will that be enough for a yacht?'

'Oh, heaps,' Alice said, 'as long as we don't have a house as well.'

I said that it sounded lovely and asked which way round the world they would be going.

'Clockwise.'

It was by now quite dark and we went into the house. Only my grandmother and Cassius were left in the library. They were completely absorbed in their game and scarcely looked up as we came in. We crept to a sofa and talked in whispers.

'Is Cassius good at chess?'

'I expect he is,' Alice said.

And I thought how wonderful it would be to have such a handsome young husband about whom one still had so much to learn. Fancy, Alice didn't really know whether he was good at chess or not.

*

Alice and Cassius spent that winter in a furnished flat in the Adelphi. It belonged to a friend of Cassius'. My grandmother and I were also in London, but as I was much occupied with getting secretly engaged to a young man called John Richardson I did not see as much of Alice as I might otherwise have done. I therefore went on believing that her marriage was an unqualified success, which it wasn't.

Cassius in the home was more than difficult. He never got up in the mornings and would lie in bed smoking cigarettes. Sometimes he wouldn't even get up for luncheon, and his friends, such as Geoffrey, began to form the habit of dropping in to see him about twelve o'clock. Cassius, dressed in silk pyjamas and a Chinese dressing-gown, would entertain them with drinks and conversation. Like Louis Quatorze he held a levee, only the trouble with Cassius' levee was that he didn't get up. He remained, after the manner of Madame Récamier, lying down.

Even so, it might have been all right if Alice had allowed for it, and arranged a domestic economy which should include a recumbent Cassius. She didn't. Her domestic arrangements aimed at being as orthodox as possible and there was a housekeeper called Gertrude. Gertrude belonged to Cassius' friends, who had only let him have the flat on condition that Gertrude remained to see that he and Alice did the least possible amount of harm to the furniture. Cassius told her that she was the serpent in his Eden and Gertrude, who was used to 'gentlemen,' rather liked him.

Alice attempted to cajole and placate her, with disastrous results. If Alice had said, 'Mr. Skeffington never gets up in the mornings, Gertrude, so the bed must be made in the afternoon, and do the bathroom whenever you like, because he's bound to have a bath just after you've finished in any case,' all might have been well. But Alice didn't. She would pretend to Gertrude that *this* morning was an exception, so Gertrude would be shooed from the bedroom to the bathroom, and then back again into the kitchen, so that in her own words, 'she didn't know where she was.' It was very annoying for her, one saw that; her annoyance made her ill-tempered, and this temper she vented on Alice. Alice, who had been taught by Nanny to have an un-healthy fear of servants, would try and make Cassius conform to the rules of living which Gertrude would have set for him. She nagged him to get up when he didn't want to. She tried to make him return to the flat in time for dinner when they had said they were going to be in. Cassius preferred to ring up Gertrude about half an hour after the meal was due to start and say that he had decided to dine elsewhere, and would she please put out a lot of glasses, because he would be bringing some friends in later. Alice would go into the kitchen and apologise to Gertrude, who was usually rude to her.

In Gertrude's opinion, a married gentleman was a gentle-man spoilt, and she told Alice as much. Alice made various at-tempts to come to terms with Gertrude.

'I'm sure, Margaret,' Alice said to me once, 'she has a most interesting personality, if only one could get to know it, but she does grumble so, and when she isn't grumbling, she doesn't talk at all, in a very marked way.'

'What are her interests?' I asked.

'Spiritualism, but it's no good trying to discuss *that* with her, because it's too sacred.'

'Did she say that?'

'Yes, apparently if she talked to me about it, it would simply spoil the whole thing.'

'I think that was very rude.'

'So do I,' Alice agreed. 'I must try and find some other inter-est for us to have in common, besides the bathroom floor, which doesn't at *all* draw us together. And then it's so awful knowing all the time that we can't get rid of her, but she can sack *us* any time she feels like it, just by writing to Cassius' friends and tell-ing them we're not being good for the flat.'

When Alice told Cassius about all the awkwardness there was being with Gertrude he only said that she had always got on perfectly well with Paul and Maurice, and allowed them to be as late or early for meals as they liked. It must be Alice who was upsetting her, as women always did, and no wonder they had such difficulty in getting servants, and anyhow, he didn't want to hear about it, as he found it very squalid indeed.

I was surprised at Cassius saying that when Alice told me about it. Personally I never found anything about the servants squalid, but always most interesting. Besides, one learnt so much more about people when one was disagreeing with them, and compared with us the servants had unbelievably exciting lives. Their world was boundless, while ours was contained within such narrow limits. I once knew a French girl of good family who said to me, 'Imagine to yourself, I now know every young man in Paris whom it is "possible" for me to marry,' and as it was, I think, true, it was sad for her. Well, in London, it wasn't as bad as that, but we were fairly narrow all the same.

But the servants! *Anything* might happen to them. They might go in a train to Woolwich and meet the love of their lives, or be murdered almost for the asking. Not that one *wanted* to be murdered exactly, but there was frustration in being denied the possibility. Ellen had met a murderer; he had lived next door to her cousins in South London. Ellen said that his eyes were really terrible, and her cousins, especially Winnie, had never liked the look of him, not from the very first, and then afterwards he had murdered that little girl, which just showed how right Ellen's cousins had been. *There* was the spice of life for you, and Ellen's cousins had only moved to the house two months before it had happened, while I had lived in Hill Street for years and years, and never a murderer had I seen. Then another thing, the servants could give notice and a month later they would be living in a different house surrounded with quite different people, and the love of their lives lurking round the corner perhaps, or beside the bandstand on a summer evening. Didn't Cassius care for such things?

But then Cassius, I thought with a shock, didn't really *like* people. He had said once that if they were seen without their defences they would be horrid. 'Love and desire and hate.' One felt Cassius was against them. He would prefer jade ash-trays and one could appreciate the preference. But could Alice, who had pursued 'real life' so eagerly through the medium of the psychology books? Alice could have enjoyed a murder in a third-class railway carriage. For Cassius, there could be no pleasure in anything that fell short of stilettos or hemlock drunk from exquisitely chased cups.

It was around November that Alice asked me and John Richardson, the young man to whom I was engaged, to dine with her and Cassius in a restaurant. We were led to a table. It wasn't a very good one as it was right on the edge of the floor. Cassius started to protest, then shrugged his shoulders, and told the manager it didn't matter. 'All the tables here are horrible, anyway; it's a horrible place.' He turned to me for confirmation of his statements.

I smiled brightly, and said, oh no, I thought it was lovely. As a guest I believed I ought to praise any restaurant to which I was brought.

'You say that, because you think you ought to,' Cassius said. 'It would be more subtle to agree with me, you know.'

'I have quite enough to worry about, without being subtle as well as everything else.'

'What a very wise remark! We all bother far too much with things that are of no importance.'

I looked at him to see whether he was laughing at me, but he appeared to be perfectly serious.

'What *is* important?' I asked. I really wanted to know. I believed that Cassius, if only he *would*, could quite easily tell me. If only I could have that question answered once and for all, everything else would be 'all right.' I looked forward to a long and interesting revelation.

'The important things,' Cassius said, 'are the things that give you pleasure.' He turned to take the menu the waiter was offering him.

The evening was only a partial success. The dancers, hemmed in on the copper floor, bumped continually into our table. At one point an American steered his girl against Cassius' lighted cigarette. Unfairly, the American became very angry. He said that the British were well known to have burnt Joan of Arc. It was evidently still a habit with them to go around burning any ladies they saw. The girl looked apologetic and steered him away.

John Richardson and I danced exhaustively. The restaurant began to fill up with people who had been to the theatre. I saw Sonia come in with a tall distinguished-looking man. Cassius knew him and said he was a member of the German diplomatic corps. He looked rather old, and I wondered whether he had fought against us during the war. That was a long time ago when we had all been quite little. It didn't matter being a German now, when we all thought internationally. We were citizens, not only of England, but of the world. The aeroplane had made a great difference. I had never been in an aeroplane, but it made a difference just the same. I felt broad-minded, and intensely international.

I watched an old man wearing glasses hobbling round the floor with a platinum blonde. I had often seen them together before. She was wearing orchids. It must be awful having to spend your evenings dancing with a man who could only hobble. I looked proudly at John, who was quite young and danced beautifully. Alice suggested we should go on to a night club and Cassius agreed, but without any enthusiasm. He seemed bored. How could he be bored when he was married to Alice? Perhaps he wished he could save her from drowning again. It must have been more exciting doing that than going to night clubs with her, and living in the Adelphi. Had there been that one moment when he had been forced to concentrate on her, and that over, had he come to regard her with the same lack of interest that he did the rest of the world? He got annoyed with her when she disturbed his comfort, and he could be petty over small things. It was all very sad, and their marriage, instead of being the union of a god and a goddess, was deteriorating into a bicker.

I felt depressed. Life was too difficult. I wished that I could go home and find my nurse waiting to put me to bed and to give me a glass of milk and a biscuit. Why had they sent her away when I was only eleven? Other people kept their nurses for *years*. I wished I could go into a Convent and be a nun. In a Convent you wouldn't have to think, or if you did, it would only be about God, and nothing awful would be happening to him. You wouldn't have to worry about him, as you did about your friends.

For Alice's marriage was not a success, and again I was frightened for Alice.

Six

THE NEXT THING that happened was that I had a row with my mother. It was in March, and I was staying with her at Tor Cross. We sat in the long drawing-room, which was filled with Captain Parsons' art treasures, and with eighteenth-century wine coolers containing flowering shrubs. My mother sat at her William and Mary writing-table, and I sat on the floor in front of the fire. Captain Parsons was out riding, and poor Jennifer, I expect, was in Sussex.

It had seemed a good moment to tell my mother that I was going to marry John Richardson. In picturing the scene beforehand, I had planned for her to be delighted. She would, as it were, receive me into the ranks of honest and godly matrons, of whom I was so soon to become a follower. She would be tender and a little sentimental. It would all be very beautiful. But it wasn't like that; my mother merely looked up abstractedly, said, 'Don't interrupt me now, darling, I'm busy,' and went on writing her letters. A little disconcerted, I waited until she should have finished. Then I told her again that I was going to be married. My mother said, 'You must be mad,' and started another letter.

'But if I'm going to be married, I've got to tell you,' I said.

'You aren't going to be married.' My mother had risen to her feet. 'You aren't twenty-one, he hasn't got any money, your allowance will be stopped, and you needn't think you can go crawling to your grandmother; *she* won't give you anything. I've talked to her about all this, and she's as disgusted as I am. I don't want to hear another thing about it.'

'I have got three hundred pounds,' I said. 'I shall learn to be a typist.'

'My God! Haven't you any sense at all?'

Afterwards it was rather awkward. Captain Parsons and I had luncheon alone together, and he said it was a pity I'd upset my mother like that, and I said, yes, and he said he hoped I wouldn't do it again, and that she was upstairs lying down. Then we didn't either of us say anything.

I didn't see my mother again until the evening, when her manner was cold, and I fancied she was treating me as if I was some kind of a mental patient. I tried to treat *her* as if *she* were one. As I said, it was all very awkward. The next day she told me that it wouldn't be convenient to spare the car to take me to the station on Monday, as had been arranged. So she thought it would be best if I left on Saturday, which was the following day. I had understood that I was to stay with her for another ten days, but didn't see that there was any point in mentioning it. My mother said that she hoped I had come to my senses and I said I was going to learn to be a typist. She said that if I was determined to wreck my life she supposed she couldn't stop me, but that learning to type would at least be better than marrying a garage hand. I said that I was going to do both, and that anyway he wasn't a garage hand. He was in an oil company. My mother said that I was not to be insolent.

'Charles has been most disgusted by your behaviour. I'm afraid that he won't want you to come here again.'

I said, 'Why don't you have Jennifer here, and lose your temper with her?'

My mother was furious, and I wished I hadn't said it.

When I got back to London I told my grandmother what had happened. She said that Hermione had always been violent. She said that girls could be very difficult. I gathered that on the whole she was displeased with me. I asked her if she would really stop my allowance if I married John, and she said yes. I told her I was going to pay to have myself taught to type and she said it would be nice for me to have an occupation. But why didn't I learn to cook instead? A lot of girls were learning to do that nowadays, and it seemed sensible. When she had been a young girl in America, she had been taught to cook, and she had never regretted it. Somehow it was more depressing than the scene with my mother had been.

I went round to see Alice and found her in a wild state of excitement. She and Cassius were going to Brazil almost immediately. Cassius, she said, had been offered a job there.

'I didn't know Cassius needed a job.'

'He doesn't particularly,' Alice said, 'if one's only thinking about the money. But he says it will be good for his morale.'

I felt sympathetically towards Cassius. Was it not mainly for my morale that I was going to learn to type?

'I think,' Alice said, 'that Cassius would have got a job as soon as he came down from Cambridge, only he got irritated by his father always talking about his future career and wanting him to go to the Bar. So he decided that he wouldn't work at all and went to China.'

Again my sympathies were with Cassius.

'But now,' Alice went on, 'he really *does* want to work. And it's all been so frightfully lucky, because he met this man in his club, who offered him this job, and it's all arranged. I can't tell you how glad I am, because Cassius is so much happier already.'

I asked what the job was.

Alice said that Cassius was going to represent a firm of motor-car engineers, of which his friend was the chairman. 'It means selling cars on commission really. But if he does well they'll bring him back to London and give him something really good.'

I said that my mother would call selling cars becoming a garage hand. Alice said that she didn't see that that would matter, and I asked her if they would go to Brazil in a yacht.

'No, in a liner.'

So Alice and Cassius went to Rio de Janeiro and I went to the Polygon Secretarial College in Baker Street. It wasn't a very expensive school, but then I only had three hundred pounds and I didn't want to spend all of it. I had interviewed other schools, which offered complete courses at something over a hundred pounds and guaranteed that I would get a job at the end of my training, and that meanwhile my fellow scholars would be gentlewomen.

These schools were large and some of them were clean. The Polygon Secretarial College was quite small and absolutely filthy. It was their prices that appealed to me, 'Three months' tuition in typing, seven guineas,' 'Three months' tuition in shorthand, eight guineas,' and book-keeping and business training were three guineas each. That sort of thing. It sounded very reasonable.

The Principal, Miss Hartley-Jones, said that she would be *very* pleased to have me as a pupil, and that she was sure I would be very happy with them. She mentioned that of course all her pupils were gentlewomen. I was beginning to wonder where really common people learned to type. Maybe they just picked it up for themselves.

Miss Hartley-Jones was a brisk, bustling woman in her forties. She reminded me a little of Miss Dent. Anyhow she too had a fiancé who lived mostly abroad. When I got to know her better she told me about him, and about the other fiancé she'd had who had been killed in the war. In return I told her about John Richardson. She was sympathetic and asked about his job and even suggested that one day he might start in business on his own and then I could attend to the secretarial side of it and do the accounts. I agreed that that would be very nice.

I started at the school after Easter, going there every day from Hill Street. Most mornings I arrived late and most mornings I took a taxi. By the end of the summer I had learnt very little. It was discouraging, but I thought perhaps I would get on better in the winter, when I wasn't going to parties every evening. Then my grandmother announced that we weren't going to *be* in London that winter—we were going to spend it in Ireland. So there we were back where we started. She said I couldn't stay alone in Hill Street with Ellen, because it wouldn't be suitable. It was all aggravating. Practically I decided to give up the typing and the idea of making my own living. Then I remembered my mother.

'What could you ever do? You're not even educated.'

In the end my grandmother gave in. I could continue at the school, provided some respectable people could be found with whom I might live. So I found Beryl Lawes, who had been head girl at Groom Place. She was now a pupil at the Polygon Secretarial College and she lived with her mother in Hampstead. My grandmother agreed to my staying with them for the winter, but she feared they were 'ordinary.'

'But it's kind of them,' I said. 'They don't *have* to have paying guests. They're very rich.'

My grandmother and Mrs. Lawes wrote to each other. My grandmother decided that Mrs. Lawes, although 'ordinary,' was respectable. She warned me against becoming too intimate with them and said that I mustn't introduce them to any of my friends.

So in September I arrived at the Lawes' Gothic mansion, which stood in its own grounds, overlooking Hampstead Heath.

When I arrived, Mrs. Lawes and Beryl were having tea in the lounge. There seemed to be a lot of tea, and rather more than the usual amount of silver. At least two cake-tidies stood conveniently near the tea-table. Under the cakes were paper doilies, rather pretty, and there were embroidered muslin table-napkins, which were rather pretty too. Mrs. Lawes hoped I had had a pleasant crossing from Ireland and went on to tell me about some very unpleasant crossings she had experienced, but stewardesses, apparently, were always so kind to Mrs. Lawes, Mrs. Lawes didn't know why. Beryl, too, had some channel-crossing experiences to relate. Mrs. Lawes, I had noticed, called her 'Girlie.' I was glad I didn't have to do that. Mrs. Lawes said she hoped I was going to feel I was one of the family. She smiled at me kindly, and I had an excellent view of her pearly false teeth. They contrived to look most terribly expensive. Beryl offered to show me my room, and together we left the lounge, crossed the extremely Gothic hall and went up the carved oak stairs. It was all smelling of Ronuk. Beryl took me into 'the spare room.' It looked every bit as expensive as Mrs. Lawes' teeth. The walls were yellow. The panels of the door were picked out in green, and a green frieze, representing some kind of leaves, ran round the room. On the yellow bed-spread was a round cushion, covered in rucked green satin.

'What a lovely room,' I said.

Beryl said that her mother always called it her 'primrose room.' 'Mother's devoted to flowers. In her own room she's got all the delphinium colourings.'

I said I'd like to see that and Beryl promised that one day I should.

The house was called 'Number Two Hundred and Seven Willow Road.' In spite of standing in its own grounds it had a number instead of a name. Life, lived there, once one got used to it, was pleasant. There were rules, of course, but what house is without them? And in spite of what my grandmother had said, the Laweses appeared to have no particular wish to meet my friends. They had plenty of their own. These friends came a good deal to play bridge with Mrs. Lawes, and on our return from the Polygon Secretarial School in the late afternoons, Beryl and I would find perhaps three or four tables set up, the lounge full of cigarette smoke, and the tea-table and the cake-tidies crowded up into one corner.

Staying with the Laweses and having Beryl to work with in the evenings, I was getting on better with my shorthand. To keep my interest going, I used to pretend that I was learning to write Arabic, but I think that was a mistake. Whoever heard of Arabs writing fast, and the point of shorthand is speed. I on the contrary used to write it very slowly, taking immense pains with the outlines, and making them as small as possible. The result, I think, was rather pretty. If Miss Hartley-Jones or any of the other teachers tried to hurry me, I got flustered, and forgot the outlines altogether.

I was getting quite a lot of letters from Alice. She seemed to like Rio de Janeiro and wanted to know all about Willow Road. I described everything for her, as she seemed so interested, and began to feel as if I myself was a traveller in a foreign land, and in a way I was. Fizzy lemonade in the claret, and a pink and chromium sun parlour loosely tacked on to the side of the house, in which to have breakfast. Had Alice had any experience more exotic than that?

In November Alice wrote that she was going to have a baby, and I wrote back conventionally and said how pleased I was, and did they hope it would be a boy or a girl? I didn't ask what they would call it, as I thought that that might sound as if I was asking for it, should 'it' later be 'her,' to be named after me. The next letter I had from Alice was written from a hospital, and she said that she wasn't going to have a baby after all.

'I was rather disappointed [she wrote], having got so far, but Cassius doesn't seem to mind a bit, he never was terribly for it as a matter of fact, and lately he had been saying things like "of course a yacht won't be much fun with a child screaming all over it," and "it's all very well for people who've got palaces to bring them up in, but if a baby was to cry in *this* house, I should *hear* it." So perhaps it's all for the best.'

She seemed to be enjoying the hospital, and I remembered how happy she had been having measles in the sanatorium at school. I told Mrs. Lawes about it, for Mrs. Lawes, as well as being devoted to flowers and bridge, was quite fairly devoted to births and miscarriages. She said that it was very sad for Alice, and that it must have been the heat. In Mrs. Lawes' experience it was always best to keep expectant mothers as cool as possible, though of course it was different for natives. Natives, however hot they were, always managed to give birth to dozens of children. That was the trouble with them really. Mrs. Lawes was rather an authority on natives, as her father had been in the Indian Civil Service. The late Mr. Lawes, however, had been something very important in the City, and had been an alderman, and if only he had lived a little longer he would have been Lord Mayor of London.

'That would have been fun,' I said. But Mrs. Lawes only shook her head and said that it would have been a great responsibility as well as a great expense.

'But a terrific honour,' I insisted. Mrs. Lawes had really been very kind to me, and I was determined to be agreeable about Lord Mayors. I only wished I knew more about them.

*

About this time the Laweses decided to give a small dance, or, as Beryl called it, 'a hop.' Music was to be provided by a gramophone in the lounge, and there was to be a stand-up supper in the hall. Mrs. Lawes' friends were to play bridge in the dining-room.

'You must ask your young man,' Mrs. Lawes said.

'I haven't got a young man,' I said.

Mrs. Lawes looked rather surprised, and as I didn't want to embarrass her, I went on hastily:

'We've just broken it off. There seem to be such an awful lot of things that we don't agree about, but I haven't told my mother yet, she'd think it was because of the money.'

Mrs. Lawes was extremely tactful. She said that too young marriages were a mistake, that there was plenty of time, and that it was better to be sure than sorry. Basely I wondered whether Beryl being unmarried had anything to do with her opinions. I was horrified at myself. I was becoming sour. Beryl was a very pretty girl (well, fairly pretty anyhow); she could quite easily be married if she wanted to be.

The night of the hop arrived. Two hired waiters had come to supplement the Lawes maids. The lounge looked bare and unlike itself. Its rugs had been removed, most of its furniture had been huddled into the little smoking-room.

The guests had been invited for nine o'clock. At seven Mrs. Lawes, Beryl and I went out to have a meal in one of the terrible local restaurants. It seemed that 'cook' was too busy preparing the stand-up supper to have time to provide us with anything to eat. Mrs. Lawes and Beryl bickered together. Mrs. Lawes admitted that a party always made her 'nervy' and upset her digestion; she was in any case 'inclined' to dyspepsia.

Beryl was merely cross and kept on saying that she couldn't see what anyone was fussing about. They were only having a few friends in to dance to the gramophone, weren't they? What was there in that to make anyone feel 'nervy.' The way Mother was going on, anyone might think they were giving a Hunt Ball or something. As best I could I agreed with both of them, and between mouthfuls of Hampstead spaghetti I remembered to call

Beryl's mother 'Mrs. Lawes' as often as possible, Beryl having previously told me that she objected to being addressed as 'you.'

We went back to Willow Road and changed. Mrs. Lawes into red lace, and Beryl, who was a big girl, into a pink taffeta sheath. I had a plain black evening dress, which Mrs. Lawes said was a pity. There would, she assured me lugubriously, be plenty of opportunities for me to wear black when I was older. I thought she was probably right, although as I wasn't engaged any more, widowhood was further off than it *had* been, but you never knew.

The guests began to arrive, red-faced men in dinner jackets, and women dressed in either red lace or pink taffeta. The older people went at once to their bridge, the younger stood about in all-male or all-female groups, and seemed shy of each other. I wondered why; they were mostly people who knew each other quite well, and came often to the house. Mrs. Lawes started the gramophone, and nobody danced. Then she put on a record and announced that we would have a Paul Jones, which, she said, would warm us up. Self-consciously we formed our two circles, joined hands and walked round the room. Mrs. Lawes stopped the record. There was a pause while she put on a dance tune and we all eyed our future partners with speculative horror. My first one was small and fat and hearty; he looked as if by rights he belonged to the bridge-room. Boisterously he jogged round to the music; his conversation was absolutely non-stop. One knew that had one been only a few years younger he would have offered, or rather insisted, on playing bears with one. The dance music stopped and the dreary rigmarole of the Paul Jones was repeated. Mrs. Lawes kept on at it for at least half an hour. Then, evidently deciding that we were now warmed up, she left one of the young men in charge of the gramophone and went to the dining-room. Thankfully we all flopped down on to the few chairs which had remained in the lounge—others of us went and sat on the stairs. I found myself with a medium-sized young man, with nice hands and nice eyes. I noticed that it was curious, the way one always thought of the Lawes friends as coming in sizes, as if they were pairs of gloves or something, and not people at all. The medium young man smiled at me. He asked if he might get me an ice. I said he might, and he got two strawberry ones and we sat on the stairs to eat them. His conversation consisted of a good deal of questions.

Did I live in Hampstead? Had I known Beryl for long? And was I sure I preferred strawberry ices to vanilla? When I thought it was my turn, I asked him about my fat partner, and he said he was an awfully decent chap, name of Green, he was in the fruit business. I said was he really? And the young man said it was very interesting. And I said, yes, it did sound most awfully interesting. My new friend—I was beginning to think of him as a friend—said yes, it was, as a matter of fact, and he wouldn't mind having a job like that himself, only the trouble was, his family had always been in engineering and his father would break his heart if he went into anything else. His heart wasn't any too good either. All the same, engineering wasn't too bad. 'It must be very interesting,' I said. It occurred to me that 'interesting' was becoming my only adjective. The young man said that he was going out to South America almost immediately on a business trip.

'A business trip?' I said reverently. It was an expression I had not previously met outside of American magazine stories.

'As a matter of fact,' the young man went on, 'it's rather a big thing, the sort the old man usually handles himself.'

I couldn't think of anything to say to this, so I asked if he would be going to Rio, and he said, yes, and that it was the most beautiful harbour in the world, except for Sydney, only he hadn't seen Sydney, and I said that that was what some friends of mine had said, and they hadn't seen Sydney either. We smiled encouragingly at each other, then one of the Lawes maids came and said I was wanted on the telephone. I got up and went into the smoking-room, squeezed and pushed past the lounge furniture, and picked up the receiver. 'Hullo!' said a voice from the other end of the wire, 'this is Sonia.'

'Sonia!' I echoed, trying my best to sound pleased as well as surprised.

'Can you come round at once?'

'Well, not really,' I said, 'I'm rather busy.'

'But this is *terribly* important. You *must* help me, we're absolutely desperate, and why are you living in Hampstead anyhow? I've had a terrible time finding you.'

I started to explain why I was living in Hampstead, but Sonia cut me short.

'Never mind about that. The point is I'm in St. John's Wood. If you get a taxi, you can be here in a few minutes.'

'But I don't think I can,' I said apologetically. 'We're having a dance, as a matter of fact. Can't you tell me what it is on the telephone?'

'I can't, it would take too long, and to do any good, you've got to *be* here. I've told you, I'm absolutely desperate, but if you don't want to help, you better say so. Surely you can leave your blasted dance for half an hour?'

I hesitated. There wasn't any reason why I should help Sonia. The few times I had met her she had not been particularly nice to me, but I didn't feel up to telling her *that*. I hesitated, and I was lost. I put down the receiver. I must go upstairs and fetch a coat. On the way I had to pass my new friend. He got up and held out a plate with an ice on it. 'I fetched this while I was waiting.'

'I can't,' I said reluctantly, 'I've got to go out.'

'Good Lord, why?'

'I don't know,' I said miserably.

'Then you can't be in such a frantic hurry.' He pushed the plate of ice-cream into my hand. 'Anyhow, you can eat this.'

Again he asked *why* I had to go out, and I told him about Sonia. He was puzzled, but said that if I had promised to go, he supposed I must.

'I've got my car outside. I'll take you.'

I protested that I could easily get a taxi and that I didn't want to bother him and spoil the party for him. He told me not to be silly, and said that there was probably a pub where he could get a drink while he was waiting. I was glad he said that about the drink. It showed that he was coming with me, at least partly, for his own sake. The drinks at the Laweses were not terribly good, and one suspected that the cup had been made with claret powder. I went on upstairs, and when I came down he was standing waiting for me at the hall door. He was wearing a tweed overcoat. Mrs. Lawes looked at me enquiringly. I told her that I had got to go and see a friend who was ill, and she looked as if she did not fully believe me. Immediately I felt guilty.

The young man's car, parked some way up the street, was a large red two-seater. I got into it, wondering whom he usually had for a passenger. A typist with a University degree perhaps, or one of those fierce good-looking girls who was always the captain of a local lawn tennis club or hockey team. It would be interesting to know, but I couldn't very well ask him, so instead I asked what his name was. It was David Mason.

'You aren't Alice's friend that she used to write to when she was at school?'

He was and I was enchanted by the coincidence. I should have liked to have gone on discussing it. But we had arrived at the address which Sonia had given me. Reluctantly I got out of the car. For a moment I stood and looked at the house. It was rather a nice house, only two storeys high, quite tiny, but detached, and there was a window on each side of the front door.

David started the engine again. 'I'll be back in half an hour, anyway,' he called. 'I know an awfully decent pub just around the corner.'

'I wish I could ask you in,' I said awkwardly.

'That's all right.' He was cheerful. I again told him not to trouble about fetching me, as I could 'easily get a taxi,' and he told me not to be silly and drove off.

I went up the path to the front door, which was thrown open by Sonia, who was wearing a white evening dress with a very full skirt. She was accompanied by a little yapping poodle, whose full name, apparently, was 'Horrid Tessie.' Horrid Tessie rushed at my ankles and tried to bite them. This, Sonia told me, was very clever of her. I couldn't see why; if she had been *really* clever, it should surely have occurred to her that as Sonia was talking to me, calling me 'darling' and even kissing me, I was really more likely to be a friend than a lady burglar. But maybe Horrid Tessie had been brought up to treat her friends the way she was treating me. She looked quite capable of having some even nastier ways of going on, which she kept up her sleeve especially for burglars. As Sonia drew me into the house I aimed an unostentatious kick at Horrid Tessie, who, although barely touched, let out a howl of pain and displeasure. Sonia turned on me at once.

'Oh, you pig, you've hurt my darling girl. Horrid Tessie, come to Mother then. Sweetie pie, did the nasty lady kick you?'

'She walked into me,' I said, not absolutely truthfully, and saw, with relief, that Sweetie pie had gone to Mother. Sonia picked her up and asked her anxiously where she was hurt. We went into the room on the right of the front door. It was a very beautiful room with a window at each end and a yellow flock paper on the walls. A low bookcase ran almost the entire length of the room, and before this, the floor about him strewn with books, knelt a man wearing a dinner jacket. He was stuffing the books into the shelves, and as we came in he spoke to Sonia. His voice was pleasant, but he sounded distressed.

'I can't remember where the damn things went.'

'Put them in anyhow and risk it,' Sonia said lightly. 'Paddy, this is Margaret who's come to help us.'

Paddy O'Brien rose from his knees.

'It's most awfully good of you,' he said, with every appearance of gratitude and immense relief. Now that he was standing up, I could see that he was very tall, he had a long face, beautifully set eyes, a long, rather crooked nose, a small silky moustache, and appeared to be about thirty. Sonia had gone over to an inlaid satinwood table which stood in one of the windows. 'Whisky do for you?' she asked me.

'I'd rather have gin, if it isn't a bother,' I said, looking first to make sure that there was some.

'Oh, there's plenty of *gin*,' Sonia said, and immediately poured me out half a tumblerful, spilling some on the table, an accident which had apparently occurred many times before. 'Do you want anything with it?'

There didn't seem to be anything but soda water, so I asked for that.

'Could I have rather a lot, I'm terribly thirsty.'

There wasn't room in the glass for a very great deal, but Sonia filled it up for me.

'You've drowned it, but of course if you don't mind.'

Paddy shook his head and returned to the books.

'I can't think why you wanted to move them,' he said to Sonia. 'They were perfectly all right in the bookcase.'

'But I've been here for months and months. I had to read *something*.'

Paddy sighed.

'And there's a lot of other things to be done; it doesn't look a bit *right* upstairs yet. Hadn't you better sort of get on? Your friend does know what to *do*, doesn't she? I must say, it's most awfully good of you.'

He smiled radiantly at me.

'She doesn't know about it yet. I'll explain to her, while I'm dealing with upstairs. As a matter of fact, you might be able to help me with *that*.'

Sonia turned to me.

'Bring your drink, though,' she added kindly.

Horrid Tessie and I followed her out of the room and up the stairs. The wallpaper here had gold stripes on a white ground, and the stair carpet was plum-coloured. I noticed that Sonia too was carrying a drink. It seemed to be rather darker than most whiskies-and-sodas. She led me into a bedroom in the front of the house. It had blue walls, the curtains were of pale grey silk, and the pelmets were draped over long brass arrows slung above the windows. The bed-spread of the extremely low double bed was of the same grey silk, and this was a mistake, as it was evident, from the large blackish smudge in the middle of the bed, that Horrid Tessie spent at least part of her time there. She jumped up on it now. There was a ragged bit of carpet near the door, certainly eaten by Tessie. The room was in extreme disorder. Clothes as well as books lay everywhere. Brushes, combs, and jars and bottles of make-up lay on the floor in front of the dressing-table.

'God!' Sonia said drearily. 'I don't know how I'm going to get it all cleared up in time, and there's such a hell of a lot of it.'

She sank on the bed beside Horrid Tessie. It seemed that the task of tidying up was going to be too much for her. I stood by the windows uncertain of what to do. I felt that some explanation was due to me, and wondered if I should have to ask for it. Sonia was tickling Horrid Tessie's feet and telling her how clever she was.

'I suppose,' Sonia said, looking at me, 'this all seems a bit crazy to you?'

'Oh, no,' I said politely, and thought again how beautiful Sonia was.

'Well, it *is* crazy,' Sonia said viciously. 'All this pretending, and you having to be Alice. It's Paddy's idea, as if his wife would believe any of it for a moment!'

I sat down on the floor, among the jars and bottles.

'Tell me,' I said.

But Sonia jumped off the bed and started cramming clothes and things into suitcases while she told me.

'Well, the beginning's pretty obvious. I've been living here ever since the autumn with Paddy. His wife was in Switzerland, and *nothing* could have been nicer, and we've been *perfectly* happy. Well, now some dreary busybody has told his wife that I'm here, and she's come back to *see* about it. So bad for her when she's supposed to be ill. She rang Paddy up just now from the Grosvenor Hotel. He didn't even know she was in England.'

'Oh,' I said. 'Was she cross?'

Sonia looked at me pityingly.

'She was simply furious, and Paddy sort of lost his head, and told her that I was only here to keep house for him, the servants having left, which they *did* actually. And Paddy told his wife that it was quite all right, because my sister and her husband were staying here too, and that her suspicions were *most* unfair. She had only to come round here to see for herself.'

'And is she coming?'

'Yes, apparently, silly fool. Only she's having something to eat with her mother first. Which gives us time to get the rooms shifted round a bit. And you *do* understand that you're Alice, don't you, darling? And that I'll never be able to be sufficiently grateful to you, not that I think it's going to do an awful lot of good, but it will please Paddy.'

She looked round the room.

'I think we'd better say that you and Cassius slept in here. That would account for it looking rather as if it had been used. Gracious! I suppose we must make the bed for her. As it's her own house she may expect to stay. Though I do think it was thoughtless of her not to have let us know this morning, by telegram or something. Then Mrs. Mathews could have done it. Mrs. Mathews is absolute heaven; she used to come in in the mornings, when they had a servant, but she comes practically all day now, and she says I'm *much* nicer than Estelle.'

Sonia went out of the room to get some sheets, and when she came back we turned Tessie off the bed and started to make it. The blankets were blue, with grey smudges. . . . Tessie again.

'If I'm Alice,' I said, 'where's Cassius?'

'Oh, he can be out,' Sonia said, 'tramping the streets looking for lodgings for you probably. *That* ought to make Estelle feel ashamed.'

'You don't think I could be out too?' I said hopefully. 'Because honestly, Sonia, I think it's going to be rather difficult.' But Sonia's mood had changed. As we came out on to the landing she said that it would all be *quite* easy so long as I kept my head and didn't say anything silly.

'If Estelle *should* ask, only I think it would be rather indelicate if she did, you can say I slept in the spare room. It's here.'

And she opened the door of the room next to Estelle's. I looked in. Obviously it was far too tidy and clean to have been occupied for a single night by Sonia and Tessie. 'And Paddy was in his dressing-room of course; that's at the back.'

'I won't be able to stay long,' I said, 'because I really ought to be getting back to the dance.'

'Oh, that doesn't matter. As soon as she's arrived you can say that you've got to go and meet Cassius at wherever he might have got rooms. The Ritz, if you like, and then just thank her for having had you to stay and go away. I say, won't Mrs. Mathews be surprised when she arrives in the morning?'

'At finding Estelle as well as you?'

'Oh, *that!*' Sonia started downstairs. 'I think I shall tell Paddy to ring up and get me a room at Claridge's or somewhere. Of course I've never met Estelle, but I've got a sort of feeling she'd be selfish over the bathroom.'

We had nearly reached the bottom of the stairs when the front door opened and a fair, rather beautiful young woman came into the hall. She was followed by an older woman dressed in black and with a riot of blue curls. Sonia stopped on the last step, and I stood just above her. The two women also paused. Insanely I wondered if we were going to start throwing things at each other, and was glad that Sonia and I had the advantage of extra height. Then Sonia went forward. At the same moment there was a terrific barking behind us; Horrid Tessie was rushing downstairs eager for fresh ankles to bite. As she passed me, I caught her up in my arms. It was the bravest thing I ever did. Magnificently, Sonia didn't even look round.

'Hullo,' she said. 'You're Estelle.'

'And you,' said Estelle, 'are Sonia Norton?'

She didn't look as if she were going to believe even this without some fairly definite proof.

'Haven't you got any luggage?' Sonia asked with interest; then she half turned towards me. 'This is my sister, Alice Skeffington.'

No one took any notice of this. Paddy came to the door of the sitting-room with a very silly smile on his face and said: 'Hullo, Estelle, it's nice to see you back.'

The lady with the blue hair said, 'Disgraceful!' and she and Estelle moved towards the sitting-room. Paddy fell back before them, and Sonia and I, with Tessie, followed them into the room.

'I expect you'll want a drink after your journey.' Paddy was obviously horribly nervous. His smile put me in mind of the Union Jack in a print called 'The Last Hope.' He turned to the older woman. 'It's nice having Estelle back, isn't it, Mrs. Sterne? You've met my friends, Sonia Norton, and her sister, Alice Skeffington.' He looked at his mother-in-law as if defying her to make a scene in front of us. Having us thus brought to her notice, the lines of Mrs. Sterne's mouth became even harder, if that were possible, and she gave us an almost imperceptible bow. Her eyes travelled round the room. It was obvious that she saw nothing but the displaced books, the marks on the furniture and the stains on the carpet. Paddy poured out two stiff whiskies-and-soda and offered them to his wife and Mrs. Sterne. They both refused, so he gave one of the glasses to Sonia, and after I had refused the other kept it for himself. We all sat down.

'This,' Mrs. Sterne announced, 'won't do.'

'I can't think *what* you mean.' Paddy finished his drink and poured himself out another. He turned to Estelle. 'I can't *tell* you how kind Sonia and her sister have been, looking after me while you've been away. Kindness itself. . .

'That's all very well,' Mrs. Sterne interrupted him. 'But why did you keep it a secret if it was all right; why didn't you tell Estelle in your letters that you had these people staying in her house?'

Paddy shifted uneasily.

'I didn't want to worry her. I mean, I know how terribly particular she is about the carpets and everything, and she might have thought that the dog wasn't doing them any good. Well, I mean dogs don't, do they? And then they sit on sofas, and sometimes they get rather dirty. Not that it was Tessie's fault.' He looked anxiously at Sonia. 'I mean, dogs are bound to get muddy feet, especially in the winter, but'—he turned again to Mrs. Sterne—'the great thing was, I didn't want Estelle to be worried. The doctor said particularly that she wasn't to be worried, didn't he?'

'And don't you think it worried her,' Mrs. Sterne said grimly, 'when she heard from our cousin Eileen that you had a strange woman living in the house?'

'Really!' Sonia got up, and went across to get a drink. 'This is intolerable.'

'But she isn't a strange woman, I know her quite well.' Paddy leant across to his mother-in-law. 'And dear little Alice too.' He smiled at me. 'I know them both very well indeed.'

Mrs. Sterne's displeased glance rested on me.

'You are Mrs. Skeffington?'

I said I was, and remembered with alarm that I wasn't wearing a wedding ring.

'I understood you had a husband?'

'Oh, I *have*.' I was enthusiastic. 'He's out now.' I looked at Sonia for support. 'I mean, he's gone round to the Ritz to see about getting us rooms.'

Sonia spoke rudely. 'It's been extremely inconvenient for my sister and her husband. They've had less than an hour to get their things packed and make other arrangements.'

Estelle turned to me. 'But surely you'll stay here tonight?'

'Oh, no, thank you,' I said urgently. 'My husband has already made "the other arrangements." In fact, I think he's probably waiting for me now. He hates being kept waiting.' I got up, hoping that now I might go.

'They can't possibly stay if *you're* going to,' Sonia said to Estelle. 'They've been using your room. I mean they had to, where *else* was there for them?'

'Using Estelle's room?' Mrs. Sterne was outraged.

'Well, they've moved,' Sonia said. 'I don't know what all the fuss is about.'

'I can tell you.' Mrs. Sterne was ominous. Standing by the door watching them, I was apprehensive. It didn't look as if Paddy and Sonia were going to get away with anything. Paddy had taken my vacant place next to Estelle. Anxiously he asked her if the journey really hadn't tired her. Had the doctor thought that she was strong enough to travel? I had the impression that he was really fond of his wife, and I was sorry for him.

'What I can't get over,' Mrs. Sterne was saying, 'is Rose's disloyalty, leaving like that, without a word to her employer.' She turned on Paddy. 'Did you pay Rose before she left?'

'Oh, yes, and gave her the most beautiful reference. Personally, I think it would have been much *more* disloyal if she'd written to Estelle and worried her behind my back.'

'Oh, to hell with all this,' Sonia shouted. 'Isn't Paddy allowed to do *anything* without Estelle's permission? Does she expect to choose his friends for him when she's away for months and months?'

'We shouldn't object to "friends,"' Mrs. Sterne said. 'But we know perfectly well you've been living here with him alone. There was no sign of your sister or her husband when my cousin Miss Jacob called here last week.'

'Miss Jacob!' Sonia said. 'Was that that terrible little woman who looked as if she'd come to sell boot-laces? Naturally I shouldn't have *dreamed* of introducing her to my sister.'

'Don't be insolent,' Mrs. Sterne shouted. 'You come and live in my daughter's house, you make an absolute pig-sty of it, and then you dare to talk to me like that. If you don't leave immediately, and take your dogs and your relations with you, I shall call the police.'

'Please, Mrs. Sterne, *don't*. It's all a mistake.' Paddy was practically wailing, but no notice was taken of him.

'Oh, I'm leaving all right.' Sonia poured herself out some more whisky and drank it at one gulp. 'If Estelle's really got T.B., it probably wouldn't be *safe* to stay.'

Paddy moaned and buried his face in his hands. Sonia looked defiantly round the room. 'That's the trouble with you blasted rich. Just because you've bought the wretched man, you think you can keep him shut up in a little box for the rest of his life.'

Paddy rocked himself to and fro. Clearly he had ceased to believe in anything that was said. Estelle sat with a smile of conscious superiority playing over her face. Mrs. Sterne turned furiously on her son-in-law and at that moment the doorbell rang.

'I expect that's Cassius.' Sonia sounded quite gay again.

'It *can't* be,' I said, and added hastily that he'd 'still got the key of the front door, hadn't he?'

For a moment no one moved, and then Sonia went quickly out of the room, shutting the door behind her. Mrs. Sterne got up and closely examined the table on which the drinks stood. 'How people can treat *good* furniture like this I don't know. This table is absolutely ruined.'

'Mother,' Estelle said, 'I think you were right. I think I'd better spend the night at your flat.'

'I think so too,' Mrs. Sterne said. 'But I don't intend that *these* people should stay here.' She glared at me as the representative of the offenders. I smiled amiably at her; after all, this whole scene was no affair of mine. Paddy, who now, in his misery, seemed mercifully able to ignore Mrs. Sterne, turned to Estelle.

'Darling, I wish you wouldn't take it like this. I've *explained* everything, you know, and I'm sorry about the furniture.' His voice trailed off.

The door opened and Sonia came in, followed, to my intense surprise by David Mason, whom she introduced as Cassius. David smiled sheepishly, and his eyes travelled round the room, until they rested on Mrs. Sterne.

'Good evening, David,' Mrs. Sterne said, and there was a horrid triumph in her voice. I sank down on the arm of the sofa and realised that I had become involved in the nightmare. But Mrs. Sterne was still talking, and I listened to her with growing horror. As well as knowing David, she also knew Cassius; at any rate she had heard of him. Her husband was the head of the firm which Cassius was representing in Rio de Janeiro. Not very successfully it seemed.

'Are you Mr. Skeffington's wife or *not*?' She spoke directly to me. Speechlessly I shook my head.

'But he is married to that person's sister?' I nodded and she went on. Sonia, Mrs. Sterne said, was not only a liar and a gold-digger, but an obvious dipsomaniac, with no idea of civilised behaviour. Alice was probably the same. Mr. Sterne's firm objected to such people as the wives of their representatives. Cassius' lack of success must be due to Alice. Mrs. Sterne was sorry for Cassius. She felt certain that Mr. Sterne would be obliged to dismiss him. All Mrs. Sterne's fury was concentrated now on Sonia, who leant against the door and regarded her with complete indifference.

As the terrible torrent of words swept everything away I glanced at Paddy, and over and over again I repeated to myself, 'I had a little nut tree and nothing would it bear, But a silver nutmeg and a golden pear.'

SEVEN

WHEN ALICE AND CASSIUS had lived in the Adelphi, in the flat belonging to Cassius' friends, Paul and Maurice, there had been a picture in the sitting-room and the title of the picture was 'The Deserted Garden.'

Alice had often said that it was one of the few pictures that she had ever really liked and I suppose somebody must have repeated the remark to Paul.

The result was that Paul, who had painted the picture, gave it to Alice.

Nothing is happening in the picture, but much has already happened and in it there is the promise, or the threat, of the future.

The plaster peels from the walls, the glass is broken in the Gothic window, the green shutter falls forward. But nothing happens; the final decay of that window and of the garden beyond is not yet. It may be that the house will be restored, that the rank grass will be mown, that the flower-pot which lies on its side will be righted and the plant it contains will flourish. What is to happen is in the future, and for the next three years nothing happened to Alice's life. Like the deserted garden, it stood still.

And during the years when Alice's future was preparing she lived with the picture.

These years began, vulgarly enough, with Mrs. Sterne. It was a beginning of which Alice herself was at the time unaware.

Alice was in Brazil and I was in London listening to the fury of Mrs. Sterne, and later I was lying in the primrose bedroom in Willow Road and wishing I was dead. I wished I was dead and I was so miserable that I didn't even bother to decide what kind of funeral I should have. Only, in passing, I regretted that I would not lie in an unknown grave.

How horrible Sonia had been and how sordid. How I hated Mrs. Sterne, and yet I could sympathise with her over Sonia and

Paddy. They shouldn't have lived in Estelle's house and let it get so dirty. And what was going to happen to Alice and Cassius? It was all so unfair.

What was to happen to Alice and Cassius? Over and over again I asked myself that question. I reproached myself and I felt frightened.

Would Alice be angry with me? Surely she would. I ought to have done something to prevent it. Catching Tessie on the stairs was not enough. There must have been something else. I must write to Alice and announce the disaster that was coming to them. But what was the point, and after all perhaps nothing would happen. Mrs. Sterne might change her mind and not tell Mr. Sterne about Sonia, or he might think that Sonia's behaviour in London had nothing to do with Cassius and Alice in Rio de Janeiro. But in my heart I knew it wouldn't do. Mrs. Sterne would never change her mind, and Mr. Sterne would certainly dismiss Cassius.

I wished the Lawes house would catch on fire. I should be burnt to death and nothing would matter. But Cassius and Alice and Mrs. Sterne would all be alive. What was the use of being dead if it didn't change anything. Perhaps Mrs. Sterne's flat would catch on fire; then she and Mr. Sterne and Estelle would be burnt to death. That would be *splendid*, and perhaps Estelle would be rescued.

How nice David Mason had been. He had seemed such a stupid young man when I sat on the stairs with him at Willow Road, and then Mrs. Sterne had happened and he had been wonderful. He had got me away from that terrible house and brought me back to the Laweses'. He had managed to placate Mrs. Lawes, who had been annoyed by my long absence from her dance. My friend, he had assured her, had been really very ill indeed, and I had been quite right to go round and see her, and of course once there I had naturally to wait until the doctor came. Mrs. Lawes had believed him, but I didn't care what Mrs. Lawes believed. I turned on the light. It was ten to seven and I had not slept at all.

* * * * *

Cassius and Alice came back to England, for Mr. Sterne had dismissed Cassius. Cassius was discouraged and at first was inclined to blame me as well as Sonia for what had happened.

They took a house in Chapel Street. 'The Deserted Garden' was hung over the mantelpiece in the drawing-room. The walls of the drawing-room were pale grey and there were no other pictures.

Alice started to collect furniture for the house. But she did not seem to get a great deal of pleasure out of it.

She was unhappy and it seemed that life, ordinary unhappy life, was in itself too much for her, and one was afraid for what it would do to her.

Again she and Cassius were surrounded by Cassius' friends. Paul and Maurice and various young men whom he had known at school and at Cambridge, and of course Geoffrey. And I knew that Geoffrey worried a good deal about Alice; but of course not consistently and not all the time, for many of the days were pleasant, and amusing, but it was all trivial, it was leading nowhere.

Once or twice Geoffrey discussed it with me, and together we tried to look at the future, the future which Alice and Cassius seemed determined to ignore.

'Something,' Geoffrey said, 'must happen. They are too young not to have a future.'

I looked at the picture of the deserted garden and was troubled. Did the deep blue of the sky and the pink of the Gothic arch hold a promise? Surely they denied the broken window and the decaying woodwork. The picture, despite its subject, was not sad and soon something would happen to arrest the process of decay.

After he had been back in England for about a year, Cassius, in a rather desultory way, became a partner in a firm of booksellers. He still regretted that he was not with Mr. Sterne's firm. Being a bookseller was not, he said, the same thing and it didn't impress his father. All the same he quite enjoyed standing at the round table in the shop, deferentially recommending books in his charmingly modulated voice, and upstairs he had an office with a mahogany knee-hole desk.

But often Cassius would not go to the shop at all. When that happened it didn't particularly matter, for there was the partner, a young man who had been at Cambridge with him, and there was the young lady assistant in a green overall and a secretary in a pink satin blouse.

Alice and Cassius still talked a great deal about buying a yacht. 'But not an expensive one,' Alice would remind me, 'because we've decided, now we're older, that we wouldn't want to live in a yacht the whole year round.'

So in the year that Alice was twenty-three they bought *Runa* for two hundred pounds. There was no possibility of going round the world in her. She was a ten-tonner and had been built on the Clyde in 1891.

They had found her in the Blythe River, on the South Coast, and while she was being fitted out they stayed down at Blythe every week-end, and most week-ends I was asked to join them.

By this time I had of course finished with the Polygon Typing School and I had a job in the offices of an engineering factory. The job had been found for me by Miss Hartley-Jones. The factory was on the North Circular Road. I found it difficult getting there on time in the mornings, and if ever I was late and took a taxi my wages for the week disappeared. In the end I bought a second-hand car. My grandmother disapproved of the whole thing. The car as well as the work. I still lived in Hill Street. I should have liked to have a flat of my own, but that would have meant such a terrific row and anyhow would probably have cost more than I could afford.

When Cassius and Alice bought their yacht, Geoffrey and I became more hopeful. Would this mean the end of the period of decay? They seemed so pleased with the yacht and their pleasure seemed to draw them together. The scene of their interests shifted from London to Blythe. The young men who abounded in Chapel Street tended to disappear. Their place was taken by people like Captain and Mrs. Murray, who owned a Dutch barge, and by George and Arthur Shaw, the joint owners of a fifteen-ton yawl.

The Murrays were amusing. My most vivid memory of them is of one particular Saturday when I had walked over to the shipyard to see how they were getting on with *Runa*. They were getting on quite well and I went and talked to Captain Murray. He was on the deck of his barge, which was moored against the jetty.

Captain Murray sat on an upturned bucket and peeled the carrots for his supper. Mrs. Murray, he said, was below.

Two ladies approached and asked if it was true that Captain Murray had some monkeys for sale. Captain Murray pushed his cap on to the back of his head, stood up, invited the ladies on board and started to enter into negotiations.

One of the ladies asked if the monkeys were tame and quiet animals.

'Quiet?' he said. 'They're perfectly quiet.'

He pointed at the two monkeys which sat dejectedly on some straw. They were chained to a kind of hatch and some of the straw had escaped and was blowing untidily about the deck. The ladies looked doubtful.

'You see,' said the taller of the two, 'we must be sure that they're quiet; they're for pets for the children.'

The ladies came closer and peered at the monkeys.

This was the test. I moved closer to the Captain and stood behind him as a sort of bodyguard. My heart went out to him. Clearly if he wished to convince the ladies and effect a sale, he must now *do* something. Gingerly he bent over the monkeys; their chains had become hopelessly entangled. He tried to disentangle them. The monkeys chattered at him furiously and one of them bit his hand. With wonderful self-control he said nothing and put the hand behind his back. The intending purchasers might not care for the sight of blood.

'Here, can you help me?' he called to me. 'They seem to have got their chains wound round each other.'

I started to do my best with them. The Captain turned chattily to the ladies.

'They're really more my wife's pets than mine; she can do anything with them. As a matter of fact, I think they're really better with women and children than with men. Wish she could have shown them to you herself. Unfortunately, though, she's got to lie up; broke her ankle last week. Bad luck, wasn't it?'

The ladies continued in silence to watch what were now my frantic efforts with the chains. The monkeys swore unceasingly.

'Funny little beggars,' said the Captain. 'You'd think they were talking, wouldn't you? I shall be sorry to lose them in a way, but we're off to sea next week. Going across to Holland and then working our way down to the Mediterranean. Not fair on them, taking them all that way. Might quite easily have some rough passages. That's why we're so anxious to find a good home for them before we leave; that's why we're willing to sell them so cheap. Wish my wife was able to show them to you; you'd *see* then.'

He had now succeeded in wrapping a handkerchief tightly round his hand.

'I think perhaps'—it was the tall lady speaking again— 'perhaps we'd better come back another time when we've thought it over.' She and her friend began to move towards the gangplank which connected us with the shore.

'Oh, I say,' said the Captain, 'we'll have them disentangled in a minute.'

'What's the matter?' asked a voice behind us. 'Doesn't anyone like my monkeys?'

The Captain swung round; the ladies stared in amazement. Peering out of the companion-way was a figure dressed in a green velveteen dressing-gown. It swayed slightly.

'They're wunnerful monkeys. I don't know *what* I shall do without them.'

Clutching at various bits of rigging, the Captain's wife started to propel herself towards us. One foot was encased in plaster and she stuck it out stiffly in front of her while she tried to hop on the other.

'Here, I say,' said the Captain, 'you shouldn't be out of your bunk, you know.' He went to help her, and taking her arm tried to persuade her to return below. I had now succeeded in freeing the monkeys and led one of them towards the ladies.

'They're perfectly quiet,' I said, echoing the Captain. 'Would you like to pat it?'

'Perfectly quiet,' said the Captain's wife. She giggled and sat down.

The ladies had made good their escape. From the shore side of the gangplank they told me that it looked a dear little thing, and that if they thought anything more about it, they would come again, when we weren't quite so busy perhaps. Feeling rather foolish, I tied the monkey up again.

The Murrays had now gone below and I crept back on shore. I made a wide detour to avoid the ladies, who were getting into their motor-car, and walked back along the side of the river to the Crown Hotel.

I found Alice and Cassius and we went into the bar together. I told them about the monkeys and about Mrs. Murray.

Cassius was full of sympathy and said that it must have been most unpleasant. 'And why,' he added, 'do they call each other "Chief" and "Pogs"?'

'They've asked me to call them "Chief" and "Pogs" too,' I said.

'Good gracious. How very disagreeable!' Cassius was shocked. 'And are you going to?'

'I suppose I'll have to. Did you know they call you "Runa" and Alice "Mrs. Runa"? They say it's a custom and saves trouble.'

Cassius said that if he'd known about the custom in time he'd have had *Runa* renamed 'Mr. Skeffington.'

'That's what Queen Victoria did. I think it was very sensible of her. "Victoria and Albert." Very little scope for the Murrays *there.* . . .'

At this point Captain Murray came into the bar.

'Ah, the Runas,' he said heartily, and sat down with us. 'What are we all drinking?'

'We're all drinking pink gins,' Cassius said coldly, 'but we won't have time for another round, we're just going in to dinner.'

'Nonsense!' said Captain Murray. 'There's always time for one more round. I've only come in for a quick one, anyhow. Got to get back to Pogs, you know. Rotten for her being laid up, but she's asleep now, and I've got the stew on. Capital thing, stew!'

So we bought the Captain a drink because we thought it would be quicker in the end.

By the next week-end *Runa* was ready for sea. The Blythe shipyard had painted her hull white. They had re-rigged her, and her engine was, as far as possible, in working order. This engine had only one cylinder and one gear and no reverse and no neutral either. It was placed under the steps leading from the cockpit, but when it was running the steps had to be removed. So to go below at such times you had either to jump over the flywheel or use the forecastle hatch. To start it you had to swing a handle, and the handle was liable to fly off, which was dangerous, and twice during the summer Cassius had his lip cut open. When there was any sea at all water came in by way of the exhaust outlet.

The first Saturday so eagerly awaited was disappointing. We got stuck on the mud in the Blythe River and spent miserable hours sitting on the inclined deck watching other yachts sailing gaily up and down the Solent. Every now and again there was a crash of crockery as more and more things slid from their shelves. At last the tide turned and at about four o'clock we cooked our luncheon on a terrifying machine Cassius had had fixed in the forecastle. This machine burnt petrol under pressure and often went up in flames. We met a man once who showed us his yacht, and when we came to the stove (which was evidently the thing he liked best) he said that it was the finest little stove he had ever been shipmates with. Cassius' machine wasn't like that at all.

For her size *Runa* had quite good accommodation. There were two berths on either side of the engine. They were comfortable, but they were so close under the decks that it wasn't possible to sit up in them, which was horrid for Cassius, who suffered from claustrophobia. Also, of course, the smell of engine oil was here particularly strong. Then there was a small saloon and forward of that was a combined pantry and lavatory and then the forecastle.

At six o'clock we were able to leave our involuntary mud berth. We motored back up the river, where we made fast to buoys belonging to the Blythe shipyard. It had been an inglorious maiden voyage.

We went ashore to have dinner and a drink at the Crown. In the bar as usual were Chief and Pogs. Pogs' foot was much better. She and Chief both wore yachting caps with white covers and appeared to be hung all over with lanyards. They both had several knives stuck in their belts, which seemed a little ferocious, only I happened to know that they mostly used them for peeling different kinds of vegetables. When we came in, the Murrays had pint glasses in front of them.

'Ah!' said Captain Murray. 'The Runas! What are we all drinking?'

We protested a little half-heartedly that this round was on us and the Murrays said would we mind if they changed to whisky?

'Cheers!' said the Captain. 'Silly expression, that. It doesn't *mean* anything. Now in Norway they say *skoal*. Splendid fellows, the Norwegians. Did I ever tell you about when I was in Norway?'

'Yes,' we said. 'You drank them under the table.'

'That's right,' said the Captain. 'Pogs did, too, didn't you, Pogs?' he added generously. 'Did I ever tell you about Gallipoli? Terrible time we had there.'

'With Pogs?' Cassius asked.

'Lord, no,' said the Captain. 'It was during the war. Sea literally thick with dead bodies.'

'*How* disagreeable,' Cassius said. 'Still, it's all over now.' His voice was soothing, but the Captain was not to be put off. He went on about Gallipoli. He had been very *brave* there, it seemed.

By the time he had finished the bar had begun to fill up. There was the fishmonger and his wife and the manager of the furniture store. There were George and Arthur Shaw. Arthur's eye shone fiery red, so it was evidently his turn to get drunk.

Soon, probably, he would offer to fight somebody, and then George would take him away, and they would spend the rest of the evening chasing each other round the public houses of the neighbourhood.

At the far end of the bar was Mrs. Bryant, who, as usual, waited for her lover. We were glad when she did not come and sit with us. We were not in the mood to listen to the story of her life. It was enough to have the Captain and Gallipoli.

Mrs. Bryant was, perhaps, thirty and not all that good-looking, but made (one supposes) the best of herself. She told us, on more than one occasion, that she always took hours of time making up her face in the morning. The first time she told us Alice had said, 'But how *awful* for you, it must be so *boring,*' but Mrs. Bryant had shaken her head and said, 'No it is really very interesting,' and Alice had said, 'But how can you possibly make it last, or do you keep on rubbing it out and starting again?' Which, not surprisingly, hadn't gone very well.

Mrs. Bryant's other name was Rosamond. Her hair was arranged in a hard scraped-up hairdo with a bun perched on top and every hair, both the black and the grey, was in place, except for a few at the back, and those were the few that made all the difference.

With her lovers Mrs. Bryant counted not the cost, but the takings. The takings were inclined to be small. Never diamonds and mink and lots of them all the time. Cassius would refer to her as 'that dreary woman,' but then Mrs. Bryant would have said that Cassius was not her type. Mrs. Bryant seldom attempted the difficult. Never the impossible.

The bar became more and more crowded. As it was Saturday there were, as well as the regulars, quite a few strangers, most of them off yachts. Out of the corner of my eye I saw that Captain Murray had managed to scrape an acquaintance with several of them. The Captain had what he called 'an eye for business' and his business was buying and selling yachts on commission. He also, from time to time, hired himself out as a glorified kind of skipper. But on such occasions Pogs was inclined to come too and that didn't always suit people.

The Captain liked Pogs to be in on things. We understood that he had had quite a lot of wives, but Pogs must have been his favourite. He introduced her now to his new acquaintance. Pogs bowed unsteadily but with dignity.

'What are we all drinking?' asked the Captain, and one of the men bought double whiskies for the Murrays. They all told each other their names.

'And this is Margie,' said the Captain, pointing at me.

'Friend of the Runas,' said Pogs in explanation.

'Ah yes, the Runas,' said the Captain.

The man who had bought the drinks detached himself from the group and came over to me. He looked vaguely familiar and remarked affably that Runa was a very unusual name.

I said that it wasn't at *all* an unusual name for a boat.

The Major—obviously he was a Major—said, 'Oh, wasn't it?'

I felt certain that he had been going on to say that he had known an awfully nice fellow in the Heythrop country called Runa and would that be any relation?

'You're Major Wordsworth,' I said.

He started.

'I met you *years* ago at a point-to-point. With Alice Norton; she's here now.' I looked round for Alice but I couldn't see her. So I introduced Major Wordsworth to Cassius, and Major Wordsworth said that he had known an awfully nice fellow in the V.W.H. country called Skeffington, and would that be any relation? It wasn't, so the Major told Cassius all about him.

Alice joined us, and she and Major Wordsworth seemed very pleased to see each other again. It was arranged that Major Wordsworth should leave his own party and come out sailing with us the next day.

The next morning I woke with the sun shining in my eyes through the open hatch. There was the slight movement and creaking as *Runa* rode to her moorings. There was the smell of engine oil and the smell of paraffin. I stretched myself in my blankets. It would have been squalid to have slept without sheets in a house; here it was delightful. I looked across at Alice sleeping in the starboard bunk. There was a sound from the saloon; Cassius was waking up. Cautiously I got out of my bunk, and went on deck. The morning was beautiful. Farther down the river, paid-hands were already swabbing their decks. I could hear them calling to each other, and the plonk of their canvas buckets as they lowered them into the water. I went forward, took off the forecastle hatch, and lowered myself into the forecastle. Here it smelt of petrol and paraffin, mixed with the musty smell of the sail bags and very faintly with the Jeyes' fluid from the lavatory. I picked up the burgee and went back on deck. If I hoisted it, the Murrays or anyone who was about would know that the sun had risen, that Cassius was on board, and that he was a member of the Blythe Sailing Club. I watched it flutter to the truck. Already the sun was hot on my bare feet. I wondered if I should bathe, but the water looked dirty. It was low tide and we were only just off the mud. I could hear Cassius moving about below. There was only room for one person at a time to wash and dress in comparative comfort. I sat down in the cockpit to wait until he should be finished. Soon I heard him pumping up the stove, so he was going to get the breakfast. I went below. Alice was still asleep. As I stood at the bottom of the companion-way she sighed and turned over. It would be lovely to sleep as long as that, but she had missed the beginning of the morning. Cassius called to know where we had put the bacon, and she woke up.

We had breakfast, we made up our bunks, we got *Runa* ready for sea. At ten o'clock Felix hailed us from the shore, and I went to fetch him in the pram dinghy. Standing on the jetty the Major looked rather nice. Old of course, he must be at least thirty-five, but good-looking and very, very clean. He got into the dinghy, and the water rose high round the stern. He must be heavy. Anyhow heavier than Cassius, but he wasn't fat.

The Major had brought a present, a book on helmsmanship, which he gave to Alice. He had happened to have it with him at the Crown; it was as good as new. Look, he called us to witness, it did not even have his name in it. Alice thanked him and asked him to write in it. He produced a gold fountain-pen and wrote an inscription. There was her name and his own and the date, the 23rd of May.

Again we were hailed from the shore. It was Geoffrey. We hadn't been expecting him to come down to-day. If he had been ten minutes later, we would have been gone. The Major had shouted, *'Runa ahoy!'* Geoffrey stood on the jetty and called for Cassius and Alice.

He had a brown paper parcel under his arm. Darling Geoffrey! I thought of how he had sat on Cassius' clothes while Cassius saved Alice from being drowned. Cassius took the dinghy and went and fetched him. He came on board a little breathless. When he had woken up this morning, he couldn't think why he was in London. It was ridiculous to be in London on a day like this. He had got up immediately and come down to Blythe. The parcel was a bottle of gin. He was sorry that he hadn't brought anything else. Cassius told him that he must take off his shoes. They had leather soles with nails in them. It was unthinkable to come on board a yacht in anything but rubber soles. The nails in Geoffrey's shoes would tear up the decks. Geoffrey was apologetic; he took off his shoes and his socks. He had beautiful long white feet. I looked at the Major; he was wearing canvas shoes. He would never have come on board a yacht with shoes with nails in them.

'There are too many rules,' Alice complained. 'The Murrays say that one must never take an umbrella on board—or a dead body, but then nobody would want to.'

'They never talk about rabbits,' I said. 'Not even when they're making a stew out of them. It's terribly unlucky.'

'Why should the Murrays care about luck?' Cassius asked. 'They never go to sea. Their barge is really a kind of houseboat.'

'They're going to sea soon,' I said. 'They're going to work their way down to the Mediterranean.'

Cassius shrugged his shoulders and said that we ought to be starting. 'We're going round the Isle of Wight,' he told the Major.

'Will you have time?' the Major asked.

'My time is my own,' Cassius said grandly, 'and it will be good practice for going round the world.'

'We're going to one day really,' Alice said, smiling at the Major.

'You'll need something a bit different from this.' The Major looked at the shrouds, as if they particularly would never get round the world.

'You mean a different shape or just bigger?' Alice asked.

'Well, stronger really,' the Major said and smiled back at her. Again Cassius said that we ought to be starting. He went below to start the engine. The Major cast off the bows and stood by to cast off the stern, as soon as the engine should be running. Geoffrey hovered beside him. Unexpectedly the engine behaved beautifully; Alice took the tiller and we started. We passed close to the Murrays' barge. Chief was on deck; we waved to him. He shouted something which we could not hear, and Pogs came up on deck and waved too. We went on down the river very slowly against the tide. What little wind there was was following and we hoisted the mainsail. Major Wordsworth explained to Geoffrey which were the main halyards and which were the other halyards. Geoffrey looked with interest and alarm at the conglomeration of cleats and coiled ropes at the foot of the mast.

'If you were to let the main go by mistake in a storm,' the Major said, 'you'd be done for.'

'If we have a storm, I don't think I shall touch *anything* at all.'

Geoffrey went back to sit in the cockpit with Alice. We turned eastwards into the Solent. Cassius and the Major set the jib and the staysail. Cassius stopped the engine, and there was peace.

There was just enough wind to fill the sails. *Runa* rose and fell gently to the small amount of swell and creaked a little and the sun shone down. Cassius showed the Major his charts in the new grey tin case. Then he went forward, stretched himself on the deck and went to sleep. I sat cross-legged on the counter, not asleep but very nearly so, and Geoffrey talked to Alice.

The Major, having been entrusted with the navigation, got busy. He spread the charts out on the table in the saloon. He fussed with the parallel rule and the Admiralty Sailing Instructions. He had a gold pencil with which he marked things off. He told Alice what course she was to keep and when to change it. He fidgeted with the sails; a fraction in or a fraction out? They never seemed to be quite right. Obviously he was completely happy. He asked us all to call him Felix. Really he was rather sweet. The morning turned into afternoon. We ate bread and cheese; we drank beer. We were off Bembridge. We had reached the tip of the Isle of Wight. In spite of everything that Felix could do, the tide was beginning to set against us. The wind had dropped almost to nothing. If we were to go the whole way round the Island, it would be to-morrow morning before we returned to Blythe. Felix went below to consult the chart; something, it seemed, wasn't right.

'Though it looks fairly right to me,' Alice said amiably to no one in particular.

Cassius rolled over and said that if Felix had lost his way why didn't we tell him that that was the Isle of Wight over there? We said that Felix knew that. Cassius opened his eyes and said then why was anyone fussing? We explained that nobody *was*, but that Felix was doing everything by navigation. Alice continued to steer with a comfortable lack of concentration. Felix reappeared on deck, just as we slowly passed a buoy marked neatly in enormous white letters, 'East Princessa.' Cassius remarked to Felix that 'if we were where we thought we were' *that* was the *East Princessa*. Felix said shortly that it *was* the *East Princessa*, and went below to have another look at the chart. Cassius shrugged his shoulders and Geoffrey laughed. Alice told them in a whisper not to be horrid. It was decided that we should put about and return to Blythe. The trip round the island would be for another day. There was, as Felix said, the whole of the summer before us.

On the way back we had to use the engine. Geoffrey steered— under strict supervision, and Alice and I helped Felix to do the crossword puzzle in *The Times*. Alice was able to supply most of the quotations, otherwise we weren't very good at it; but then neither was he. We looked at Felix's book on helmsmanship and he found what he considered the best bits and read them aloud to us. He said that it was an extraordinary thing, but that practically nobody could sail a boat properly when she was close-hauled. The book, it seemed, agreed with Felix, and added that no woman could sail a boat as well as a man, and there Felix agreed wholeheartedly with the book. The author compared sailing to playing the violin, and Felix said there you were, look at Kreisler, and Alice said, 'and Yeli D'Aranyi,' and Felix said triumphantly that that was exactly what he'd meant.

It was after nine when we got back to Blythe. I had to be at the office the next morning. Geoffrey and I, invited to dine on *Runa*'s stores, had an extraordinary meal of baked beans and sardines and very strong tea. The others would be able to get something at the Crown. We drove up to London in convoy. Always one seemed to have too many cars or too few.

I put my car away in the mews and let myself into Hill Street. It was two o'clock. I went quickly up to my room and was surprised to see a light on the landing above mine. I heard my name called and Ellen came downstairs.

'Hullo!' I said. 'Is anything the matter?'

'It's your mother,' Ellen said.

'Is she dead?' Surely nothing except death could have kept Ellen up and fully dressed until two in the morning. It would be easier for Ellen if I asked the question. Then she could just say 'Yes,' and she would have told me.

'Good Gracious, *no!*' Ellen was shocked. 'It's *that* Jennifer, she's going to run away with a priest.'

'How very extraordinary!'

'Of course he isn't a Catholic,' Ellen went on. 'That wouldn't be allowed, would it? And he's got ever so many children.'

'Then it's bigamy?'

'Oh, no, his wife died. In childbirth, I shouldn't wonder. It was only to be expected.'

'Ellen,' I asked, 'are you sure you feel quite well? Hadn't you better sit down or something?'

'If you came up to my room,' Ellen said, 'we could make a cup of tea on the gas-ring. I have to have it for the iron.'

So I went up to Ellen's room and sat on the floor and looked at the ugly furniture while Ellen made the tea.

'Those trousers could do with a good press.' Ellen turned to look at me severely as she took the cups out of the wardrobe.

'It doesn't matter,' I said. 'Tell me about Jennifer.'

'There's been a to-do,' Ellen said grimly.

'But why *here*? Jennifer hasn't got anything to do with *us*.'

'But she's *here*.' Ellen put her fingers to her lips.

'Oh, God!' I said. 'Does Grandmamma know? And where's the priest? Is he here as well?'

'Now you don't think I'd have allowed that. I didn't like to let *her* be here. Let alone a clergyman after *midnight*. And anyhow, he's in Ireland.'

It was too difficult. I felt bewildered and exhausted. I thought of myself standing on *Runa's* deck and the warmth of the sun on my bare feet. And Cassius and Geoffrey teasing the Major. Ellen measured the tea into the pot. She was so obviously enjoying herself. She had waited up until two o'clock to tell me this story and she was not to be hurried.

'There's only you and me knows she's in the house. Luckily, as it happened, I answered the door to her myself. The pantry must have been gallivanting off somewhere, because the bell rang twice and they didn't seem to hear it. She's asleep now in the spare room; at least I *suppose* she's asleep. I peeped in just before you came back and there wasn't a sound from her.'

'But why did she come here?'

'She came to see you.' Ellen handed me my cup. 'Your mother's been and turned her out of the house, because of her taking up with this clergyman, I suppose.'

'But I thought Jennifer lived in Sussex,' I said stupidly. 'With her aunt; they do raffia work and sell it in the village. They're both terribly rich and people buy it out of charity.'

'Well, she must have given that *up*,' Ellen said, 'because just lately she's been living with *them* in Regent's Park.'

'Them' were presumably my mother and Captain Parsons.

'There's been a bust-up,' Ellen went on, 'and I don't think Mrs. Parsons was very nice to her and Miss Jennifer wants you to make it all right. She was ever so upset, and talk about crying! Why, she was nearly in hysterics. I quite thought Mrs. Boswell would hear her. She would have too, if I hadn't of shut the window. And I always thought that Jennifer was one of the reserved ones.'

'Did my mother throw anything at Jennifer?'

'I think it was a jug—with hot water in it.' Ellen put more sugar in her tea. 'And Jennifer ran out of the house and came round here, and then as you wasn't in, she said she would wait. And then when it got to one o'clock, I said that she'd better go to bed in the spare room, and gave her one of your old nightdresses that you used to wear at school. Well, I mean to say, she couldn't go to a hotel, not at that hour, and with no luggage and crying like she was?' Ellen looked at me enquiringly, and I realised that she was asking for my approbation of what she had done. I must be getting really old then, or perhaps Ellen was. Until now she had always told me what to do, with complete faith in the superiority and infallibility of her judgments.

'You were quite right,' I said, and thus accepted responsibility for 'poor Jennifer.'

'What I think funny,' Ellen said, 'is her carrying on so. After all, she's of age, and I understand she's got her own money. She can marry who she likes, even if it is a clergyman. She doesn't have to have Captain Parsons' permission, let alone your mother's.'

'Jennifer was always stupid,' I said, 'and perhaps she hasn't had things thrown at her before, though I can't think why *not*. I'll go round to Regent's Park in the morning and get her luggage. Then she can go to Sussex or Ireland, or anywhere she likes.'

'You can't do that; it'll make you late for that office.' Ellen was assuming control of me again.

'I can telephone to them,' I said.

'Perhaps we ought to telephone to Regent's Park; they may be thinking Jennifer's got run over.'

Ellen was determined that the smallest possibility of drama should not be overlooked.

"*You* telephone if you like,' I said. 'I'm going to bed.'

Ellen was hurt. Then she brightened.

'Wouldn't you say that was a coffin?' She handed me her empty tea-cup. 'And tears too. It's as plain as anything.' She leant over my shoulder and pointed out the little mass of tea leaves that was supposed to be a picture of the coffin.

'I wonder who it is,' she said speculatively.

'You can always get tears,' I said, 'by not drinking all the tea.'

'You can't always get a coffin. I haven't had a coffin for *years*. But then'—Ellen got up—'there probably isn't anything in it. Though the woman who lives next door to my cousins at Bromley is really wonderfully good. She sees ever so many things and they come true. I'll try and get her to come over one evening and tell yours for you.'

'Well, I'm going to bed,' I said. 'Thank you for the tea.'

'Will you look in at Jennifer? She may be awake again,' Ellen said hopefully.

'I think I'll leave her till the morning. And Ellen, I suppose she'll have to have some breakfast.'

'I suppose so. I only hope the kitchen are going to be agreeable about it.'

I went down to my own landing very quietly. I didn't want to wake Jennifer and have to listen to the whole story of the clergyman and my mother and the jug all over again. I was sorry for Jennifer, but she was a bore.

I undressed and switched off the light. Then I drew aside the curtain and stood at the window in my nightdress while I brushed my hair. It was a white satin nightdress. Poor Jennifer slept, or lay awake in the next room, wearing one of the cotton nightdresses I had had at school. It had been chosen by Miss Partridge. How I had hated Miss Partridge. Now I was rather sorry for her. It must be awful having had to put up all these years with my mother's temper. People were frightened of my mother. Jennifer must have been frightened. That's why she had rushed round here for me to protect her. Had she been frightened of my mother, or of the violence? I didn't know. You so seldom knew what people were frightened of. But you knew when the fear was there; you could feel it. There was something in the Bible about casting out fear. If you could cast out fear, everything would be all right. But you couldn't do it. Too many people were frightened of too many things.

I thought of Alice and Cassius. Were they lying on board *Runa*, looking at the moonlight and feeling afraid? And Major Wordsworth at the Crown. What was he afraid of? Perhaps of not feeling always superior. That was what made him say things like 'No woman can sail a boat as well as a man.' And I thought of myself and of the shaming fears which I experienced at the dentist's; and of the time when I had slipped and thought I was falling from a cliff.

Then very clearly I saw Alice, and her eyes were wide with fear, and I knew that she was afraid of something tremendous. The time of the Deserted Garden was at an end. My mother and the dentist were the fears of children. Jennifer and I would never have to contend with the terrible fears that beset Alice, for Alice was afraid of life itself. Life, like the winter sea, against which no man could stand. 'There are those who from their birth are doomed to greatness.'

Abruptly I drew the curtains across the window. I turned on my bedside light and got into bed. Ellen had said that the woman from Bromley could look into empty tea-cups and see things that came true. It was ridiculous. No one could foretell the future; it wasn't possible for a moment. I pulled up the sheet. On the corner of it in red cross-stitch were my grandmother's initials and a date—'1884.' What was there to be frightened of in a world where sheets lasted for more than fifty years?

EIGHT

IF WE HADN'T MET Mrs. Bryant, if Felix had never come to Blythe, would the next few months have been so very different? I don't know. I think only the details would have been different; everything else was probably inevitable.

At first they seemed unimportant, and Felix anyhow was quite pleasant and a welcome addition when it came to sailing the boat.

On the first Saturday in June, *Runa* was entered for a handicap race for 'yachts of fifteen tons and under.' Felix, because of his greater experience, was to sail her. Cassius, Geoffrey, Alice and I were to act as crew. It was all very exciting, but right from the beginning we didn't have any luck. We made a bad start; that was Cassius' fault; he had been stupid with the stopwatch. We went on being stupid and also clumsy. Not unnaturally, Felix became annoyed. Half-way round the course he gave the tiller to Alice and went forward.

'What the bloody hell do you think you're doing?' he shouted.

Cassius, poised elegantly on the bowsprit, turned round.

'I am,' he said, 'tying my own bloody balloon jib into bloody knots.'

Felix asked Cassius how he expected us to make the next buoy with no blasted wind and no blasted sails either, and why the hell had Cassius let the jib go before he had the balloon ready. Cassius said that if there wasn't any wind, it surely couldn't matter less about us not having any sails. Felix swore again. The leading boats, which had made the buoy, were beginning to come back past us. The tide was with them, and there seemed to be a nice breeze going in their direction.

Geoffrey chose this moment to ask Felix, very politely, if there was anything he could do.

'Let's stop racing,' Alice said, 'because really I don't think we're going to win.'

'Yes, do let's,' Geoffrey said. 'Then we could anchor and have tea. That's rather a nice place over there.' He pointed vaguely in the general direction of Freshwater Bay. 'And we could bathe. I've been longing to bathe all day.'

Felix said that if anyone was going to bathe with this tide running he wouldn't be responsible for them.

I was sorry for Felix. Geoffrey and Cassius really were being more than usually aggravating. They knew nothing about sailing and he knew a great deal. He was doing Cassius a favour in sailing the boat for him. Now we were going to give up and bathe and have tea. It was very disappointing. My sympathies were with the Major. He was not even going to be allowed the small satisfaction of completing the course.

'Never mind'—Alice made an attempt to comfort him— 'perhaps we won't be so stupid next time.'

The Major shrugged his shoulders. Probably he had decided that 'next time' he would not be with us. Alice smiled at him. He smiled back and said:

'Er, what, yes. I'll *murder* them.' The Major was always going to *murder* people, but we thought it might be only an expression. Anyhow, he was smiling. Obviously he *would* come with us next time and any other times that Alice invited him.

On Sunday morning Alice and I went down to the Crown about ten o'clock to have our baths. Cassius and Geoffrey remained on board *Runa*. We were all under the impression we were tired. We wouldn't bother to go sailing until the afternoon. The weather was perfect.

Baths at the Crown cost a shilling and included a clean towel. When I had finished I joined Alice downstairs. We decided to take our beer into the garden. The garden was empty, except for Mrs. Bryant, who sat alone surrounded by a circle of chairs. On the table in front of her was a portable wireless tuned in to Radio Normandy. She called to us to join her. There was no choice but to do so. Mrs. Bryant sat neatly in the middle of her chair. Mrs. Bryant asked us if we had won our race the day before, and we told her 'no.'

'You don't mind the wireless?'

We assured her that we liked it and listened in silence to the advertisement for Bile Beans.

'It's new,' Mrs. Bryant said. 'Harold brought it down from London with him last night.' Harold was Mrs. Bryant's lover.

'How very kind of him,' Alice said.

Mrs. Bryant smiled.

'Oh, well'—the smile ended in a simper. Soon we should be hearing the story of her life. How she had had to leave Mr. Bryant, though he had been terribly 'attractive.' Mrs. Bryant didn't believe in marriage. It was better to be free. I remembered that Ellen didn't believe in marriage either. A lot of people didn't, if you came to think of it. All the same, I thought I should get married, but not until I was at least twenty-five. I was happy at the factory. I was happy during these week-ends with Cassius and Alice. If I was married my husband might want to do something else. There was plenty of time.

'Of course,' Mrs. Bryant was saying to Alice, 'I married far too young. Out of the schoolroom. I was only seventeen.'

'I was eighteen,' Alice said.

Mrs. Bryant sighed sympathetically.

'But you weren't in the schoolroom,' I said.

'Oh, no,' Alice agreed, 'I was in the sea.'

'Like Aphrodite rising from the waves,' I said. 'I never thought of it like that before.'

Mrs. Bryant stirred. The conversation was drifting away from her. Men, she said, were very foolish. Take Harold now. She and Alice took Harold for a bit. It seemed that he was 'foolishly' fond of Mrs. Bryant. When his divorce came through he wanted her to marry him. But Mrs. Bryant didn't think she would. She was afraid it would spoil their relationship. In the meantime he was useful. He paid the rent of her flat in London, and they had a great deal of fun together. He was paying for her to spend the summer down here. She had been very ill during the winter. Harold had been wonderful to her. She gave us a long resume of the various details of her illness. They sounded very unattractive, but apparently they had interested the doctor. It was extraordinary how good Harold had been about it. Most men were bored by illness, but Harold had been wonderful. All the same, she didn't think she would marry him.

'Perhaps he won't get his divorce,' Alice said.

'Perhaps he won't,' Mrs. Bryant said.

'I suppose,' Alice went on, 'people often say they want to marry people when they can't. When one of them's married already, you know.'

She seemed to be talking to herself. I had noticed that Alice had taken a habit of doing that lately. I watched Mrs. Bryant's face; she was offended. I waited for her vindication of Harold, but it didn't come. Instead she said that no man liked being played about with. Did Mrs. Bryant think she knew everything about men?

'And it isn't fair to them,' she was saying. 'It isn't fair to take everything and give nothing.'

So she was talking about sex.

'But sometimes it can't be helped,' Alice said. 'I mean, a person mayn't want to take anything, and it may still be given them.'

Why must she say that to that horrible woman?

'That's ridiculous.' Mrs. Bryant was authoritative. 'You can't play about with a man of his age if you don't mean to have anything to do with him.'

This was horrible; it was getting worse.

'And I think you're making a great mistake. He absolutely worships you. That's the sort of thing you only appreciate when you've lost it.'

Alice sat quite still. It seemed that she was fascinated by Mrs. Bryant. She looked as I had imagined her that night when I stood at the window in Hill Street. But she *couldn't* be frightened of Mrs. Bryant. It was too silly. I remembered how she had attacked Beryl Lawes at school. I longed for her to hit Mrs. Bryant. If that happened, would Mrs. Bryant cease to look self-satisfied?

'You must forgive me for being so outspoken.'

Detestable woman. She didn't believe that there was anything to forgive. She didn't know she was unforgivable.

'I see quite a lot of him during the week, when you and Harold are away. And he's absolutely pathetic. I don't think you *can* know how much he adores you.'

Did Alice know? She gave no denial, so perhaps she did. But then, why should she discuss Felix or anyone else with Mrs.

Bryant? And *lots* of people adored Alice. David Mason did for one, and Geoffrey, and heaps of others. I only wished Harold Cunningham would. That would put Mrs. Bryant in her place.

I got up off the grass. 'We ought to go,' I said to Alice. 'They'll be waiting for us.' I didn't mind if I was rude.

'Oh,' Mrs. Bryant said, 'I thought you were asleep.' She turned to Alice. 'You'll stay and have another drink? I can't think where Harold and Felix can have got to.'

'Harold and Felix!'—'Rosamond Bryant and Alice'; it was intolerable. Alice hesitated, and Mrs. Bryant said would I be an angel and ring the bell for the waitress, it was there, just by the garden door.

Alice smiled apologetically at me and said to Mrs. Bryant that we mustn't be long. It was true, they would be waiting for us.

I moved away from them, towards the door of the hotel. Perhaps, after all, Mrs. Bryant was right. Perhaps Alice was silly to take no notice of Felix who adored her.

I lingered by the door. I would order the drinks and pay for them. Ivy, the hotel waitress, answered the bell. She was a tall girl who wore pince-nez. She suffered from varicose veins which she concealed, even in the hottest weather, under black woollen stockings. But she liked to discuss them. Why did people with varicose veins always consider them a fit subject for conversation?

This morning Ivy was cross. I had disturbed her while she was helping with the beds. I offered to go and get the drinks myself. She thanked me. She said that it was the standing that *did* it, she wasn't fit to be on her feet all day the way she had to be, and disappeared again. I got the drinks; gin for Mrs. Bryant (it was the only thing that did her blood-pressure any good), and beer for Alice and myself.

Mrs. Bryant was telling Alice about the lovely week-end she had spent in Prague some years ago, with a young man called Valentine Bruce. 'It was so lucky his surname beginning with a "B,"' it made Mrs. Bryant's monogrammed luggage and hairbrushes so much less noticeable in hotels. I had seen Mrs. Bryant's brushes. They were ivory with black initials; not blond tortoiseshell and gold. And they had had a wonderful room, with balconies overlooking the Moldau, or perhaps they had gone to Budapest, and had a wonderful room with balconies overlooking the Danube, it didn't matter.

Mrs. Bryant had unpacked her brushes at once, so that the chambermaid could see the 'B's' on them, and so conclude that Mrs. Bryant's name was Mrs. Bruce. And then as she finished, the manager sent up for their passports. Mrs. Bryant hadn't known that the hotel would ask for their passports. It had been perfectly all right. The manager hadn't said a thing. But it had been funny, especially as Mr. Bruce had been so insistent that they should be given such a really beautiful room with a double bed in it.

That was Mrs. Bryant's life. Double rooms with balconies, and hotel managers who were discreet about passports with different names on them. And the service flat in London, of which she was not always able to pay the rent. But no, I looked at Mrs. Bryant. When she was unable to pay the rent, she would move to a cheaper flat. Mrs. Bryant would never have debts; and she would always know where the string was and the stamps and the writing-paper. As a way of life it was amusing, even practical. Superficially Sonia lived like that too. But Sonia would never care *what* was written on her hairbrushes, and if anyone paid for Sonia's flat, she would merely spend her own money on some delightful extravagance. When things were going badly, Sonia would come round and see you and try to borrow a pound. Mrs. Bryant wouldn't. She knew it was tactically a mistake.

Were Sonia's and Mrs. Bryant's lives much more amusing than Alice's and mine? They had variety certainly, and Mrs. Bryant, anyhow, seemed to think that she had the best of two worlds. One way and another Mrs. Bryant had got away with a lot.

We got on to Mrs. Bryant's elder sisters. She confided that they disapproved of her. But then they were so ugly, poor things. It was as much as they had been able to do to get themselves husbands at all, and very dull husbands they were too. In spite of myself, I found I was despising the sisters. Poor things, with only one husband each, and not a lover between them! I looked at Alice. Was she also despising Mrs. Bryant's sisters?

Then I saw Mrs. Bryant as she really was. She was evil.

The moment passed. I watched Felix and Harold coming towards us across the garden. Harold was a heavy man of forty-five or so. He had a thick moustache. I thought of him looking after Mrs. Bryant when she was ill. Had he taken her temperature and run her up milk puddings? Or had he merely tiptoed about a darkened room and then gone out to his club so as not to disturb her?

I looked at Felix with a new interest. Mrs. Bryant had said that he 'absolutely worshipped Alice.' He said good morning to us all. Then he went and sat down by Alice and asked how she was.

'Not tired or anything, what!'

It didn't sound particularly ardent. He told Mrs. Bryant that Alice had the makings of a 'first-class sailor. Really remarkable for a woman!'

With the arrival of the men Mrs. Bryant's manner had changed. Now apparently she could only speak if her head was turned on one side. Her mouth was smaller and primmer.

'Did you have an interesting walk?' She looked at Harold. Was she consciously trying to 'put her whole soul into her eyes'? One had read of it being done. But it seemed a little old-fashioned.

Harold said that the walk had been all right. Presently Alice said that we must go. She gave no invitation to Felix, but he walked with us as far as the shipyard, where reluctantly he left us.

'What have you done with that poor dear Major?' Geoffrey asked as soon as we were back on board.

'We have left him for Mrs. Bryant to make mince-meat of,' Alice said.

'Oh, dear!' Geoffrey was concerned. 'I don't think he'll like that.'

'It'll make a change for us,' Cassius said, 'not being told all the time what to do. Though he *is* useful for pulling the sails up and down. And he looks after the boat very nicely during the week.—Keeps it clean and all that,' he explained to Geoffrey.

'Very good of him,' Geoffrey said.

'Mind you, I think he's a roué,' Cassius went on. 'I shouldn't be at all surprised to hear that he keeps opera girls and drinks champagne out of their shoes. He's the type, don't you think?'

'He might be,' Geoffrey agreed. 'I can just see him sitting in their dressing-rooms saying, "Er, what, yes, I'll *murder* them."'

'As a matter of fact'—Cassius turned to Alice—'I thought he *was* coming out with us to-day. Didn't you ask him?'

'No,' Alice said indifferently, 'I thought *you* would have, if you'd wanted him.'

'It doesn't matter,' Cassius said. 'Shall we not go out at all? There isn't any wind, and I've got rather a good book actually. Geoffrey and I have been reading it aloud to each other. The matron has just been found murdered in the gym, and a quiet girl in the lower fourth has been suspected. But we don't think she did it.'

'Can't have,' Geoffrey said. 'The music-master every time, if you ask me. Just a nice healthy *crime passionel*, with no nonsense about it.'

'Why don't you ever read a sensible book?' Alice said to Cassius. She spoke rather crossly for her.

'How can I?' Cassius said. 'I sell them, and that does put one off so.'

'I wonder what the Major reads,' Geoffrey said. 'Terrible spy stories about the war, don't you think? And those expensive books about hunting.'

Alice said that he read ordinary books like other people.

'*Not* just "The place where the old horse died"?'

'That isn't a book, it's a poem.'

'But it's a good "sensible" poem. The Major might easily read it,' Geoffrey insisted.

'You don't know anything about him. He reads Housman, and T.S. Eliot.'

'Educated, you see!' Geoffrey said.

We spent the rest of the day at Blythe. We sat about on deck and argued a little. We went down to the pub for meals and drinks. In the evening we returned to London.

On Monday, after dinner, Felix rang me up at Hill Street. He was staying at his club. Would I come to luncheon with him next day at the Ritz? Alice was coming. Could I be there by one o'clock? He had some friends coming early for drinks, whom he wanted us to meet. I said I couldn't, as I should be at work. He said, surely I could get some time off once in a way. I said I would try. Felix said that was 'perfectly splendid,' and rang off.

Mr. Saunders, the chief buyer, who was the head of my department, said I needn't come back in the afternoon.

'Though I hope you're not going to make a habit of it, Miss Boswell. Most of you blasted women think about nothing but time off for this and time off for that. I suppose you're going to lunch with your boy friend?'

'That's right, Mr. Saunders,' I said.

'Well, be careful,' Mr. Saunders advised. 'And don't, whatever you do, get married.'

This was a joke; I laughed dutifully. Mr. Saunders, unlike Mrs. Bryant and Ellen, *did* believe in marriage. He had a cosy peroxide-blond wife whom he brought to staff dances. They lived in Hendon and had three splendid kids who were 'doing well.'

When I arrived at the Ritz I went straight to the cloakroom. It contrasted so pleasantly with the one at the factory. The attendants in their black dresses, talking in low voices to their regular clients. 'Really, madam, *very* hot in Berkshire?'—'The *seven* o'clock train? That is an early start.' And taking the dogs into custody. 'Oh, yes, madam, she'll be quite all right with us. She remembers me, don't you, Judy?' And Judy would either growl and back away, or wag her tail and jump on to the sofa which was provided for customers who might feel faint.

And the ladies would laugh and answer the attendants in high patronising voices. For were they not charming, and were they not democratic? 'With always a kind word for everyone,' and probably they were bloody to their own servants at home.

At the factory the old crone in the cloakroom would stand at the door in her overall and shout, 'Hurry up there, you girls, you've been quite long enough, and the bell's gone.' And the place smelt of disinfectant instead of scent, and you didn't have to tip her.

I left the cloakroom and met Alice, who was just coming into the hall.

'Hullo, am I late?' Alice asked anxiously, and her eyes travelled to the clock. Alice often asked whether she was late. Actually she very seldom was. It was exactly one o'clock. Together we crossed the entrance hall.

I asked Alice whether Geoffrey was coming. She said no, and that she was rather glad. Geoffrey, Alice said, was becoming rather a bore, and he was always so silly about Felix.

We were standing on the steps which lead up to the gold-fish when I picked out the Major. He was leaning forward in his chair, his hands grasping its arms. His face was screwed up with laughter. The man and the girl with him were smiling. All three seemed happy in each other's company. For the first time I saw the Major as part of a group. With these people, anyhow, he was not on the defensive; for the first time I saw him happy. Then he turned and saw us. His eyes rested on Alice; he smiled a welcome, got out of his chair and came towards us. Did he know that he had been happier before we came? Now he had to worry as to whether Alice was going to like his friends. Whether *they* were going to like *her*. He smiled a welcome, but he had been made less happy by our coming.

I felt sorry for him; but I realised his pretentiousness.

Felix introduced us first to the girl. Later he whispered to us that she was brilliant. The man was a Conservative M.P. He was very informative and inclined to be confidential. Among other things he told us that he had been in Germany when the Germans were not allowed to wear uniforms. So they wore dark blue suits. He had seen thousands of them at a meeting and all dressed exactly the same—what was that but a uniform?

'Like uniform with this volume,' Alice said.

The brilliant girl sat silent, smiling occasionally at Felix. Presently we went in to luncheon.

We had a table near the door. I remembered my mother telling me, when I was quite little, that those tables were the best in the room. It was grander to sit there than at any of the other tables. I wondered if Alice knew that; I would tell her after luncheon. We drank white wine and then burgundy; they were both good. Evidently the Major knew about wine. It was when we had got to the coffee and brandy that I saw Cassius. He was sitting at a table in the corner with a very handsome woman. Not young but very distinguished-looking. He saw me and waved. I waved back. Alice looked up and he waved to her too, but he didn't come over to us. I wondered who the woman was. A rich client probably, if booksellers had them, which I supposed they did.

'Good Lord, Cassius!' Felix had seen him now. 'I didn't know he was free in the middle of the day, what?'

As if Cassius was *ever* not free! But I suppose that Felix meant it as an apology for not having asked him to luncheon.

A week later Cassius left Alice. He walked out of the house, saying that he was going to get a taxi, and he didn't come back. Three days later he wrote to her. The letter said that he would continue to support her. He would, if she wished, provide her with evidence on which she might obtain a divorce. And he was sorry for any inconvenience he might have caused her. The letter was signed, 'With love from Cassius,' and there was a postscript, in which he gave her *Runa* as a present, as he wouldn't be doing any more sailing that summer.

As far as I know, Alice saw no one but Geoffrey during those three days when she waited to hear what had become of Cassius. Geoffrey had been there when Cassius went to fetch the taxi. He had been dining in Chapel Street and the three of them were to have gone to a cinema. At first Geoffrey and Alice had thought that Cassius must have forgotten them and absent-mindedly gone to the cinema by himself. Then at twelve o'clock they had become alarmed and telephoned to the police. It was no good. Cassius, it seemed, had completely disappeared.

I made Geoffrey promise that he would let me know the moment there was any news. The news came on the third day in the letter from Cassius. The letter had been postmarked in Maida Hill. It seemed an unlikely district. There was nothing to do but wait. Two days later the letter was followed by a picture postcard of a lady with a diamante hair ribbon and a ballet skirt made of mauve crêpe-de-Chine. She had been photographed against a background of roses. On the back was written:—

"*Friday*. Sailing to-day for South Africa. Hoping to contact opium-smuggling friends. Have quite good cabin with port-hole. Have just won the jackpot on the fruit machine in the bar, *only* fifteen shillings, which is *bad*. Lots of love from Cassius."

It wasn't satisfactory. We decided that the part about the opium smugglers couldn't possibly be true. Geoffrey now said that Alice must be cheered up and took parties of mutual acquaintances round to see her in Chapel Street. They would arrive about six o'clock and sit about drinking Alice's gin and talk loudly to each other. Alice would sit in the midst of them, frightened and wretched. After a few days of it she asked me to go and stay with her. I had offered to when Cassius had first disappeared, but she had obviously so hated the idea that I had not suggested it again. But now she seemed glad of any company that was sympathetic.

I arrived on a Wednesday evening after work. The drawing-room, as usual, was filled with Geoffrey's friends. Alice took me up to the spare room and told me that Mrs. Norton had arrived in London.

'She's staying in a hotel in Knightsbridge. I had to go and have luncheon and spend the afternoon with her, and she was very cross.'

'What about?' I asked, and began to unpack.

'Florence will do that.' Alice sat down on one of the two white painted chairs. I went on unpacking; had I not come to be helpful?

'What was your mother cross about?' I repeated.

'About Cassius, of course. She said I was irresponsible, and that Anthony was no better, because he isn't getting "on" in the army.'

'What has that got to do with it?'

'Nothing,' Alice said. 'Mummy's like that. She said she was terribly worried about *all* her children. I wish I was dead.'

'But it wasn't your *fault* about Cassius. After all, you didn't leave *him*.'

'But I *might* have,' Alice said.

I didn't answer. There didn't seem to be anything to say to that.

'Though actually, I suppose I never would have.'

I agreed that it was unlikely that Alice would have left Cassius.

'You see,' Alice said, 'I really do love him, and we enjoyed the same sort of jokes and all that sort of thing. And I thought he loved *me*. He never said he *didn't*. And I just sort of thought we would go on for ever. Like Mummy and Daddy, only having more fun.'

'Perhaps he'll come back,' I suggested diffidently.

'He won't,' Alice said with conviction. 'I know for certain that he won't do that.'

We were silent again. Alice seemed embarrassed at having said even so little about herself and her feelings. But she went on, speaking so softly that I could hardly hear her. 'If nothing's permanent, I don't see the good of being alive. What's the *point* of being hurt all the time? If there was something that would last, then it wouldn't matter. But the way things are, one is tortured for no reason.' She got up abruptly. 'I'm being stupid. I know I'm being stupid. I think self-pity is perfectly disgusting.' She went towards the door. 'Hurry up with that, and come and get a drink.'

I was kneeling on the floor, arranging my jerseys in the bottom drawer of the chest of drawers. Like the chairs, the chest was painted white, as was the iron bedstead. It struck me that this furniture had come from Alice's bedroom at home. I stared up at Alice as she stood in the doorway. She was no longer embarrassed by her mood and words of a moment before. She had completely forgotten them.

I got up and walked downstairs behind her. As we reached the drawing-room, the telephone started to ring. Geoffrey answered it and turned to Alice.

'It's *that* Mrs. Bryant, dear.' He put his hand over the receiver. 'She's up in London. She wants to know if she can come round and bring that poor Harold with her?'

'Tell her I'd love to see them.' Alice sounded quite sincere.

'Very well, dear, if you say so.' Geoffrey shrugged his shoulders and spoke again into the telephone. 'They'll be here in ten minutes,' he said as he put down the receiver. 'And I think I'd better warn you, that she's likely to "delve."'

'Who cares?' Alice went over to the table which had the cocktails on it. She poured one out for me, but I noticed that she helped herself only to lemonade and soda water. Florence, Alice's house-parlourmaid, opened the drawing-room door. I was expecting her to announce Mrs. Bryant and Harold, but she was followed into the room by Sonia.

'Darling!' Sonia rushed across to Alice and kissed her on both cheeks. Although she and Alice had not met for months, she seemed perfectly sure of her welcome. 'Darling, why didn't you *tell* me? I had no idea that anything had happened, until Mummy rang up in a most frightful flap. Really, Mummy is *impossible.*'

Alice gave Sonia a drink, and left her to talk to Geoffrey and me. She did not introduce her to any of the cheering-up party.

'Well!' Sonia turned to Geoffrey. 'It's a very long time since I've seen you.'

'Not since you ran off with young Yorke,' Geoffrey agreed sweetly.

Sonia looked surprised. 'Good Heavens! Is it really as long ago as all *that*?' I turned away. Geoffrey was quite capable of dealing with Sonia, but I wondered why she had come.

Mrs. Bryant and Harold arrived. Mrs. Bryant was wearing a yellow dress which didn't suit her.

'But where is Felix?' Mrs. Bryant asked in a loud voice, looking round the room.

'We very much hope,' Geoffrey said, 'that he is down at Blythe polishing the brass and getting those nasty black marks off the paint.'

Rosamond Bryant raised her eyebrows.

'But he's in London,' she said, looking at Alice. 'Didn't you know?' And her mouth set into its primmest lines. Really, she was remarkably like an egg. An egg which she spent an hour and a half painting every morning. It was fantastic.

Sonia and Mrs. Bryant already knew each other. They sat together on the sofa. Harold went across to the fireplace and spoke to the most presentable of Geoffrey's friends, a golden-haired young woman wearing a large black hat. The young woman appeared delighted to see him.

Mrs. Bryant talked to Sonia, but at the same time she managed to keep Harold under constant supervision. When it was time for the young woman to leave, I heard Harold inviting her to have luncheon with him the following day. He told her that he was a member of quite an amusing little club, and suggested that she might like to go there. The young woman accepted with evident pleasure. I glanced at Mrs. Bryant. She was no longer looking at Harold. Her conversation with Sonia had become sensibly more animated. There was no expression on that face which might betray that she had overheard the invitation. I was quite sure that she had done so and that Harold would be dealt with later. With the departure of the young woman, and with Harold safely talking to one of the men, Mrs. Bryant was able to drop a little of her animation. She called to Alice to join her and Sonia on the sofa.

Geoffrey came over to me.

'I've had a letter from Cassius,' he said.

'What did he say?'

'He said he'd realised during the last few weeks that Alice didn't like him, so he thought it would be better to go away. He isn't coming back to her.'

'It will be all right,' Geoffrey said. 'Of course it will be all right,' but I knew that he did not believe what he said.

NINE

I REMAINED with Alice for several weeks, and it was while I was there that Jennifer got married to her clergyman. The wedding was at St. Columbia's, Pont Street, and Ellen and I went to it together. Captain Parsons gave his daughter away. All Jennifer's female relations were there wearing their raffia hats; amongst them had sat my mother, looking elegant and distinguished. Involuntarily one had felt how lucky poor Jennifer was to have such a stepmother.

Poor Jennifer had looked hot in straining white satin.

'She doesn't make a very pretty bride, does she?' Ellen had whispered to me during the service.

'Perhaps she'll make a good wife,' I whispered back. Ellen sighed and glanced at the clergyman's three children, who sat in the front row on the other side of the aisle.

'Captain Parsons looks nervous.'

I looked at Captain Parsons' back; it seemed much as usual.

'But then men don't enjoy weddings the way we do,' Ellen whispered complacently and folded her hands in their white kid gloves.

I got back from the wedding to find Mrs. Bryant sitting in the drawing-room with Alice. Mrs. Bryant seemed to be continually in the house now. She came up from Blythe to spend the day, the night, in London. She had appointments with her dentist, her hairdresser, and with the woman who sewed for her. I would come back from work, or in this case from Jennifer's wedding, to find her with Alice. Always confiding, always giving advice; and now Alice listened to her. Now Mrs. Bryant was never 'that dreary woman.' She wasn't even Mrs. Bryant. She was 'Rosamond,' and 'rather amusing when you got to know her.'

I suggested that perhaps she was rather coy.

Alice said, no, Rosamond wasn't coy. So I left it. I told myself that it was good that Alice should find that anything was amusing, even Mrs. Bryant whom I thought of as evil, and perhaps I was wrong about Mrs. Bryant.

Obviously that wasn't how she thought of herself. She sought to do neither harm nor good. She was detached, intellectual and artistic. She read American books which had been banned in England and English books which had been banned in America. She belonged to the Arts Club and the Gate Theatre, and so had the opportunity of seeing translations of French plays which had been banned in both England *and* America. These plays seemed to deal always with the Eternal Triangle and the Eternal Tart, with the added complication of almost Eternal Incest.

I went with her and Alice to one of these little theatre clubs. It was in North London and was called the Troubador Theatre. Mrs. Bryant assured us beforehand that they never put on anything but 'interesting' plays. As Harold simply hated 'interesting' plays, Mrs. Bryant arranged that we should go by ourselves and meet him and Felix and Geoffrey afterwards. We dined in Chapel Street and during dinner Mrs. Bryant told us that this evening the principal actress as well as the play would be interesting.

'That will be nice,' I said.

'You've probably heard of her,' Mrs. Bryant said, 'Honoria Winston; she used to be quite well known before her marriage.'

There was a pause, during which Alice and I failed to recognise the name of Honoria Winston.

'Wasn't she in musical comedy?' Alice said doubtfully.

I could see at once from Mrs. Bryant's face that that wasn't right.

Honoria Winston had been a Shakespearean actress of great promise. Then she had married and gone and buried herself in the country. She had had several children. Her husband had gone mad and had tried to strangle her. He was shut up now and Honoria wanted to return to the stage.

'But how awful!' Alice said, and I agreed.

Rosamond reminded us that *her* husband had tried to poison her.

'And he wasn't even shut up.' Alice was sympathetic. 'I do think it's a shame.'

Mrs. Bryant smiled sadly and went on about Honoria.

'Of course, it's terribly difficult for her to get back after all these years. That's why she's at the Troubador.'

'Doesn't she like it?' Alice asked.

'It suits her in a way because naturally she's able to play much more interesting parts than she would in the commercial theatre, but it's terribly badly paid, of course.'

It all sounded very sad. I imagined Honoria Winston starving in a garret. Every Friday she probably bought small postal orders and sent them to the orphanages in which her children were being brought up. Art, true art (anyhow according to Mrs. Bryant) went unappreciated in England. The English public had appallingly bad taste. As a result wonderful actresses like Honoria Winston appeared at the Troubador Theatre, which couldn't afford to pay them properly. Feeling thoroughly depressed, I followed Alice and Mrs. Bryant into a taxi and we started on the drive to North London.

The tiny foyer of the Troubador gave one at once the sense of brave endeavour rather than of gaiety. It was lit by naked bulbs hanging from the ceiling. The walls were painted a serviceable dark green. There was a wide door, leading into the auditorium and three smaller doors labelled respectively 'Ladies,' 'Gentlemen' and 'Bar.' On the one marked 'Bar' someone had painted two small wine-glasses leaning towards each other at an angle of forty-five degrees. In the box-office was an earnest young woman wearing a green knitted sweater. She didn't appear happy. One felt she was getting into a muddle with the tickets. When we arrived the foyer was full of people, many of whom seemed to know each other. Young women with unbrushed hair wearing sweaters and tweed skirts and sandals. Young men with unbrushed hair wearing flannel trousers and strangely checked shirts. Although it was a perfectly fine evening, they seemed, without exception, to have brought their mackintoshes. The rest of the audience was composed of middle-aged couples in navy blue and little groups of women in dark clothes and unfashionable hats.

We were shown to our seats by a young woman who appeared to be a replica of the one in the box-office. She sold us programmes which consisted of a single unfolded sheet of paper. We read that the play was called *L'amie de Papa.* 'Father's friend' was printed underneath in brackets. There were only five characters. Rosalie: Honoria Winston. Obviously this would be father's friend. Monsieur Jacques Poiret. Madame Poiret *(sa femme),* Guy Poiret *(son fils)* and Yvonne. Yvonne was the only unknown quantity. We could be sure, even before the curtain went up, that Monsieur Poiret and Guy *(son fils)* were both the lovers of Rosalie. Probably, though, they wouldn't know it themselves until near the end of the play.

We were in the front row. The mauve casement cloth curtain was within a few feet of us. To judge by its agitations the stage manager of the Troubador Theatre had left the arranging of the scene until the very last moment.

We waited. Somewhere out of sight a gramophone was playing very softly. At last the house lights were lowered and the curtains parted. Honoria Winston as Rosalie lay on the tiny stage in what was probably a Louis Seize bed. She was very good-looking. Within a few minutes she and Yvonne had told us that she was a drug addict. Obviously she was going to die very painfully and before our eyes in the last act. It all happened the way one had thought it would, with the splendid addition of Yvonne turning out to be the intimate friend and confidante of both Rosalie and Madame Poiret. As she was not anyone's illegitimate daughter, it was inevitable that she should be concerned with unnatural vice.

When the play ended, Mrs. Bryant said that she *must* go round and see Honoria 'Just for a minute.' Would we like to come too?

'She won't mind?' Alice asked. Mrs. Bryant assured us that Honoria would *love* it. We found one of the young ladies in green sweaters and she grudgingly took us round to the back. I had once or twice before visited actors or actresses in their dressing-rooms. It had never been a success. It was not now. Honoria Winston, still in the dressing-gown in which as Rosalie she had so lately died, received us politely but without enthusiasm. Obviously, poor thing, she was tired and wanted her supper. We said we had enjoyed the play. She said she was so glad. Mrs. Bryant praised her acting and Honoria thanked her. Alice and I smiled fixedly and inanely, hoping to identify ourselves with Mrs. Bryant's remarks. We had been brought round to 'see' Honoria, much as one had been taken to 'see' a particular animal at the zoo. But we could not just stare at her in peaceful silence, nor could we give her buns. Convention demanded that we should find words of praise. I looked round the dressing-room. It was small, stuffy and unglamorous and exactly like the others I had seen, differing from those in larger theatres only in the absence of running water. With relief I heard Mrs. Bryant preparing for our departure. It was sweet of Honoria to have seen us. They must have luncheon together very soon, or would Honoria, if she were doing nothing else, like to have supper with us this evening? We were meeting some friends at the Savoy. Honoria hesitated. Was she weighing Mrs. Bryant's invitation against a kipper eaten alone in her garret, or against fish and chips with Monsieur Poiret? It can't have been against anything very exciting, because almost at once she accepted.

We went into the passage to wait until she should be ready. We were passed by 'Yvonne' arguing with a young man in horn-rimmed glasses. They looked at us with some amusement, as we stood in a row leaning our backs against the wall opposite the door of Honoria's dressing-room. The man broke away from Yvonne and asked us if we had enjoyed the show. We said, oh yes, very much, and he said it was tough on the actors having such a very small stage. Mrs. Bryant got in something about the interest of the production, and the young man went away.

We continued to wait. At last Honoria Winston joined us. She was wearing a black dress, and furs and a small black hat. She looked just like an actress and I was glad. I had been afraid of sandals and a tweed skirt and a jersey. We left the theatre, and there was a real stage doorman, who said, 'Good night, Miss Winston,' and smiled. Outside it was not so good. There were no taxis. We walked a short distance and got on a bus. Somewhere in Holborn we got off it and found a taxi. By the time we got to the Savoy Miss Winston had stopped being an animal at the zoo and had turned into an ordinary person.

In the little lounge off the grill-room we found Harold Cunningham, Felix and Geoffrey. Mrs. Bryant introduced them to Miss Winston and told them how simply wonderful she had been in the play. Harold, although thus prevented from uttering his prepared jokes about the absolute awfulness of interesting plays, seemed nevertheless quite pleased to meet Miss Winston. He even recalled that he had once seen her as Ophelia, and beamed at her, obviously expecting to be highly praised for this endurance, and for now recalling it so readily on meeting her.

We went in to supper. It seemed to be Harold's party and he sat between Honoria and Mrs. Bryant. I sat on Honoria's other side. As we sat down Mrs. Bryant leaned across Felix and spoke to Alice. Alice laughed, a laugh in which Felix joined; for a moment the three of them were isolated from us by their amusement.

But Mrs. Bryant could not bear isolation, even in laughter, for long. She turned to Harold, only to find him deep in conversation with Honoria. It seemed that he had a good deal more to say about Ophelia. I caught a flicker of determination on Mrs. Bryant's face. She drew Harold's attention to the fact that he had not yet ordered what we were to eat. Then he had to order the wine. Mrs. Bryant leant across him and, in the most friendly way, talked to Honoria. Honoria was amused. The smile on her beautiful mouth was derisive. She could not fail to know that she was being ordered off. Eventually, with a shrug, she turned to me.

'I think life is *fascinating*, don't you?' Honoria said. I said I supposed it was.

'Rosamond has told you, of course, that my husband tried to strangle me?'

'Well, yes,' I began, wondering where this extraordinary conversation was going to lead us.

'You needn't look so embarrassed. Rosamond always tells everyone that. She considers it to be the most interesting thing about me. And who knows, perhaps it is? Rosamond likes things to be interesting.'

'I suppose so.'

Honoria looked quickly round the table. 'She managed to tell me in the bus that Mrs. Skeffington had just been deserted by her husband.'

'But it's true,' I said.

'So is it true that I was nearly strangled but I do not think that that is the first piece of information that should be given about me.'

I said I saw that one but felt compelled to add that Mrs. Bryant had also told us what a marvellous actress Honoria was.

'In my *day*,' Honoria said. 'She must surely have mentioned that it was "in my *day*"?'

I laughed and gave up all pretence of being loyal to Rosamond.

'It's a curious thing,' Honoria was saying, 'how many of Rosamond's friends have trouble with their husbands. And she's always so wonderfully sympathetic about it.'

'You mean . . . ?' I said.

'Oh, not the usual thing. She doesn't "steal" them. In fact, she prides herself particularly on *not* doing that. Making it quite clear all the time that she is being very chivalrous in not attempting it.'

'Men seem to like her all right,' I said.

'But *she* likes power, and she gets it by interfering in other people's lives,' Honoria said. 'Rosamond can tell a wife that she's not happy with her husband and never suspect herself of acting from any but the most disinterested motives. Unconsciously, of course, she wants the men to be left free. She doesn't *admit* that is her motive, because she doesn't know it. I don't know the facts, but didn't something like that happen with the Skeffingtons?'

Honoria's enormous burning eyes were fixed on my face. It was impossible that she should feel so intensely for a stranger. There could be no doubt that this woman felt that Rosamond had interfered in *her* life. Honoria's eyes now rested on Alice. This evening Alice was quite lovely, gay and animated; but somewhere, though indefinable, existed a hardness that had not been there before.

'Yes,' I said. 'Alice has altered; that's why Cassius left her.' I had been unaware until now that I knew this.

'That's how she does it.' Honoria turned to me again.

'But how?' In spite of the heat of the room I felt cold.

'It isn't very difficult. She shows them how dull their lives are. She intimates that their emotions remain unfulfilled. Then she holds up her own life as an example of what *could* be.'

'But her own life's beastly.'

'She is able to make it sound quite pleasant, and for sensitive people it has one supreme advantage. Rosamond, you see, is *never* hurt.'

'But why not, when she's so horrid?'

Honoria shrugged her shoulders. 'Because, if you like, she's sold her soul to the devil; or because she never had one.'

I began to object and then fell silent, thinking how difficult people were, how mean and ungenerous. I looked up to find that Honoria was talking to Harold. Geoffrey was watching me.

'You're very depressed, dear.'

'I was thinking how nasty everything is.'

'That's not a very gay thing to think at a party.'

'I can't see that there's any point in Mrs. Bryant.'

Geoffrey considered her. 'She's quite useless certainly, but don't talk so loud, she'll hear you in a minute.'

'I don't care if she does,' I said recklessly.

We reached the end of supper. Mrs. Bryant suggested that we should go on somewhere and dance. Alice agreed that it would be wonderful to go to a night club. Honoria Winston said that she was far too tired, and Geoffrey and I said we wouldn't go either. We left the Savoy in two taxis. Geoffrey dropped Honoria and me home. Honoria lived somewhere in Primrose Hill. The taxi stopped, as far as I could see in the darkness, at a pleasant small house. Even if she was lodged in the garret, it was probably a nice one. She said that there was no matinee the following day and would we come to tea with her? We said we'd love to, and she said we were to be sure and bring Alice with us.

* * * * *

The next morning when Florence called me she said that Mrs. Skeffington hadn't been home all night. She managed to make it sound incredibly disreputable.

'What an extraordinary thing,' I said brightly.

'It seems very funny,' Florence agreed lugubriously. 'Of course, in this house, we're used to people going out and not coming in again.'

I tried to look repressive and Florence left the room. It did seem perhaps a little strange that Alice should not be back yet. I ate my breakfast and got up. It was twenty to nine. If I didn't leave in a few minutes, I should be late for the office. It seemed silly to ring up the police. Besides, we'd had rather a lot of that sort of thing lately.

When I got to work, I remembered that I might telephone to Mrs. Bryant. I was answered by a sleepy and distinctly cross voice.

'Who is it? Who?'

I said again who I was.

'Well, what do you want?'

I said I wanted to know where Alice was.

'How should I know? I don't go following my friends around to see who they sleep with.'

She rang off. I put the receiver down and hoped that our telephone operator hadn't been listening-in.

Later in the morning Alice rang me up.

'Darling, I've only just got in. I can't tell you how snooty Florence is being. I do hope you weren't worried.'

'Not at all,' I lied. 'Honoria Winston has asked us to go to tea with her, and I said we would. Will you be able to come?' Alice said where did she live? I gave her the address.

'Wait while I get a pencil to write it down.'

I waited under the disapproving eyes of Miss Grimthorne, the senior woman in our department. Miss Grimthorne thought that all private telephone calls, even incoming ones, were unnecessary; and mostly they were. Alice came back to the telephone. I repeated the address.

'How do you spell the person's name?' Alice asked. Wondering a little, I spelt out Honoria Winston for her. 'And I'll meet you there about a quarter-past five?'

'Yes,' Alice said, 'I think I shall go and lie down now. I do wish Florence wasn't being quite so awful, I must say.'

I arrived at Honoria's very late. Miss Grimthorne had found me several last-minute jobs; jobs which should rightly have been done by the office girl. But then Miss Grimthorne quite liked the office girl and wouldn't, if she could possibly avoid it, keep her at work a moment after five o'clock.

'There's no reason why you shouldn't finish the post, Miss Boswell. *You've* got your car to go home in. Poor Miss Clarke has to wait for the bus.'

Poor Miss Clarke, aged sixteen and with protruding teeth and her unbridled passion for Mr. Saunders. Somebody ought to buy her a bicycle; then she could finish the post herself. And at the week-ends, she could have a nice lot of healthy exercise, which might help to keep her mind off Mr. Saunders.

As I rang the bell in Primrose Hill, I was still possessed with the garret idea. The door was opened by a pleasant, rather untidy-looking woman. She had red hair, and wore a dark blue skirt and a green blouse. She had pink ear-rings which might have been coral.

'Miss Winston?' I began.

'Is she expecting you, do you know?'

'Oh, yes, she asked me to tea.'

'Then she's in the studio.' The woman retreated down the hall and opened a door on the right. I was shown into a largish room. The walls were distempered in cream. There was linoleum on the floor. The curtains were of pale embroidered Chinese silk. Honoria, who had been sitting in the farther window, jumped up at my entrance.

'How wonderful of you to come!' She took both my hands. 'But you haven't brought Alice.'

As she dropped my hands Honoria looked disappointed.

'She ought to be here any minute now.'

'Never mind. We'll have tea.' Honoria went to the door and shouted, 'Winifred!' There was no answer. Honoria, standing with one hand on the door-handle, shouted again. This time there was an answering shout from the basement.

'But the kettle ought to have boiled *hours* ago, oughtn't it?' She turned to me for corroboration.

'Geoffrey isn't coming, after all; apparently they're stocktaking at the museum.' Before I could answer her, she had left the room.

When she came back she was followed by Winifred carrying the tea-tray. Winifred slammed the tray down on the table. She was obviously 'put out.'

'She's a treasure,' Honoria said as Winifred went out, slamming the door after her. 'You wouldn't think it, but she's a treasure.'

On the tray there was an earthenware teapot, china cups which were all beautiful but did not match, and a lot of cosy-looking cakes and buns. For Honoria there was an egg in a silver egg-cup.

'It's to prevent my getting hiccups in the first act. Would you like one?'

I said no, but ate largely of everything else. Half-way through the meal Alice arrived.

'I'm sorry I'm late,' she said.

She looked very sad. I wondered whether Mrs. Bryant had been wrong in thinking that Alice had spent the night with Felix. There was nothing triumphant about her. She was sad and depressed and horribly nervous.

Most of the talking was done by Honoria and me. That evening I was dining out and going to a theatre and soon it was time for me to go. Alice got up when I did, but Honoria put a detaining hand on her arm.

'Don't go unless you have to, or are you dining early, too?'

'Oh, no,' Alice said, 'not until about nine.'

'Then stay and talk to me. I shan't go to the theatre until seven.'

I got back to Chapel Street about twelve that evening. The drawing-room was empty, but as I went upstairs I saw a light under Alice's door. She called to me to come in. Alice was in bed, a book lay open on the eiderdown.

'Hullo,' I said, 'you're early.'

'Yes,' Alice said. 'I didn't go out to dinner, after all. But I had a most lovely evening in Honoria's dressing-room and afterwards we went back to her house and Winifred gave us a delicious supper. I've only just got in. Do you think it would be a good thing if I went on the stage?'

'Aren't you rather old?' I said, sitting down on the bed.

'Well, I thought I was, but Honoria says that's nonsense. And there's a wonderful school one can go to—not the Royal Academy, another one. It's run by a frightfully good woman who's a great friend of Honoria's. . . .'

Alice, sitting up in bed, looked flushed and eager.

'Margaret, you *do* think it's an idea, don't you? I mean, I must do something and I would *like* to be an actress, and Honoria says it's possible. There wouldn't be any harm in trying, would there? Or do you think it's silly?'

'I don't know anything about it,' I said, and immediately Alice was disappointed and ready to abandon the scheme.

'I didn't mean not to try,' I said hurriedly. 'And it would be wonderful if it was a success, and why shouldn't it be?'

'Success only happens to other people,' Alice said gloomily. I told her not to be silly and glanced down at her book. It was Shakespeare's tragedies. I picked it up. It was open at *Romeo and Juliet*.

'Even if one was only a Woman Relation to Both Houses, it would be something to *do*. . . .'

'When will you be able to start?' I asked.

'Honoria says that the new term doesn't begin until September. But she made an appointment for me to go and see Miss Iliffe tomorrow.'

'How frightfully exciting!'

'She probably won't even accept me as a pupil.'

'She's bound to,' I said.

'Then why does she want to see me?'

'To make sure that you don't look like hell and that you haven't got adenoids or thick ankles.'

'And I haven't, *have* I?' Alice became more cheerful. 'Oh, Margaret, it *is* fun and Honoria says that after I've been accepted by Miss Iliffe I must try and get some work in repertory for the summer, as anything at all, you know. She says even an amateur company would be better than nothing.'

Again Alice was eager and enthusiastic.

My mother and Captain Parsons were in London. The next evening I had to go to dinner with them. It was annoying. They had a perfectly good house in Devonshire; why couldn't they spend the summer there? I was dressing gloomily when Alice knocked at the door of my room.

'Come in.'

Alice came in and shut the door behind her.

'Isn't it *wonderful*? Miss Iliffe liked me.'

'I thought she would. I wish my mother was going to like *me*.'

'Perhaps she will if you agree with everything she says,' Alice said absently.

I crossed to the wardrobe and took out a rather unbecoming dress which usually I didn't wear.

'Tell me all about Miss Iliffe. Did she make you recite to her?'

'No, of course not.'

Alice was looking critically at herself in the glass.

'She asked me a lot of questions about why I wanted to go on the stage, and whether I could afford to be trained by her.'

'So it's all settled?'

'Yes, she's an extraordinary old woman. She didn't look as if she could act at all. Now I must find a repertory company. Miss Iliffe says there are heaps of them up and down the country. Where do you think it would be nice to go?'

'Brighton, then if you got bored you could sit in the Pavilion.'

'Or Wales,' Alice said. 'I've never been to Wales. I wish we'd had a telephone put in this room. I want to ring up Rosamond and say I can't have dinner with her.'

'Isn't it rather late to do that?'

'Not if I'd got a really bad headache which had come on suddenly. I think Rosamond's rather a bore, and *very* limited.'

'That's what Honoria said.'

'Did she? Well, anyhow I agree with her.'

I was now ready. If I didn't start for Regent's Park I should be late.

'I think I shall go to bed and ask Mrs. Browning to give me an egg on a tray,' Alice said. 'Florence will be furious at having to carry it up. When I'm on the stage, I'll have a servant like Winifred whom I can shout at. I think one servant's heaps, don't you, and I shall live in a much smaller house and be economical.'

'Perhaps you'll get married again.'

'Oh, I do hope *not*. Anyhow I'm not divorced so I can't, and everyone says that divorces take simply *ages*.'

So I went out to dinner. As I left the house, I heard the telephone ringing.

I arrived in Regent's Park. The staircase was very beautiful. If I was going to be bored, I could at least enjoy the beauty of the staircase. I was shown into the drawing-room, furnished with art treasures of a later date than those at Tor Cross. On the floor was a Savonnerie carpet; over the mantelpiece there hung a picture by Winterhalter of a woman in a blue dress. On her rounded arm was a heavy gold bracelet. Captain Parsons was in the room. With him was a young man. They got up as I came in.

'Your mother isn't down yet.'

I asked after poor Jennifer. Captain Parsons sighed and said he believed she was well. Poor Jennifer became very remote.

'Or as well as can be expected.'

So poor Jennifer was going to have a little clerical baby. But it was of no interest either to me or Captain Parsons. I looked at the young man. He wasn't as young as I had thought, probably thirty-five.

'Don't you two know each other?' Captain Parsons seemed surprised. 'My step-daughter Margaret Boswell, Commander Penrose.'

We shook hands. My mother came in and we went down to dinner. My mother was in a very good temper. It was all pleasanter than I had expected. A month later George Penrose and I were married.

But that was the future. This evening I sat in my ugly dress and thought about the situation I had left behind me in Chapel Street. When I was alone with my mother in the drawing-room, she upbraided me for my silence during dinner.

'You might make some effort to try and appear entertaining. What's the matter with you, and why do you always wear such awful clothes?'

'It's not very nice, is it?' I looked down at my bunchy black taffeta dress. My mother, looking wonderful in grey chiffon, fingered her diamond and ruby necklace.

'You're not elegant,' she complained.

'But spotlessly clean,' I said.

'I should hope so. Is it true that Alice is getting herself involved with that dreadful Felix Wordsworth?'

'He isn't dreadful. Besides she isn't involved.'

'He was mixed up in the Bexhill divorce case.'

'With that terrible old Lady Bexhill and the Bishop?'

'There was no Bishop,' my mother said, 'and I think Alice is behaving very unwisely. If she isn't careful she won't get her divorce.'

'I don't think she wants one particularly.'

'That's nonsense. Of course a young woman in her position wants a divorce.'

I let that go, and from divorce we passed easily to marriage, and why wasn't I married? We were now on familiar ground. We remained on it until Captain Parsons and Commander Penrose came upstairs. When it was time to go, Commander Penrose said he would take me home. I liked him. He asked me when I would have dinner with him, so perhaps he liked *me*, and probably he hadn't noticed the black taffeta enough to be put off by it.

I let myself into Chapel Street. On the hall table there was a letter for me. It was from Alice. Wondering rather, I picked it up. So Alice hadn't managed to have her supper on a tray.

Something had happened and she had gone out leaving a letter for me. I started to walk upstairs as I read it. It was in pencil and had evidently been written in a hurry.

DARLING [it began],

Sonia rang up just as you were leaving. She said that I wasn't being fair to Felix and I do see what she means, so I have gone down to Blythe with him.

We shall stay on board *Runa*.

With love from Alice

It was terrifying. It was so casual, and yet it was inevitable. Mrs. Bryant would have advised Alice to go away with Felix. Mrs. Bryant had been discredited by Honoria, so Sonia rang up and told Alice that she was not being fair to Felix. Immediately Alice decided to go away with him. Did Alice love him, did she feel anything at all about him?

I went into the drawing-room and switched on the lights. The sofa cushions were still crumpled; there were cigarette ends in the ashtrays. Felix had been here, and then he and Alice had gone to Blythe. It couldn't be very long since they had left. Probably they hadn't even got as far as Basingstoke. Felix would be driving and Alice would be sitting a little sideways looking at him, watching his profile, seeing his hands on the wheel, as they were lit up by the headlights of oncoming cars. How often from the back seat of a car had I seen Alice watching Cassius as he drove. Felix's hands on the wheel would look stronger, thicker, less beautiful than Cassius'. Would Alice compare their hands, thinking regretfully of Cassius? It was more likely that she would be glad of Felix's devotion.

And Felix, how would he feel? Triumphant perhaps, or a little puzzled. Happy that now at last he had Alice to himself. Being Felix, he would have to complicate it, be able to feel that he was taking her away from the confusion she had made of her life, and from the conflicting voices, the conflicting advice.

Again I looked at the room. It was as if I saw it for the first time. Soon it would disappear altogether. These tables and chairs and lamps would no longer form part of a single whole.

Together they had made a background for Alice and Cassius. Cassius and Alice no longer existed.

Ten

THE NEXT MORNING Florence, not knowing that the house had ceased to exist, called me as usual.

'It's raining.' She stood at the window in her crumpled overall. 'It's raining very hard,' she repeated; evidently she felt that bad weather was a personal triumph. 'And Mrs. Skeffington isn't here.'

'She's gone down to see about the boat,' I said.

Florence sniffed. 'I wish she'd told me before; none of her underclothes were ironed.'

I didn't answer.

'Mrs. Browning wants to know if you'll be here for the weekend, because if so, she'll get something in.'

'Oh, no,' I said hurriedly. 'I shall be away.'

'You won't be wanting luncheon?'

'Certainly not.'

Florence left the room, and I was left to contemplate the burnt toast she had set before me. It was Saturday. I didn't have to go to work. By giving way to Florence, I had left myself with nowhere to stay for the next two nights. But if Alice wasn't coming back, there was no point in remaining. Alice, I thought crossly, had been inconsiderate. But I knew I was being unreasonable. I heard the telephone ringing. It went on and on. Florence and Mrs. Browning must have been struck deaf, or, more likely, have decided not to answer it. I got out of bed and went down to Alice's bedroom and took off the receiver.

Who on earth was it? Standing in my bare feet (I had been unable to find my slippers), I felt cross. Over the line, I could hear those confused noises that precede a long-distance call. Metallic voices assuring each other that they were Bristol and Winchester. The operator told me not to ring off. I hadn't thought of doing so; now I wondered if it wouldn't be a good idea. Then I heard Alice's voice.

'Darling, is it you?'

'Yes,' I said grudgingly.

'We're in Yarmouth,' Alice said. 'Will you have all my letters sent on to the post office in Weymouth, and not tell anyone where I am?'

'All right,' I said. 'But I'm going away for the week-end, and after that I shall be at Hill Street.'

'Oh, very well,' Alice said. 'Florence can forward the letters, but I always think a post office is such a very compromising address.'

'Are you coming back?' I asked.

'Yes, of course. I want to get rid of the house and I shall have to give Florence and Mrs. Browning notice. I suppose you couldn't do that *for* me. I've never given anyone notice before.'

I said I should adore to give Florence notice, and asked Alice why she was in Yarmouth.

'To buy some bread and to telephone. It's a perfectly wonderful day. We're going to go to Poole and then to Weymouth on Sunday. If Mummy should ring up, you might say I'm with friends. It might easily be true, mightn't it? I hope Sonia's not going to be indiscreet, though.' Already Alice was sounding worried.

I said to leave Sonia to me. I had no idea what I meant, but Alice seemed pleased and we rang off.

I sat down on Alice's bed and rang up Hill Street. My grandmother was in Ireland. Ellen answered the telephone.

'Ellen, will it be all right if I come back for the week-end?'

Ellen said that of course it would, and if I wanted any lunch, she had a lovely bit of fish. I felt comforted. Ellen was the nicest person I knew. No one else was so consistently on my side. Gratefully, I tried to think of something to say that would give her pleasure.

'Poor Jennifer's going to have a baby.'

'Really! Still, I suppose with so many step-children, she won't notice the difference.'

'It's bound to make a bit of difference,' I said. Ellen laughed and asked how many months 'Poor Jennifer' was 'gone.' I said I didn't know.

'Never mind, we shall soon see. You remember the woman who lives next door to my cousins at Bromley?'

'The one who tells fortunes?' I asked uncertainly.

'That's right. Well, she's coming over to have some supper with me on Sunday. We may go to the pictures first, but I'll get her to tell your fortune either before or after.'

'I hope she'll see something nice.'

'She'll tell you whatever it is,' Ellen said darkly.

'Well, I must go and pack.'

'If they aren't even going to do *that* for you,' Ellen said, 'don't you go giving those girls a lot of money. It isn't necessary, and they won't think any the more of you. Though it's nice to be generous,' she added as an afterthought.

Feeling altogether happier, I went and had my bath. The water wasn't hot. I went back to my bedroom, where I found Florence wondering, she said, if it was worth while to put any sheets back on the bed. I told her no, and that Mrs. Skeffington was giving up the house, and wanted her and Mrs. Browning to take a month's notice. Florence glared and said she wouldn't have been staying long anyhow. And she supposed Mrs. Skeffington had gone off with that Major Wordsworth.

An hour later I was in Hill Street. Florence and I had parted frostily. I had given her an enormous tip because I hated her so much.

As it happened I remained in Hill Street until I was married. Ellen was delighted. It was, she said, ridiculous having that big house with nobody in it, and anyhow I was somebody to talk to besides Annie, who was no better than a half-wit, and a great waster of scrubbing soap. All Ellen's under-housemaids, since the time she first came to us, had been half-wits and had wasted scrubbing soap. Most of them had been called Annie.

After a week Alice came back to London. She had, she told me, to settle up her affairs.

'I have been to a house agent and a lawyer and they are both going to see other lawyers and house agents. I'm afraid that it's all going to be rather complicated. And I've had a letter from a lady in Golders Green asking if Florence is discreet. I think it would be untruthful to say "yes," don't you?'

It was not yet dinner-time. We were sitting in the little room at the back of the drawing-room in Hill Street.

I had been delighted and surprised to find Alice there when I got back from work. She was only in London for two nights. She had left Felix in Weymouth. He was quite happy, as he was going to 'do' the decks properly with spirits of salt and mend a hole in the staysail.

'Mending sails is much more fun than sewing,' Alice said. 'I suppose it's because one can pretend one's Drake and Sir Walter Raleigh.'

I said that when I sewed I always pretended I was the Brontës. 'Especially Anne, because she sewed much better than the others.'

'Felix pretends that sort of thing too,' Alice said. 'It's one of the reasons I like him. When he does the brass, he's always a very old sailor in a windjammer. You know, he's quite different than we used to think. All that "er, what yes, I'll murder them" wasn't him at all.' And Alice looked at me, anxious that I should accept Felix as a human being.

'What about the stage?' I asked. 'I suppose you won't be doing that now?'

'You don't understand,' Alice said. 'Felix and I aren't going to tie each other down in any way. I'm going to go to Miss Iliffe's when the term starts and Felix has got some friends who are at a summer theatre in Cornwall. He's written to them to see if they couldn't fit me into it; if they could it would be great fun and we could take *Runa* down there and live on board. It would be wonderful if it came off, but it does sound so much too good to be true, and it would be awful if Mummy found out.'

'Why should she?' I said. 'And I don't see it would matter if she did.'

'She'd be cross,' Alice said, 'and if people are cross it spoils things.'

'Tell me about Felix,' I said.

Alice hesitated. 'I'll tell you about the night we went down to Blythe. I'd never meant to go away with him and if it hadn't've been for Sonia, I never would have. It's the only helpful thing that Sonia's ever done, and she only did that by accident. Do you remember all those years ago, how she behaved over Martin? I could have killed her then. I mean *really* killed her. I knew *exactly* how murderers feel.' Alice looked at me and I saw in her eyes the hatred which had been there five years before and which, at the time, she would never have allowed *anyone* to see.

'After Sonia had telephoned,' Alice went on, 'I went and packed and wrote that note to you and then Felix came round and we sat in the drawing-room and talked, not that there was very much to say, because I'd decided by then that I was going with him, so it was mostly a conversation about petrol and paraffin and how many tins of sardines were left in the locker. That sort of thing. And then Felix said that he supposed we ought to be starting and he looked quite shy and that made him suddenly awfully nice, and we went down to the hall and I called to Florence and told her that I was going to Blythe unexpectedly, and she sounded cross, so I didn't ask her for a loaf of bread like I'd meant to and we left the house.

'It was a wonderful evening, and on the drive down I thought about how wonderful everything was going to be now, if only nothing happened to prevent it, and then I thought about Felix and I hoped *he* was going to be happy. Because he's really had rather a horrid time in spite of being rich. You knew that his wife left him about six years ago and he divorced her and she's married to an Australian and wears washing silk dresses, but I was telling you about Felix.

'When we got to Blythe it was cold and there wasn't a moon. We couldn't find *Runa* at first because the shipyard had moved her and we went stumbling about falling over things, and I wished I hadn't come; but Felix was marvellous and in the end of course we found *Runa* and got on board. It was terribly dark and everything was damp and I had that awful feeling as though I wasn't there. Then Felix lit the lamps in the saloon and got the primus working and said that we'd have a cup of tea, and suddenly it was all right again. We sat in the saloon and the lamps smoked a bit, you know the way they do, and it began to get warm and I thought how horrid it would be to have a yacht which had electric light, and I was happy and I wished it would stay like that for ever. I do wish things didn't have to go *on*, don't you?'

I said that if things didn't go on one would be dead.

'I suppose so,' Alice agreed, 'but it's a pity. Anyhow we sat there for a long time just enjoying it and Felix told me a lot of things about himself. How he was wounded right at the end of the war when he was only eighteen and how he'd married that awful woman when he was still so young. He didn't say she was awful, but she obviously was and years older than him. Then he told me about that divorce case he'd been in and said how he hated living in his club and asked me to marry him again.'

'And are you going to?'

'No, I don't think so,' Alice said. 'I want us to stay as we are now.' She paused a moment and then went on. 'The next morning everything was still lovely and we sailed over to Yarmouth and I rang you up.'

'Didn't you see the Murrays?'

'Oh, yes, they were messing about on their barge and we shouted to each other. I don't think they'll ever go to the South of France, do you?'

I agreed that they probably wouldn't.

'I like them,' Alice said. 'They're so silly. They've got a wonderful scheme now for starting a club outside the three-mile limit, and they think they're going to make a lot of money.'

Alice went to her summer theatre in Cornwall. On the way down there she and Felix nearly drowned themselves in Portland Race. Alice wrote that it had been interesting. In her next letter she said that the theatre was interesting and that they were playing to full houses. 'It isn't really a theatre but a hall which belongs to the Women's Institute and the audience sit on kitchen chairs,' the letter went on. 'The whole company is very young and last week we did *The Breadwinner*. Felix is being very sweet, but he gets cross sometimes. Mummy has found out where I am.'

I wrote back and told Alice that I was going to marry George Penrose. As George had been ordered to the Mediterranean, we were married almost immediately and there was no time to arrange an elaborate wedding. We went down to Devonshire and I was married from Tor Cross, but to please Ellen I wore white and a bridal veil and George produced two small nieces to be bridesmaids. They were ugly little girls with wide mouths and straggling fair hair. Ellen told me afterwards that they had fidgeted the whole way through the service. She was probably right. I had been too nervous to notice.

We went for our honeymoon to Scotland where it rained. By the middle of September George had sailed and I was back in Hill Street. We didn't know how long his appointment was to last, but like all naval officers he was hoping to get a spell at the Admiralty and we planned that our permanent home should be in London. George left it to me to find a house and to furnish it. He thought that he might be back by Christmas. If not, I was to come out to Malta or Cyprus or Gibraltar.

Alice and Felix came up to London. They took two service flats in the same building; an arrangement which was intended to deceive Mrs. Norton as well as the King's Proctor who, it was hoped, would soon be concerned with Alice's affairs. It was a *vain* hope; pre-war divorces moved with all the slow stateliness of life at the German Courts during the last century. The term began at Miss Iliffe's school of Dramatic Art.

'Il faut souffrir,' Alice said, 'pour être better.'

She sat in front of the dressing-table and put combs in her hair, drawing it tightly back from her forehead. She frowned at herself in the glass.

I turned from Alice to the room in which we sat. It was typical of any of the service flats off St. James's Street. The furniture was dark and so was the wallpaper which was supposed to look like tapestry. The curtains, also tapestry, were drawn across a window which looked out upon a well. The neighbourhood was 'good'; the room and everything in it was 'bad.'

Felix came in from the sitting-room without knocking and sat on the bed.

'Haven't you finished *yet*?' he asked. 'The drinks are getting hot.' He sounded cross.

Alice turned round with a smile which ought surely to have disarmed him. 'You shouldn't have mixed them so soon, I'm not ready.'

'But your guests have already arrived.' Felix looked at me and I felt the chill unwantedness of the guest, that so often unwelcome supernumerary.

It was the end of November; Alice had now been at Miss Iliffe's for over two months.

'Who else is coming?' Felix asked.

'Only Sonia and Paddy and Geoffrey,' Alice said. 'Surely you remember, and we're going on to Honoria's afterwards?'

'Geoffrey!' Felix said. 'Why do we always have to cart him around?'

'But don't you *like* him?' Alice was genuinely surprised.

'Intellectuals!' Felix said. 'Talking a lot of rot. *I* don't want to know what he's been doing at his beastly museum.'

'Then I don't expect he'll tell you,' Alice said.

'He's all right of course.' Felix got off the bed. 'But boring, don't you know. Let's go and get a drink.'

We went into the sitting-room, which was furnished in the same dismal style as the bedroom. In the middle of the room was a large dining-room table; the walls were covered in plywood stained to that colour known, for some reason, as 'oak.' The mantelpiece was 'Tudor' and beside it was a small sofa and a stuffed chair, both were upholstered in 'tapestry.' A tray of drinks stood on a heavy sideboard.

Alice and I sat down on the sofa. She offered me a cigarette from a box which stood on a low surgical table.

'It will be nice,' she said, 'when we don't have to live here any more.' She looked at the loudly ticking oak clock.

'It's perfectly bloody.' Felix handed me a drink. 'And damned nonsense living in two flats.'

'The King's Proctor,' Alice said. 'I wonder if he knows how expensive he makes things for everybody?'

Felix repeated that it was damned nonsense, and it wasn't even as if Alice's divorce had started yet.

The valet, obviously love-nest trained, tapped on the door and on being told to come in, announced Geoffrey.

'Darling Geoffrey!' Alice jumped up.

Geoffrey came into the room looking charming. I saw him, as I had so often done before, as a bulwark against that which was disagreeable, raw and not quite civilised.

'Dearest Alice'—he kissed her on both cheeks—'and dearest Margaret.' He turned to Felix. 'I simply adore this room.'

Felix said, 'Oh, yes,' and gave Geoffrey a drink. He was always suspecting, quite wrongly, that Geoffrey was 'getting' at him or was being 'clever.' And yet Felix was not a stupid man and he was not insensitive.

'And how is Miss Iliffe?' Geoffrey asked Alice.

'She's very well,' Alice said, 'and she's teaching me how to be Portia.'

'That seems rather advanced, dear.'

'Oh, it's only practice,' Alice said. 'Everyone's being Portia this week.'

Geoffrey drew up one of the dining-room chairs. It had a bright red leatherette seat. 'And will you be having an end-of-term play, and are we all going to come to it?'

Alice was prevented from answering by the entrance of Sonia and Paddy.

Sonia at nearly thirty was as beautiful as ever and looked extremely young.

'Darling!' As she kissed Alice and Alice returned her embrace I remembered that Alice had known '*exactly* how murderers feel.' Only that had been years ago and because Sonia had taken Martin Yorke away from her. Alice didn't hate Sonia now, she was indifferent to her, or she admired her because she had, so far, come through her life unscathed. Like Mrs. Bryant, Sonia had 'managed.' Unlike Mrs. Bryant she was generous and not particularly calculating. She turned now to me.

'You remember Paddy?'

Paddy bowed and said, 'We last met in rather trying circumstances.'

I thought of the 'trying circumstances,' of the house in St. John's Wood, of Mrs. Sterne with her blue curls and of the dim Estelle. Was he still married to Estelle, and if so how had he escaped from the vigilance of Mrs. Sterne? I smiled uncertainly; it seemed more tactful not to ask after his relations. I wondered why he had remained so consistently in Sonia's life among all the muddle of lovers and service flats and jobs in flower shops and race meetings, and *his* marriage to Estelle. Estelle was rich; Sonia had found it convenient for Paddy to have a rich wife. I remembered I had been shocked when Alice had told me about that. Other people had behaved like Sonia and would do so again, only it was better not to think about it, better to imagine that Paddy and Estelle and Sonia were an exception, a deviation from the natural order of things.

I looked across at Alice. She was talking to Geoffrey and Sonia. Felix had joined them. He stood, as it were, apart from them on the fringe of their society. Sonia turned and included him in her conversation. Sonia was the link which joined him with Geoffrey and Alice.

'My mother-in-law,' Paddy was saying, 'thought you were so charming.'

I started. 'She didn't seem to at the time.'

'Oh, that was nothing,' Paddy said. 'She was a little distrait, you know, and then thinking you were Alice confused her. Then there was that nice David Mason. What have you done with him?'

'Nothing,' I said. 'I believe his father's dead now and he runs the factory.'

'Does he?' Paddy said. 'I must go and see him. I have an invention; it's rather neat really, but it might be difficult to carry out.'

I asked him what the invention was and he said it was a new kind of camera. 'Once it gets going the film people will be falling over themselves to get hold of it. What a pity that Alice isn't going to be married to David instead of to that old man.'

I said that, as far as I knew, Alice wasn't going to marry anybody.

'Now don't get me wrong,' Paddy said. 'I wasn't *only* thinking of my camera.'

The waiter knocked on the door and said that dinner was ready. We trooped out of the flat and down the corridor to Felix's flat. His sitting-room was an exact replica of Alice's. His dining-room table was laid with the unconvincing silver and inadequate napkins belonging to the flats. It was like a table in a shop window, and rather a cheap shop at that. One had the impression that real food would never be served at that table, real people would never gather round it and talk and eat and exchange opinions. I sat beside Felix and on my other side was Paddy. Dinner began badly with a watery soup. Felix was soon caught up in conversation by Sonia. He still looked cross. It wasn't important. People were often irritable and cross. When that happened one mustn't be frightened, one must remember that it was natural, that they had indigestion and that it would pass. One had only to wait and they would become agreeable again. I looked past Paddy at Geoffrey and Alice. They at least were not frightening.

'Mind you,' Paddy spoke confidentially into my right ear, 'I should be the last person to advise anyone to marry.'

I told him that I had been married two months before.

'I had heard that too,' Paddy said, 'and your husband, if I may say so, is quite delightful.' Paddy spoke with great conviction although he had, I knew, never met George. 'But,' he went on, 'I wasn't thinking so much of that; it's Alice I'm worried about. That old man's doing her no good at all.'

I looked fearfully to see if Felix had heard. Fortunately Sonia was keeping him fully occupied.

'Now don't get me wrong.' Paddy put up a hand to silence an objection which I had not made. 'I *know* that it has nothing to do with me, only you mustn't forget that Alice might easily have been my sister-in-law and naturally I take an interest in her.'

'She's all right.' I said it to convince myself.

'And this David Mason,' Paddy went on as if I had not interrupted, 'would make a wonderful husband. I have it on the best authority, reliable, hard-working, everything you could want.'

I told Paddy not to be silly. Alice hadn't seen David for years, and, 'Anyhow,' I said, 'you've made him sound much *too* good.'

'You've got it exactly.' Paddy swung round to face me. 'These girls won't have anything to do with people who are too good, and then what happens? They marry people like me, and is it a success? No. Look at poor dear Estelle.' When he mentioned Estelle, Paddy hung his head. He seemed to feel a real sympathy for his wife.

The soup was replaced by limp pieces of white fish. I turned to Felix, meaning to make some innocuous if banal remark.

Suddenly he glared down the table at Alice. 'Did you order this dinner?' His voice was rough, not quite controlled.

The waiter, who was coming into the room with a bottle of wine, paused.

Alice looked at Felix with surprise. 'No, I don't think I ordered it,' she said. 'I just told Williams we would be six.' She smiled at the waiter, as if to exonerate him from any share of blame in the badness of the dinner.

'It's quite uneatable.' Felix pushed the fish about his plate in disgust.

'I'm sorry,' Alice said mildly.

Felix turned on the waiter, who still stood in the doorway.

'Who's responsible for this food, what?'

'It's sent up from the kitchens, sir.' Williams remained imperturbable, disinterested. One felt that had the kitchens chosen to send up nothing but potato peelings he would have served them with detachment and without comment.

Felix flung down his fork. 'You can take this away, I can't eat it.'

The waiter removed the plate; the rest of us went on with our fish.

Felix turned on me. 'These flats are abominable. I don't know why we're here. If Alice didn't go off to that damned school every morning she might be able to do something about it. It's no good leaving everything to servants.' He glared at Williams, who was filling his glass. 'Has this been properly iced, what?'

Williams said that he thought it had.

Geoffrey, dearest Geoffrey, was talking loudly to Alice.

Sonia said something across the table to Paddy. Paddy, who for the last few seconds had been sitting in apprehensive silence, responded nobly. He was reminded of something that had happened in Dublin to a friend of his. He told the story at some length. It called for excursions into dialect and the brogue, even for action.

Desperately I started to inflict Felix with a second-hand description of the scenery to be met with in the island of Cyprus. After I had run on for some time, Felix said, 'Oh, yes.' A vein which swelled and throbbed at the side of his forehead showed no sign of subsiding. There was going to be another outburst. I was sure there was going to be another outburst. Why would Sonia do nothing to help? I looked across at her and at the same moment she stopped attending to the Irish story.

She turned to Felix with the most charming smile. 'I think,' she said, 'that your behaviour is perfectly horrible.'

Williams paused in his service, and I saw a slow grin spread over his face. So he wasn't as detached as one had supposed.

'Your manners,' Sonia went on, speaking distinctly and still smiling, 'are uncouth in the extreme.'

I glanced at Alice's end of the table. They were all listening now, she and Geoffrey and Paddy. I had an insane idea that Geoffrey was going to clap. I didn't look at Felix; he might be going to explode, to do something terrible. For a moment there was silence and then to my surprise he laughed. Not the shamed laugh of someone who is trying to carry off a situation, but a hearty amused laugh.

'These people,' he told Sonia, 'needed something to think about.' He looked round the room impartially. We were left in doubt as to whether it was Alice, or the now perfectly serious

Williams who needed to be given something to think about. The dinner-party went on. This time the crisis had been averted.

'My mother-in-law,' Paddy fingered his chin, 'is thinking very seriously of divorcing me. She and Estelle are going to the West Indies or Switzerland, I forget which. They are shutting up the house before they leave.'

I said that was a great pity, and Paddy said that indeed it was, as Estelle's house was so much more comfortable than Sonia's flat.

'And Horrid Tessie?' I asked. 'What has happened to her?'

Paddy said that she was in a maternity home, and that if only she could manage to have *five* puppies she would show a profit.

We went to Honoria's party, which had evidently been intended to be gayer than it actually was. For a very short time there was champagne and then we were down to beer. We sat about on the floor and various people played the piano, usually songs of their own composition. One woman tried to make us join in her choruses.

Most of the guests belonged to the theatre. Amongst them I noticed the young woman from the box office of the Troubador; she still wore her green jersey and she still looked worried. Mrs. Bryant was there. When we arrived she rushed across the room and was very effusive to all of us, while keeping a watchful eye on Harold who, as usual, was busy making new friends. The others sheered off and I was left alone with her.

'I haven't seen you since you married.' She smiled her encouraging experienced smile. 'And your husband's a sailor and he's gone abroad *already*.' It was not clear whether she was congratulating me on my marriage or on George's absence. In a moment she would be arranging my life, advising me how to 'manage.'

I looked round for a way of escape. For the moment there was none.

'Isn't it splendid about Alice and Felix? And he's done Alice so much *good*.' Mrs. Bryant was complacent. I looked at her mouth, covered in thick red paint. 'But I don't think Alice is altogether wise in trying to go on the stage.'

'Why not?' I asked, but I didn't care *what* Mrs. Bryant thought. I only wanted to get away from her.

Mrs. Bryant paused and rearranged one of her combs. I noticed, with satisfaction, that a few hairs at the back of her neck still escaped from the general architecture of her coiffure. 'Well, it leaves Felix rather a lot alone, doesn't it?'

'He has the waiters to talk to,' I said, 'and then there must be all those dreary men at his club.'

Mrs. Bryant looked pained; for her men could *never* be dreary. They were her life's work, and she was an energetic woman. She said that what Felix wanted was a home; he wanted to be free, but at the same time he needed a home. I thought of Mrs. Bryant's arid flat, of the ball of string in its proper place. Did she seriously think that that was the sort of thing that *any* man wanted? It was very strange.

With relief I saw a young man coming towards us and with him was Beryl Lawes. Mrs. Bryant, obviously equally relieved, turned immediately to the young man. She put out her bony jewelled hand. I noticed she had a new ring; it was a zircon.

It seemed years since I had seen Beryl. I wondered why she was at this party. Probably someone had brought her. It was the kind of party to which people took their friends.

Beryl seemed pleased to see me. I asked after her mother and wondered if Mrs. Lawes still had her delphinium room. Perhaps by now she had had it done over to look like a rose or a hollyhock. Beryl was wearing a nice bright blue evening dress. She told me that she had got a very interesting job. I couldn't quite make out what it was, but I said I was glad.

She talked about the Spanish war and I was ashamed I knew so little about it.

'David Mason is going out there to fight.'

Beryl said that there was going to be an International Brigade and David was going to join it.

'Isn't that Alice over there?' Beryl was looking at a large group in the opposite corner of the room. In the midst of it were Alice and Sonia. They were both laughing and taking very little notice of the lady who was playing the piano. Alice looked happy and I was glad to see that Felix appeared to have completely recovered his temper.

'She doesn't seem to have changed much since she was at school,' Beryl said. 'She was always wild then. Do you remember the terrible time she used to give poor Madame?'

I agreed vaguely. It was so like Beryl to come to a party and spend her time remembering what people had been like at school. I wondered if she was thinking of the time Alice had beaten her up with a hairbrush. Beryl had looked very funny then.

'Sonia was always a bad influence, of course.' Beryl was still musing, still living in the past where she had been head girl at Groom Place.

'I don't think people do things because they're influenced,' I said. 'I think they do them either because they *want* to or because they're frightened.'

'But what is there to be frightened of in modern life?' Beryl looked boldly round the room.

'I think life is very frightening indeed,' I said stubbornly, and found that my instinct to contradict Beryl was as strong as ever.

'But you can't be frightened of *life*, it's too big.' Beryl was derisive.

'If you come to think of it,' I said patiently, 'being *big* doesn't make a thing less frightening.'—I felt that I could have done with a hairbrush.

The woman at the piano crashed down on a last chord. Everyone stopped talking and clapped. Honoria said that supper was now ready in the basement. Slowly people began to leave the room. I found myself next to Geoffrey. He told me that in a fortnight's time we were all going to Brighton for the week-end to see Honoria in her lovely new play.

I said that that would be fun. 'Yes indeed,' Geoffrey said, 'and I am so glad that Honoria will be going to the seaside after spending the whole summer in that stuffy little theatre. We shall stay in one of those beautiful plate-glass hotels and in the afternoons we will walk on the pier.'

* * * * *

So it was arranged that we should go down to Brighton, and two weeks later I met Alice and Felix on the platform at Victoria. Felix was quite easy to pick out from the other travellers. He was dressed entirely in checks. Instinctively one looked for his gun-cases and for the retrievers which he should surely have been seeing into the van. Fortunately he seemed to be in a good humour.

The train drew in and we got into a Pullman car. It is with these cars that the charm of Brighton begins. Brighton and the Regency. Brighton and the Metropole. The rich ladies with their dyed hair and their extraordinary figures. Figures which surely *cannot* be built around the normal skeleton.

We kept a seat for Geoffrey who was late. I looked round the car. Already we were surrounded by people who exist only in Brighton and only at the week-end.

'Miss Iliffe said she might be on this train.' Alice peered out of the window into the dingy December afternoon. 'Do you think we ought to look for her?'

'Now, don't *fuss*.' Felix sounded impatient. His good humour then was only on the surface. 'Miss Iliffe is quite old enough to travel by herself.'

'Yes, of course.' Alice smiled.

The attendant passed through the car; from either side he was given orders for pink gins and whiskies-and-soda.

A figure hurried down the platform. It was Geoffrey, desperately looking for us and failing to see us. The train started.

'What does Miss Iliffe want to come down for?' Felix asked Alice.

'She's an old friend of Honoria's,' Alice said, 'and I suppose she wishes her well. It is quite a thing for Honoria, you know, to have got this part in a play which is going to the West End.'

'You mean she isn't very good, what?' Felix said with some satisfaction.

Alice was spared having to go into explanations by the arrival of Geoffrey.

'My *dears*, I couldn't think *what* had happened to you. I've been through every coach on the train.' He sank into the empty seat opposite mine. 'I had such a time getting away from the Museum. I can't tell you. A dreadful old man came into my office just as I was leaving. He's studying the middle period of Byzantine Art and its influence upon something which I couldn't quite hear and he wanted my advice. Such a dreadful old bore and he was wearing sandals.'

'I thought they all wore sandals,' Alice said.

'Well, yes *and* no, dear.' Geoffrey lit a cigarette. 'Of course there is that woman who wears sandals and a mackintosh cape and nothing else at *all*. So very uncomfortable for her, poor dear, and she isn't as *young* as she was either.' Evidently exhausted, he leant back in his seat.

The journey was over almost before Felix had finished his second drink. We collected our suitcases and followed the other occupants of the Pullman on to the platform. We were just in time to see Miss Iliffe descend from a third-class smoker. She waved her stick at Alice. 'My dear, you will be able to help me find a taxi.' Her voice was deep. She enunciated each word clearly, giving it its proper value.

'Yes, of course.' Alice introduced us all to Miss Iliffe as we walked towards the barrier. When it came to Geoffrey's turn he offered to carry Miss Iliffe's string bag for her. She appeared to have no other luggage and she surrendered the bag with the air of a queen giving her first-born into captivity. She was not in the least impeded by several impatient travellers who, in their unseemly hurry, bumped their fibre suitcases against her legs.

We all got into one taxi. We dropped Miss Iliffe at some bow-fronted lodgings in a side-street and then drove along the front to our hotel.

When we had left London it had seemed late afternoon, almost evening; here the daylight had lingered and the sun set over a steel-blue sea. The lights of the two piers twinkled dimly.

'Wonderful air,' Felix said contentedly and inhaled cigarette smoke.

We arrived at the doors of the hotel. Page boys sprang forward and were followed by directing hall porters. At least three men conducted us into the hotel and across to the reception desk, where many clerks helped us to register. We were shown up to our rooms by two managers. It was all very expensive and exactly as it should be.

That evening we went to the first night of Honoria's play. It was one of those very 'advanced' plays, in which every other scene takes place on some brightly lit steps which are to represent Heaven. In the intervening scenes life is shown as going its humdrum way. Whenever it looks as if anything at all exciting, such as rape, is about to happen, a visitant arrives from the other world in order to prevent it. Honoria inevitably was the mother who, not yet having passed over, appeared only in the earthly scenes. The hero, as far as one could make out, was St. Peter. He wore a pale blue dressing-gown and looked very cosy.

When it was all over we went round and saw Honoria and told her how good she had been. She seemed depressed, which wasn't surprising when you thought of the play. Miss Iliffe was there, explaining, with the help of her stick, exactly where St. Peter had gone wrong.

Mrs. Bryant and Sonia and Harold and Paddy were also there. I hadn't known that they were in Brighton.

Mrs. Bryant, it seemed, had enjoyed the play and although, as an agnostic, she didn't of course 'hold' with St. Peter or the steps of Heaven; it had all really meant something quite different and had been, in fact, a very beautiful portrayal of the sub-conscious.

'A very *pure* sub-conscious, surely?' Geoffrey said, and Mrs. Bryant laughed salaciously.

Some of the other actors began to drift into the dressing-room and then there was a kind of bustle and two men in dinner jackets were ushered in. It was whispered that they were London managers. We outsiders huddled in the corners. The effect somehow was the same as when the police make way for the Royal Party at a race meeting. We judged that the moment had come to leave.

'Dearest Honoria, how wonderful you were!'

'Dearest Honoria, I am sure that the play will run for ever in London!' And we were in the passage outside the dressing-room, and with us were Mrs. Bryant and Sonia and their two escorts. Inevitably, we must go to one of the hotels and have supper and dance.

The next morning, by appointment, we met Honoria and Miss Iliffe on the Palace Pier. They had arrived first and we found them sitting on a silver painted bench. Between them sat one of the London managers. He wore a soft black hat and a black overcoat with an astrakhan collar. He had greying hair and a long grey face, he was smoking a cigar, and he was *exactly* one's idea of a theatrical manager.

Honoria jumped up as we approached. 'How nice to see you all! Sonia and the others are already attacking the machines.' She pointed farther up the pier to where Sonia and Mrs. Bryant, Harold and Paddy stood together.

The morning was perfect. The sunshine was brilliant. It glittered on the roofs of the buildings at the end of the pier, on the windows of the majestic hotels and on the windows of the Regency houses. There was just enough wind to ruffle the sea, to fleck it with blue and silver, and to cause Mrs. Bryant to have a scarf tied tightly over her head. Beneath it her face showed mauve through its make-up. She had her arm through Harold's, and Harold stood beside her smiling; but his smile was directed, not downwards at Mrs. Bryant, but at Sonia and Honoria and the world generally and especially at any pretty women who might be passing. This is mine, he might say of Mrs. Bryant, but I am quite free, you know, if you have anything better to offer me. I can leave her in a moment, there will be no difficulty at all, and there is no reason why you should not compete with the rest.

Sonia and Paddy waved to us; they shouted that we were to come and try the rifle-ranges, the skee-ball alleys.

'Very expensive,' Paddy said, 'but well worth the money.'

We turned to Miss Iliffe. As we expected, she was uninterested in rifle-ranges, but with the help of her stick and the theatrical manager's arm, she would walk a little way out to sea. She motioned Alice to her other side. Miss Iliffe was being very regal again this morning, and surely there was some royal figure whom she *did* resemble, some decayed princess or other, who like Miss Iliffe was hung with ropes of pearls and pieces of lace, and who, with the help of an ebony stick, walked a little beside the sea. I puzzled to think who it could be, to put a name to the princess, and then it came to me that what Miss Iliffe most reminded me of was a Christmas tree. She was the same shape.

Slowly we moved along the pier. The nucleus of the party was formed by Miss Iliffe with the theatrical manager tethered firmly to her side.

Geoffrey and I stopped by a fortune-telling machine. Geoffrey put a penny into it and after some electric bulbs had switched rapidly on and off, it produced a printed card which Geoffrey picked up and read with careful attention.

'It says that the future holds more than the past, and that I will shortly meet an interesting person of the opposite sex.'

'Perhaps it means the lady in the mackintosh cape,' I suggested.

Geoffrey looked at the card again and shook his head. 'No, I think not, but we shall see. It says that they are likely to become my life partner, provided, that is, that I am not already married. How extraordinarily tactful these machines have to be. I wish Cassius was here. I had a postcard from him yesterday morning. *Rather* a nice picture of a feast day in Capetown.'

'What's Cassius going to do? He can't live abroad for ever.'

'I don't see why not, thousands do. But I expect he will come back *sometime*. He still has his interest in the bookshop.'

'He should never have left Alice,' I said resentfully.

'I see what you mean, dear. Do you want to have your fortune told?' Geoffrey produced another penny.

'No,' I said crossly.

'Then perhaps a photograph of your future husband?' Geoffrey had moved on to the next machine. 'Oh, I'm sorry dear, I'd forgotten you were married. How about a picture of your future baby?' He stopped in front of the third machine and put the penny in the slot. This machine had no electric lights; it merely rumbled internally and gave up two cards. Geoffrey handed them to me; on one was a drawing of a white baby and on the other a black baby. Geoffrey said he thought it must be a joke.

'You mustn't think too hardly of Cassius,' he said. 'When he found that Alice preferred even Felix to him, he did the only possible thing in leaving her.'

I started to protest. 'It was all the fault of that beastly Mrs. Bryant.' I was angry and I would vent my anger on somebody.

'No,' Geoffrey said. 'It wasn't even *her* fault. She precipitated it but it would have happened in any case.'

What did Alice want? When she was eighteen she had loved Martin Yorke, but surely, with their completely different tastes, they would never have been happy together. Besides, Alice was too intelligent for a Martin Yorke. There had been the early friendship with David Mason, but I could not believe that that had meant or could ever mean anything to Alice.

Then there had been Cassius. I saw him in my mind's eye, and what I saw was a Greek god, young and beautiful and heroic. He was a warrior, a poet, the embodiment of a noble idea; but Alice had never loved him.

Now there was Felix, masterful, bad-tempered, but probably possessing great physical attraction. It wasn't enough.

Alice wanted security. She wanted to be made safe from the fears which surrounded her.

Would she be happy in the theatre? I could only hope so.

I thought of the picture of the deserted garden; there, I thought, was what Alice wanted. Time standing still under a blue sky; anything may happen and yet nothing does.

For the moment time stands still and we are able to build our own world within the world, safe and secure and perhaps happy. Could Alice, who was so afraid of life, find any lasting happiness in life itself?

A shadow passed across the sun; the sea ceased to sparkle and the roofs to glitter. I shivered and we walked quickly after Miss Iliffe and the others.

We were joined by Sonia and Paddy. They came up some steps which led to a lower part of the pier.

'You ought to go down there,' Paddy told us confidentially. 'There's a *wonderful* little rifle range, much the best in Brighton; mind you, it isn't everybody I'd be telling about it.'

Sonia regretted that Horrid Tessie was not with us. It seemed that if there was one place that Horrid Tessie enjoyed more than another it was the Palace Pier.

'You heard she pulled it off?' Paddy said. 'She has five puppies, bless her, so co-operative, and just as soon as they're sold we'll be living in luxury for the rest of the winter.'

'Isn't it all rather bad luck on Tessie?' Geoffrey asked.

'Oh, no,' Sonia said positively. 'She *loves* having puppies—a most extraordinary taste, but there it is.'

We came face to face with Miss Iliffe and her party, who were returning slowly along the pier.

Miss Iliffe waved her stick. 'Mr. Zwemburgh has been telling us about a most unusual play he saw in Manchester. It was being performed by an amateur dramatic company, if you can imagine such a thing.' Miss Iliffe spat out the words 'amateur' and 'dramatic' as if they had been the husks of beechnuts. 'But apparently they had got hold of this play which nobody in London would look at and it's really very remarkable. Isn't that so?' She turned to Mr. Zwemburgh who said, 'Yes,' and looked unhappy.

We smiled encouragingly and expectantly and Mr. Zwemburgh looked more unhappy than ever and said nothing. We formed into one group and walked towards the shore. Mrs. Bryant and Harold joined us. Alice dropped behind and I found myself walking between Honoria and Miss Iliffe. Miss Iliffe held firmly on to Mr. Zwemburgh, who seemed to be in the deepest gloom.

Miss Iliffe couldn't leave the Manchester play alone. 'Imagine,' she said to me, 'a play in twenty-four scenes dealing with the life of the Empress Eugénie. You wouldn't think there were any possibilities in *that*, would you?'

I said I wouldn't and wondered why not.

'But Mr. Zwemburgh says it's tremendous. There they were, amateurs in Manchester with no scenery and no actors to speak of, and it was one of the most moving things that he has ever seen.' Miss Iliffe turned on me triumphantly as if I had argued with her and she had conclusively proved me to be in the wrong.

'Their *Eugénie* was very good,' Mr. Zwemburgh said suddenly. 'She is a typist in a government office. When I talked to her about bringing the play to London, with a professional company of course, but keeping her in the lead, she told me she had her career to think of.' Mr. Zwemburgh bit on his cigar and relapsed into silence.

Honoria asked who had written the play.

Miss Iliffe thought that it was a young man whom nobody had heard of, even *two* young men whom nobody had heard of.

They talked on and on about the play. Very soon I had ceased to listen and probably I would not have remembered the conversation, only, as it happened, months later Alice appeared on a London stage as the Empress Eugénie.

ELEVEN

MONTHS LATER one could pick up any weekly illustrated magazine and find a photograph of Alice wearing a crinoline. The photograph that I remember best had a surround like a valentine or an elaborate cake paper, very correct, very nineteenth century, and in the middle of this valentine was the photograph. In it Alice sat on a tightly buttoned sofa, with her hands clasped in her lap. She was looking upwards, a wonderful parure of pearls and diamonds encircling her neck; the light fell on her hair, which was arranged in bands. Her lips were parted (for that is the way photographers prefer lips). This, you felt, is an Empress, not an actress impersonating an Empress; but the Empress herself at the height of her beauty. Underneath the picture was a caption explaining Alice as a talented society girl who was to make her first stage appearance in a principal part; it was recalled that she was descended from the famous Mrs. Ashdown (which was a posthumous leg-up for Mrs. Ashdown). It was claimed that she was a discovery of Mr. Zwemburgh's. It was claimed that the play was sensational. This was advance publicity.

A number of causes were responsible for the part of the Empress being given to such an inexperienced actress as Alice, although it was not of course true that this was to be her first stage appearance.

To begin with, there had been the typist in Manchester who had refused to come to London in the part as she had her career to think of. Then a well-known young actress was engaged; but no sooner had the play, after many delays, gone into rehearsal than this actress became ill and was ordered to a sanatorium. No other leading actress who would have been at all suitable happened to be available. Alice already, through the influence of Miss Iliffe, had a small part in the play, a lady in waiting, or something of that kind. So the producer was in a position to know that she could act, and her gaiety and elegance which he admired coincided with the picture he had made of the character of the Empress. Eugénie, of course, had been dark and Alice was fair; but that was a matter which could be put right.

Alice, who had spent the summer with a touring company, came to see me one afternoon in the autumn. She had just begun rehearsing *Eugenie* and she was happy and elated.

I was by then living in Victoria Walk, Kensington. George had been home for a short leave and had been again ordered to the Mediterranean. My grandmother had given up Hill Street and now lived entirely in Ireland, and Ellen had come with me to Victoria Walk.

'But Ellen, it won't be grand enough for you!' and Ellen had replied that at her age she had done with grandeur, and that one must move with the times. We must try and get a nice little cook who would 'do' her own kitchen, and then with the help of a charwoman we would probably be able to manage.

It all sounded to me unnecessarily elaborate.

Alice and I sat in my tiny drawing-room and gossiped, mostly about the play.

'It's so wonderful,' Alice said, 'that I just can't believe it.' The firelight lit up her face, her hands were clasped as they had been in the photograph, and here again was the Empress. Even the blue sofa was right, for the fashion for Victoriana had begun.

Ellen came in with the tea-tray and there were crumpets.

'Well,' she said to Alice, 'we've been seeing all about *you* in the papers.'

'Isn't it exciting?' Alice beamed at Ellen.

Ellen agreed that it was and started to draw the plaid curtains. 'I suppose you have to wear stays. My aunt always said that the stays were the worst part, but that it was lovely when you got them off at night.'

Alice admitted that as the Empress Eugénie she did wear stays.

'Oh, well.' Ellen gave the curtains a final tug. 'It's all got to be just right, I suppose.'

'How's Felix?' I asked as Ellen left the room.

Alice's face clouded. 'He's all right.' For a moment she didn't speak and then she told me that she was worried about Felix. 'He's drinking rather a lot and it makes him most awfully cross.' Alice drew her legs up on to the sofa and stopped looking like the Empress Eugénie. 'He wants us to get married as soon as the divorce is through, and the lawyer says that it's practically *certain* to be heard this term.'

'It will be six months after that before you can marry again.' It was all the comfort I could offer.

'It upsets me,' Alice said. 'I always told him that I didn't *want* to marry him. I don't want another failure, and anyhow there's no *point* in it.'

Suddenly I felt an intense pity for Alice.

'I wish,' she said, 'that he would find somebody else. I like him and I want him to be happy; but it's too difficult, and I haven't got time.' She looked immensely tired.

'Why don't you leave him?' I said.

'He says that if I do his life will be over.'

'That isn't true,' I objected. 'He didn't have a life before he met you. His life's been over for years.'

Alice looked uneasy and repeated that she was fond of Felix. It seemed to me that she was also afraid of him, but perhaps it was only a fear that she might hurt him.

'It's the play that's upsetting him really,' Alice said. 'He wants me to be a success, but with all the excitement and the rehearsals he feels neglected.'

'But it's ridiculous,' I said. 'He hasn't got any claim on you at all.'

'He's very good in bed,' Alice said inconsequently, 'and then he's always been particularly nice when I'm discouraged. Oh, Margaret, won't it be awful if after all I'm not a success?'

I reminded her that it was only just over a year since she had been afraid that Miss Iliffe would refuse to accept her as a pupil.

'I know.' Alice smiled. 'I suppose it is that I'm *used* to things not being a success.'

'But that's silly.' I was impatient.

'Well, school wasn't,' Alice said, 'and neither was Martin nor Cassius, and as for *Felix* . . .' She shrugged her shoulders.

No, Alice's life had not been a success, and again I felt that intuitive fear which Geoffrey and I had so often felt before. If Alice had not minded so much, these things would not have mattered, but as it was. . . . Involuntarily I shuddered. I tried to throw off my fear. I told Alice that I had been seeing quite a lot of Beryl Lawes. Beryl was working now with Spanish Medical Aid. She hoped to go out to Spain. We talked about Spain and the war. It seemed that we knew more of politics than we had done the year before. We were indignant against Franco. We had awoken to the fact that we were threatened by war. We were restless. We were no longer satisfied with the Conservatism we had always taken for granted. Our opinions swayed towards the Left.

'I don't believe that anything will ever be nice again.' In spite of the fire Alice shivered.

'It will be in the end,' I said without conviction. I was not sure whether she was thinking of Felix or the international situation.

'To live in the world as not of the world,' Alice said. 'That always sounded so nice, as if one had a little world of one's own floating about inside the big one.'

'That isn't supposed to be a good thing,' I said. 'It's not being a realist.'

'But who wants to be?' Alice asked. 'It would be so frighten-ing. *And* if you were truly a realist, you'd have to think all the time about dying instead of making nice cosy plans for to-mor-row and deciding what you were going to have for luncheon.'

I said I saw what she meant and that of course one mustn't overdo things.

'The world inside the world,' Alice said, 'looks like a doll's house and has lace curtains.'

'I know, and one's afraid it will *stop* floating or be broken up.'

'As soon as you're born,' Alice said, 'they dress you and say it's a dear little girl, and when you die they talk about the corpse, and in between you lead this extraordinary life and pretend that things are important and are going to go on for ever.' She got up and examined the clock, ticking under its glass dome. 'They've got one like that in the last scene only it doesn't work. I hate that scene and I have to have cotton-wool in my cheeks to make me look old.'

'Doesn't it taste horrible?'

'It does rather, but I pretend I'm too old to notice it. They say I shall get used to it, but I don't see how anyone *could*. I suppose I must go now,' and I thought she looked at the clock regretfully.

'Don't,' I said, 'stay and have dinner. I shall be all alone this evening.'

'I wish *I* was going to be,' Alice said, 'but Felix and I are dining out.'

When Alice left I went and stood by the mantelpiece. With the pride of possession I looked at the clock. I moved the can-dlesticks which stood on either side of it; they were French and must have been made at the time of Eugénie's birth. In spite of the success which was coming to her, which must come, I was worried about Alice.

I thought of her on that summer night at Groom Place, when she had looked at the stars and said that nothing mattered. I thought of that other summer night, when Geoffrey and I had sat in the house in Belgrave Square, with the sound of dance music coming to us from the floor above and the couples pass-ing us as they went up and down stairs. Then I had seen Alice's fear as in a kind of vision. For a moment it had been my fear, the bursting lungs and the agony which would last for ever. And then I thought of Alice as she had been a few minutes ago. 'To live in the world as not of the world.' To live in a doll's house with lace curtains and to know that that small world was a prettily contrived pretence, and that at any moment it might disappear, leaving nothing but death and violence and unknown terror. I thought of winter seas and of their frightening inevitable force. I rang the bell for Ellen. I went over to the telephone. I no longer felt that I wished to spend the evening alone.

Who should I ring up? Geoffrey? It was usually Geoffrey in times of stress. I dialled his number and heard the telephone ringing in his empty flat—or perhaps the flat was not empty. Perhaps this was one of the evenings when Geoffrey was not answering his telephone. Discouraged, I put down the receiver.

Who else was there? Mentally I went through the list of my acquaintances; there was nobody I wanted to see.

Ellen came into the room.

'Ellen, I'm feeling depressed, who shall I ring up?'

Ellen said, unhelpfully, that if my mother hadn't been in Devonshire, I could have gone round and seen her. 'There's always plenty of excitement *there*, I should imagine.' Without saying anything else Ellen carried the tray out of the room. She was evidently cross about something, or perhaps it was merely a depressing evening. Perhaps my fears for Alice were aroused only by darkness and the suggestion of fog which hung in the air, which had equally affected Ellen making her gloomy and unfriendly.

Then I thought of Beryl Lawes. I had had a letter from her, saying that she wanted to see me. I would ring her up and ask her to go to a cinema with me. Fortunately she was in; she would like to go to a cinema and she suggested that we should first have dinner together at her club.

I put down the receiver and went and told Ellen that I should be going out.

She said that that would mean a nice bit of sole going to waste.

I said to tell the cook to give it to the cat, and Ellen looked offended. There was no doubt that it was one of her bad evenings.

I arrived at Beryl's large and gloomy club. She was already
there. Beryl was very excited about Spain. When she talked of
it she became quite animated. I reflected how strange it was
that Beryl, of all people, should be working for a left-wing organisation. It contrasted so abruptly with Willow Road and the
cake-tidies and the pink and chromium breakfast-room.

I asked Beryl when she would be going to Spain.

'Next week, I hope. David Mason is out there, you know. He
is fighting with the International Brigade.'

I said I remembered. She had told me at Honoria's party.

Beryl said that she thought it was wonderful the way David
had thrown up everything to go out to Spain. Her voice had all
its old unctuousness. Was she never to grow out of being head
girl at Groom Place?

There was a pause and Beryl asked after Alice. 'What's
happening about that man she was with at Honoria's, Felix
Wordsworth?'

'Nothing,' I said.

Beryl hesitated. 'You know that David Mason is terribly in
love with her?'

'But he hasn't seen her for years.' I didn't want to discuss
Alice with Beryl.

But Beryl, sipping her glass of sherry, was not to be put off.
'He told me all about it. He was in love with her when he was
still at school. They used to write to each other.'

I nodded.

'It was a terrible shock to him when Alice suddenly married
Cassius. He had thought that she would wait until they were
both twenty-one and that Alice would marry him.'

'But had he asked her?'

'No,' Beryl said, 'he was too proud to ask her until he was in
a position to marry, and his father would never have allowed it
until he was of age.'

'But after all these years?'

'He feels exactly the same. But he would never ask her to marry him unless he was sure of being accepted. I don't think he would have told me about it if he hadn't been going to Spain, and then I've known David since he was a little boy. I've been wondering for weeks if there was anything I could do about it.' Beryl fell silent and I was silent too, wondering if this wasn't the solution for Alice. David who loved her long ago and who still loved her. I found myself wishing that he might marry Alice, take her away from Felix, for with David she would be safe. He was good and dependable. He had ideals for which he was prepared to fight. Even though he might never share it, he would protect that world within the world which belonged to Alice.

But what could I do? There is a point beyond which it is not permissible to interfere in the lives of others.

Beryl asked me what cinema I wanted to see.

During the next few weeks I hardly saw Alice at all. She was very busy with rehearsals, and her spare time was devoted to Felix, who was getting more and more difficult.

Then one morning Ellen called me as usual at eight o'clock and said that Mrs. Skeffington was downstairs.

'She looks very upset and I've made her a nice cup of tea, but she says she won't have anything to eat.'

My first feeling was one of relief. For some time I had been afraid that something, I could not define exactly what, was going to happen to Alice; and now it must have happened, and Alice was alive and if not well, at least uninjured and drinking a cup of tea in my drawing-room. I jumped out of bed.

'Now then,' Ellen said, 'you're never going downstairs. I haven't had time to get the fire lit yet and it's *bitter*.'

Her words reminded me that the night before I had gone to bed with a temperature of a hundred and what Ellen called one of my colds. I discovered that I still had a cold and probably a temperature. I got back into bed, and Ellen said that she would go and tell Mrs. Skeffington that I was awake.

'I'll put a bit of extra toast on your tray. Perhaps if she sees you eating, she'll be able to fancy something herself.'

I lay back on my pillows. How nice Ellen was not to gloat over other people's troubles.

Presently Alice came into the room. She sat down on the armchair with her face turned away from me, but I could see that she had been crying.

'I'm sorry it's so terribly early, but I've left Felix.' Alice seemed to be addressing a small painting which hung on the wall opposite the end of my bed.

I said that it wasn't early, and that I was glad about Felix.

'I have left him for *ever*,' Alice said firmly to the painting. Then she turned round and looked me directly in the face. 'Do you know, he beat me up!' As she spoke her eyes filled with tears.

I thought I detected a swelling on the side of her forehead. The tears ran down her cheeks, but she kept her eyes fixed on mine. I was so appalled that I could think of nothing to say.

'I have *never* been so surprised,' Alice went on.

Ellen came in with the breakfast-tray, put it down on my bed, and went out again without saying anything.

The telephone rang and it was Felix. He asked if I knew where Alice was.

I said that I had no idea and rang off.

'I never want to see him again,' Alice said.

'I should hope not.' I buttered a piece of toast and offered it to Alice. She reached over and took it and began to eat.

'You will come and stay here,' I said.

Alice nodded. She seemed unable to speak.

'I suppose all your things are at the flat? Ellen can go and fetch them.'

'And not tell Felix I'm here,' Alice said.

'Are you supposed to be rehearsing to-day? If you are, I'll ring up and tell them you're ill.'

'But I'm *not* ill,' Alice said, 'only tired. Do you know, he came into my flat—he's got a key—at two o'clock this morning. I was asleep; he woke me up and I thought he was going to kill me.' Alice looked at me questioningly. She seemed astounded, unable to believe that this thing had happened to her.

'I thought it was going to go on for ever and ever. It was terribly humiliating. And then in the end I screamed, and he stopped.'

Alice got up and began walking about the room.

It was an appalling story.

'Will you go to bed,' I said. 'The spare room is ready and Ellen will bring you a hot-water bottle.'

'No,' Alice said. 'I must think.' She fingered her forehead where the swelling began to show plainly.

The next few days were very painful. Felix made continual attempts to see Alice. We had had to tell him that she was staying with me in order to prevent his going to the police. He rang up the house and the theatre at all hours of the day and night, and he called continually at both. It got so that we never answered the front-door bell without first looking to see who was there, and most of the time we left the telephone receiver off. At the theatre he was dealt with by the stage doorman. He had little sense of shame and no feelings of reticence. His one idea was to see Alice in order that he might 'explain.' It was, as I said, very painful.

Weeks passed. Alice's bruises slowly faded, and as the first night of *Eugénie* approached it seemed that the very memory of Felix faded as well. It was obvious that she had been badly frightened by him and had really thought that he would kill her. But her chief feeling had been humiliation. She had thought that he would kill her, but he had not come near to her ultimate fears. She had been safe from his attack, because he did not know what he attacked.

Long afterwards I came to think that here was the key to what Felix had done. He suspected the existence of something which he could not get at, and he thought that by using physical violence he could batter his way through to the thing that was Alice. He was impatient, he was undisciplined, and his tragedy was that he loved Alice. Had he been less sensitive he would not have known that he did not possess her entirely.

Eugénie was due to open at the beginning of December at the Diplomats Theatre, London. There was to be no try-out in the provinces.

The play had first been produced the year before by the amateur company in Manchester, where it had been 'discovered' by Mr. Zwemburgh. The fact that it had been previously submitted in manuscript to every London manager, including Mr. Zwemburgh himself, in no way lessened its importance as a discovery.

The first night was to be on a Tuesday. The play had been given enormous publicity. Extracts from it had been printed in the evening papers and, as I said, for weeks beforehand the weekly illustrated papers had been filled with photographs of Alice. Almost the whole interest was centred upon the Empress. The relatively well-known actor who was to play Napoleon III had been practically ignored. Tight trousers and imperials have nothing, pictorially, when compared with crinolines.

Alice had remained calm and confident. I had been to several rehearsals and it seemed to me that she was extremely good. I think that was the general opinion.

Away from the theatre she seemed to have withdrawn into herself. I had the feeling that she lived with something tremendous, something which needed her whole attention. During these last few weeks we continued to live in Victoria Walk, seeing practically no one.

After giving it a good deal of thought I told Alice what Beryl had told me about David Mason. Alice seemed pleased though incredulous, and I wrote to Beryl, who was now in Spain, telling her that Alice and Felix had parted. I thought that she would let David know, but I received no answer. Later I learned that it was months before my letter was received.

Occasionally Geoffrey came to dinner with us, and once or twice Sonia and Paddy, who were living now in great discomfort in a flat in Earl's Court. Estelle was still in Switzerland and still threatening to divorce Paddy. Mrs. Bryant had rather faded from our lives. I wondered if she ever thought of the time when she had advised Alice to be 'fair' to Felix. Mrs. Norton was in the country. She had written to say that she would be coming to London for the first night.

It was Sunday. It was Monday and at last it was Tuesday morning. I woke up extremely early, feeling nervous and excited. It would be all right; of course, it would be all right. I told myself this over and over again as I waited for it to be time to get up. Finally I turned on the light and tried to read Gibbon's *Decline and Fall.* 'Augustus rested his last hopes on Tiberius.' I had been reading without knowing what I read. And now, here was Augustus with his last hopes. On what could I rest mine? This was becoming ridiculous. It was not a question of last hopes. Alice was extremely good. As far as success can be assured in advance, hers was assured. It existed already. I got out of bed. I wondered if Alice too was lying awake. I crept to the door of her room and opened it. She was still asleep.

Throughout the day Alice was calm. It was Ellen and I who seemed to suffer from nerves and from stage fright. For the sake of our own anxiety, we insisted upon treating Alice as if she were a sort of invalid. We planned light meals for her, and kept her out of draughts. During the afternoon Ellen came into the drawing-room with a woollen shawl which she made Alice wear round her shoulders. We didn't care for her to go out. As much as possible we prevented her from answering the telephone.

At tea-time Ellen changed her tactics and put a boiled egg on the tray. The hours before a first night had become confused with the hours following a day's hunting.

'There!' Ellen put the tray down in front of Alice. 'I expect you could do with an egg.'

With beautifully controlled patience Alice thanked her.

'I always say it's better to face things on a full stomach.' Ellen turned to me for confirmation of this gloomy theory, and a first night now became confused with a Channel crossing.

At six o'clock Alice and I drove to the theatre and went straight to her dressing-room. Her dresser was already there, and at her suggestion Alice immediately made-up and put on the dress she was to wear in the first scene. As soon as that was finished the dresser said that Alice would feel better if she loosened her stays, so she was partly undressed again. Napoleon III came in, said that he was feeling sick, and went away. Alice sat in an armchair with a dressing-gown round her and remained calm. The dresser went on fussing. Like Ellen and me she plainly suffered from stage fright and was disappointed that there were no signs of it in Alice. The Prince Imperial came in and said he was feeling very sick indeed. He told me that it was always worse if you weren't on until the second act; then he too went away. The dresser told Alice that she had the smelling-salts 'all ready.' '*And* a drop of brandy,' she added persuasively.

Alice said that she would rather have a cup of tea and the dresser went away to get it. 'Louise was beginning to be annoying,' Alice said. 'Do you think I shall have to drink the tea? I really don't want it at this hour of the evening.'

'Then be like Napoleon and say you feel sick.'

'What's the time?' Alice asked.

I told her and it was only seven o'clock.

'Another hour and a half. I think I had better read.' Alice reached for a novel which lay on her dressing-table.

There was a knock on the door.

'Please tell them that I can't see anybody,' Alice said without looking up.

Before I had time to get to the door, it was thrown open and Mrs. Norton came in, evidently thrusting her way past someone in the passage who would have barred her entrance.

'Darling! and how do you *feel*?' Mrs. Norton, in her usual flowered evening dress, rushed at her daughter and kissed her. One was reminded of a black and white hen hurrying across a farmyard with its wings outstretched.

'I feel all right, thank you,' Alice said, disentangling herself from Mrs. Norton and laying down the book.

'Not nervous or anything?' Mrs. Norton straightened herself as if there might be nervous fears crouching in the corners or under the wash-basin.

'You remember Margaret?' Alice said.

'Oh yes.' Mrs. Norton remembered me and we shook hands. Then she turned back to Alice. 'Darling, I had such an awful journey up, the train was *packed*, and I met the Gladstones and they were so interested and asked after you and said they wanted to come to-night.'

'That was nice of them,' Alice said.

'But the thing *is*, darling, that now they can't get tickets, and I said I'd see you and arrange it. That stupid man in the box office says that they haven't got any left.'

'I expect he knows,' Alice said.

'But darling, I should have thought you could have done something. After all, you've known the Gladstones since you were a little girl and . . .' Mrs. Norton went on at great length, and Alice looked at her and said 'yes' and 'no,' and I could tell by the expression on her face that she was trying hard not to listen.

'Daddy sent you his love and wished you every success.'

'Is he still cross?' Alice asked.

'Well, you know how he feels.' Mrs. Norton sighed. 'He doesn't *like* the stage, but then of course it was all very different when he was a young man. Have you seen anything of Anthony?'

'He telephoned the other night. He's bringing some of his friends and he's got a box.'

'Isn't he sweet!' Mrs. Norton smiled indulgently as she spoke of her son.

'He didn't *pay* for it,' Alice said.

Louise came in with the tea and was introduced to Mrs. Norton.

'There was a lovely queue for the gallery,' Louise said, and Mrs. Norton went pink in the face.

So under all the talk about the Gladstones and Anthony she was proud of Alice.

Alice was to vindicate the hopes that she had had for her children. She would have preferred that success should have come in some other manner. She would have wished for brilliant marriages for the girls, for a brilliant military or political career for Anthony. She would never have chosen that success should come to the Nortons through the theatre. But it seemed that success was coming to one of them and Mrs. Norton could not but rejoice and feel happy and excited and get on Alice's nerves.

Success seemed now to be hurrying. Time, which for the last hour had passed so slowly, began to gather tempo.

Louise was kept busy by knocks on the door. She took in flowers and telegrams and messages. She denied all personal callers. Miss Norton was 'resting and could see no one.'

'You're looking pale,' Mrs. Norton said to Alice. 'Oughtn't you to put some more rouge on?'

Alice sprang out of her chair. 'Can't you leave me alone for one minute.' She shook her fists in the air.

Mrs. Norton was appalled. Louise went quickly to Alice; she patted her on the back, she called her 'dear,' she administered the smelling-salts. On Louise's face there was a look of great relief.

'I can't go on,' Alice sobbed. 'I can't possibly go on. I can't remember a single word of my part. I've even forgotten the first line.'

'There, there.' Louise sat down on the arm of the chair and put her arm round Alice. 'They always feel like that, really they do, and if it isn't that, they're sick. You'd be surprised.' Louise was evidently a dresser of great experience.

'Darling,' Mrs. Norton said, 'you mustn't upset yourself like that.'

'Leave me alone.' Alice's voice rose to a scream.

'I think it would be best to leave her.' Louise spoke to Mrs. Norton, who stood looking helplessly at Alice.

Still Mrs. Norton hesitated and I got up to open the door.

'It will be all right,' I whispered. 'The curtain will be going up in twenty minutes and by then it will be all right.'

There was a rap on the door and it was thrown open. Miss Iliffe marched in, followed by Mr. Zwemburgh, who looked unhappy. Mrs. Norton, harassed and uncertain, left the dressing-room.

Miss Iliffe took in the scene that confronted her and sat down firmly on the dressing-stool. She placed her hands on top of her ebony stick and rested her chin on them. Mr. Zwemburgh stood by the door. Alice stopped whimpering and looked timidly at Miss Iliffe.

'You have forgotten your lines?' Miss Iliffe spoke as though this could have no real importance.

Alice nodded.

Miss Iliffe turned to Louise. 'What has she had to drink?'

'Nothing, and she didn't even touch that cup of tea.'

'Well, good heavens! Send somebody round to the bar at once and tell them to get a bottle of champagne and two glasses; then come back here and finish dressing her.'

Louise scurried out of the room.

'Nobody else need stay,' Miss Iliffe said, looking at me and Mr. Zwemburgh.

Rather sheepishly we left the room, Mr. Zwemburgh giving himself just time to say good luck, and he was sure she'd be splendid.

The passage was full of people. I met Louise, who passed me without a word. She went into Alice's dressing-room and shut the door after her. She had all the importance of a midwife at the moment of birth.

Amongst the hurrying figures I saw Mrs. Norton standing uncertainly at a turn in the passage. I went and joined her.

'I don't think there is anything we can do. Shall we go and find our seats?'

Mrs. Norton was distraught and seemed grateful that any suggestion should be made to her. 'I've upset her,' she said pathetically. 'I've ruined it all by upsetting her.'

'It wasn't you,' I said as we made our way to the pass door, 'and anyhow it was a good thing. She was much *too* calm before, and that's supposed to be much worse. Everybody says that it's better to have your nerve-storm and get it over.'

'Are you sure?' Mrs. Norton was still anxious. 'I'm sitting in the third row by myself. I felt I should be too nervous if I went with anyone else.'

By this time we had reached the auditorium. The stalls were almost half empty. I looked at my watch. It was twenty past eight. In ten minutes the curtain would be up.

Mrs. Norton said that she ought to telephone to the Gladstones. 'I promised I would, and they've known Alice since she was a little girl.'

Thinking it a good thing that Mrs. Norton should have some occupation, I watched her go in search of a telephone. Whether she found one, and whether she got through to the Gladstones I never learnt.

I was dismayed by the emptiness of the house. Could the box office possibly have made a mistake? Or had people bought tickets and decided not to come after all? I went to the foyer to find Geoffrey, as we were sitting together. The foyer was full of people. They were packed tightly together and there were photographers with flashlamps. Everyone was talking, explaining, gesticulating. Peering between heads and shoulders, I could see the entrance doors and part of the striped awning. At every moment more people were arriving, walking up the steps and being photographed. A crowd had gathered to watch them; occasionally the faces in this crowd showed for an instant as a cameraman used his flashlight.

I turned back towards the theatre. I wondered how Alice was, alone in her dressing-room with Miss Iliffe and Louise. Had they managed to calm her? Had she drunk the champagne?

'Everyone has nerves on a first night, it is only to be expected. They always disappear as soon as the curtain goes up.' But supposing Alice's nerves remained with her. Supposing she really forgot her words, and remained there on the stage not able to say anything. What would happen then? I found that my hands were clammy with fear. Alice had had so little experience; they had said that too. With experience you could get through anything, and experience was exactly what Alice had not got.

I found my seat—B 14. Thank goodness it was at the end of a row. If anything awful happened, I should be able to go away. The stalls were beginning to fill up now; the bell must have gone. It was twenty-five to nine.

'Good evening, dear, you don't look very happy.' It was Geoffrey. He sat down in the seat next to mine.

I told him that Alice had forgotten her part.

'But they have a prompter, dear,' Geoffrey said comfortably.

'But she's forgotten it *all*,' I said desperately.

'Well, never mind, dear.' Geoffrey opened his programme. 'I'm sure it won't be as bad as you think.'

'Perhaps that's why they're late starting.'

'First nights always begin late,' Geoffrey said. 'It's part of the general sort of fuss.' He settled himself in his seat. 'I've been talking to some critics I know, and they say that this play will be absolutely terrific, if it isn't a flop of course; and Alice's name will be made.'

Slowly the lights dimmed, the curtains quivered. The auditorium was a confusion of late-comers finding their seats and disturbing those who were already there. We were in complete darkness. I thought I should cry out or faint.

Then the curtains parted. On the brightly lit stage two ladies sat and sewed. We were in the Governor's rooms at the Conciergerie. A girl ran into the room; she was very young, hardly out of her teens. One of the ladies stopped sewing and spoke to her. The other crossed to the window and called to the girl to join her. They stood at the window and looked down on the Prince Louis Napoleon, who was being brought to the Conciergerie as a prisoner. We, the audience, could not see him, but the girl smiled and waved, for the Prince had looked up at her. The girl turned from the window. She was excited and flattered. It was the year 1836; Eugénie de Montijo and the future Napoleon III had seen each other for the first time. Or it was a hundred years later and the girl was Alice Norton and she had not forgotten her lines.

Scene followed scene in rapid succession; they were all magnificent, although of course in the nature of things many of them were little more than backcloths. It might have been said that this was a scene-shifters' play, Alice's and the scene-shifters'. Nobody else was of any importance. Not Napoleon III or Von Bismarck or Queen Victoria.

For three hours or for a lifetime we lived with the Empress, with her gaiety and her despair. We saw her strange smile and felt that we knew its secret.

This was different from anything that had happened at rehearsals.

During the interval I remained in my seat. I felt that I could not trust myself to speak. Geoffrey went away and came back to say that they were 'fairly eating it up.'

I reflected that Geoffrey must be very much moved to make use of such an expression.

Again the lights were lowered; but this time there was no fear. The darkness was only the preliminary for the return of a dream.—And at half-past eleven the dream was over. The curtain had come down for the last time, the hitherto unknown young authors had made a joint speech thanking Alice and thanking each other, and Alice had made a speech thanking the scene-shifters.

During the playing of the National Anthem I happened to look up to the level of the dress circle. A face detached itself from the others. It was Cassius, looking very beautiful and a little quizzical. Excitedly I whispered to Geoffrey.

'Oh yes, dear.' Geoffrey was quite calm. 'He arrived back in London on Saturday.'

Now everyone was moving, searching for their hats and coats, and suddenly I was surrounded by faces which I knew and recognised.

There was Martin Yorke, and there, for an instant, was Felix. I found myself talking to Mrs. Norton; she seemed quite incoherent. Sonia and Paddy and Honoria joined us, and Mrs. Bryant and Harold. Now we were all moving towards the door. We were going to see Alice; we were going to see the Empress Eugénie. We were at the turn of the passage where Mrs. Norton and I had stood earlier in the evening. I saw Ellen and her cousins from Bromley.

The door of Alice's dressing-room opened, and there, already surrounded by a mob of people, was a girl dressed as an old woman.

* * * * *

There was no doubt as to the success of the play. The critics, almost without exception, were enthusiastic. They had, indeed, 'fairly eaten it up,' and Alice was hailed as another 'Sarah,' or alternatively, another Ellen Terry. Mrs. Patrick Campbell's sudden rise from obscurity was recalled, and it was predicted that Alice's equally sudden appearance would, like Mrs. Pat's, be followed by sustained success.

As Alice and I read these notices, we continually reminded each other that these comparisons with Ellen Terry and 'the great Sarah' are by no means unusual.

We wandered about the dining-room in our dressing-gowns. We were delighted with the notices and tried to discredit them. The telephone rang almost continually. In the end we left off the receiver.

We had both woken very early. Alice, whose calm confidence *before* success had seemed almost pathological, was now not only excited, but extremely nervous. She admitted that she had slept for only two or three hours.

Ellen came in with the breakfast-tray and banged it down on the table. 'What we need in this house is a "valley" to answer the door. It's been ring, ring, ring ever since I got up this morning.'

'We could get a parlourmaid perhaps,' Alice suggested tentatively.

'And where would she sleep? In the coal-cellar?' Ellen went out and banged the door after her.

'Oh, dear,' Alice said, 'I'm afraid she's upset.'

'It's the excitement,' I said doubtfully, and supposed that after all Ellen must be missing Hill Street.

Alice and I decided to get a daily servant who should be exclusively Alice's and answer the doorbell.

'We could say she was a social secretary,' Alice observed. 'I've always wanted to have one and it would save all that disagreeableness about caps and aprons.'

The remark showed, I thought, a very just understanding of Ellen.

Gradually we settled into a routine. Alice, of course, went to the theatre every evening and we formed the habit, when I was not dining out, of having a meal about six o'clock.

This, I pointed out to Ellen, was very nice for her and the cook; they were able to 'finish' earlier. Ellen only replied that it seemed 'funny.' She implied that dinner eaten before eight o'clock constituted a lack of dignity and was in fact 'common.' After a few weeks though she relented and we became cosy again. In the end she even tolerated the social secretary, whose first introduction she had viewed with the greatest resentment. One evening, when I had rather cravenly complained of Miss Peters, hoping thereby to curry favour with Ellen, Ellen told me sharply that there was nothing wrong with the woman that *she* could see, and she had her work to do like everybody else.

The chances of my going out to the Mediterranean to join George seemed to come nearer and then receded again. I decided that I would go back to work, anyhow for the time being. I rang up the factory. Yes, there was a vacancy in the buying office; yes, Mr. Saunders would be very pleased to have me back. Just before Christmas I started work and was much happier.

Considering that we lived in the same house, Alice and I saw relatively very little of each other during the next few months. Occasionally, of course, we met at high tea, but she seldom came home until after I was in bed, and was seldom awake before I left in the mornings.

Once she complained to me that she was still sleeping badly. 'It's been like this ever since the first night. Do you know, I hardly ever get to sleep now until an hour or two before I'm called.'

I said, 'Why be called then?'

'I have to write my letters,' Alice said.

'Can't Miss Peters do that?'

'No, not really,' Alice said thoughtfully. 'She always wants to say such extraordinary things.'

I suggested sleeping-pills and getting another secretary, and Alice said she would think about it.

Another time, Alice told me that she was having difficulty with Felix.

I was startled. 'I didn't know you ever saw him now.'

'He keeps on ringing me up,' Alice said, 'and trying to get round Miss Peters, and he tries to see me at the theatre.'

I told her that she must be firm and that she couldn't possibly see him after what had happened.

'I know, but he's been terribly insistent and he sends me flowers. Do you think I'm being unkind?' And Alice looked guiltily at the enormous bowl of roses which stood in the corner.

I said no of course she wasn't, and that she mustn't allow herself to be upset.

'I don't,' Alice said, 'really I don't, but it's all very distressing.'

I sympathised as well as I could and was vaguely worried.

In February, Alice's divorce came up for hearing. The lawyers had managed to complicate the case owing to the fact that the necessary evidence of adultery, supplied by Cassius, referred to incidents which had taken place in South Africa.

Just before we went into court, Alice's lawyer warned her that the result was 'by no means in the bag.'

'You mean, we may have to start all over again?' Alice sounded tired and not particularly interested.

The lawyer pursed his lips and remarked that we had an excellent counsel.

The proceedings, once they started, were quite gay. Alice gave her evidence clearly and with good elocution. Afterwards she told me that she had enjoyed herself very much in the witness-box. When she had finished an usher conducted her back to Geoffrey and me, who as prisoner's friends were sitting in the front row of the audience. The judge said a few words. Alice's solicitor picked up his hat and stick and we followed him out of the court.

'Well, have we got it?' Alice asked as soon as we were outside.

The solicitor looked rather hurt and said, 'Yes.'

Alice thanked him and looked round for the counsel, who had disappeared.

We left the Law Courts and took a taxi to the Diplomats. In Alice's dressing-room there were several bottles of champagne and Louise was in attendance. The leading members of the cast were already there and we drank to Alice's health and the health of the judge. Alice said that it reminded her of a wedding reception after the bride and bridegroom had left.

The divorce was reported in the evening papers under the headline 'Actress Gets Decree,' and there was a photograph of Alice arriving at the court 'with a man friend'—Geoffrey.

February passed away and most of March. The 31st was Alice's birthday and we decided to celebrate it with a supper-party. There were to be ten of us; Geoffrey, Sonia, Paddy, Honoria, a man friend of Honoria's and I were to dine at the Savoy, and Alice was to come on from the theatre with her understudy and Napoleon III and the Comte de Morny.

As it happened, I didn't go home at all during the day. Honoria, whose latest play had just come off, was having a cocktail party earlier in the evening, so I took a suitcase to work and later changed at Honoria's house.

Dinner was rather fun. At about half-past eleven a waiter placed an iced cake in the middle of the table. This had been Geoffrey's idea and was to be a surprise. The cake had 'Alice Norton' in small pink letters round the edge and the figures '25' in the middle. Geoffrey looked at it complacently and called to everyone to admire it, and we all did and told him how clever and thoughtful he was. Then he asked the waiter to bring a clean tablecloth—everything must be perfect—and some more champagne must be put in an ice bucket, so that we were quite ready. At the table next to ours some young people from the provinces sat and drank champagne round an iced cake which they had already cut. Their table was decorated with the cardboard effigies of doorkeys. I saw Geoffrey looking at them with some disapproval.

'Very macabre, dear.' He shuddered and turned away.

I said not to let it upset him, and reflected that I was always telling people not to let things do that to them.

'I thought "Alice Norton" would be more tactful than "Alice Skeffington," and after all it is her stage name, so if she likes she can think that that is the reason.' Fussily Geoffrey shifted the position of the cake.

I said again that it looked very nice and asked whether Geoffrey had seen Cassius at all.

'As a matter of fact I have. He's back in the bookshop, as you know, and he's got charming rooms in Half Moon Street. Really, he's very happy.'

'So *that's* all right.'

'Orchids!' Geoffrey said suddenly. 'I should have got her orchids.' He looked wildly round.

'They sell them in the hall,' I reminded him.

'There should be orchids waiting for her.' Geoffrey got up and as he did so we saw the two actors and the understudy being conducted towards our table. Alice was not with them.

She had not been to the theatre that evening.

The publicity given to Alice's disappearance was enormous. Her photograph was published in every paper, and every paper carried the story in headlines. It seemed that if she were still alive she could not have failed to have been seen and recognised. The search for her was intensive and was spread over the whole country. The theories as to what had happened to her were innumerable and fantastic.

After two days I personally was certain that she was dead. Once before she had tried to drown herself. Now she had tried again and had succeeded.

David Mason arrived back in England. Beryl had at last received my letter and he knew that Alice was free. He had loved her since he was sixteen and now he would ask her to marry him.

He learnt about her disappearance casually as he read the paper in the train coming from Liverpool. Naturally he was terribly upset. When he got to London he came straight from the station to see me.

We had not met for six years. He had changed very little, only he looked sad and care-worn.

'But, they *must* find her, a person can't just disappear in the middle of London like that.'

I told him of everything that had been done. I told him of the horror in which we had lived and in which we were still living. Of the nightmare ending of the party at the Savoy, of the interviews with the police.

'When she didn't turn up at the theatre, the stage manager rang the house, but got no answer. I suppose there must have been something the matter with the telephone, because Ellen was in all that evening. They weren't terribly worried at the theatre. They thought that Alice must be ill and that there had been a message which had not got delivered. Maurice Jackson, that's the man who plays Napoleon III, thought that when they got to the Savoy I would give them some perfectly ordinary explanation.' I spoke mechanically. It seemed I had told the story hundreds of times before.

'It all sounds so casual,' David said impatiently. 'When was she last seen?'

'At about six o'clock the day before yesterday. She and Miss Peters had been having tea together at the Dorchester. Alice said that she would walk to the theatre and they parted at Stanhope Gate.'

'But why did she walk,' David asked, 'and if she meant to go straight to the theatre, wouldn't she have arrived there much too early?'

'She enjoyed walking and she generally went to the theatre early. She used to change for the first scene and then lie in her dressing-room and read a book. She said it composed her mind.'

'I can't bear it.' David moved about the room. 'I wanted to marry her.'

The clock on the mantelpiece struck six. 'Forty-eight hours,' David said, 'forty-eight hours since she was seen by anyone.' He continued to move about the room. A terrible silence fell between us. To distract him I asked about Spain.

He smiled and sat down. Now he was sorry for me as well as himself. Spain, he said, had been tiring.

I found it difficult to reconcile this gentle creature with the toughness of the International Brigade.

'My mother,' David said, 'was very angry about the whole thing.' Again he smiled.

I tried to remember what Alice had told me of David's mother. A rich woman in a Rolls Royce. A jolly woman with vehement though unoriginal opinions. She had all her jewellery reset every year and thought that other people did the same.

She had been devoted to David, less so perhaps to David's father. I had had the impression that somewhere, discreetly in the background, there had been a lover. But although she had been a widow for several years now Mrs. Mason had not remarried, so it might be that the lover was after all only a friend of the family.

'My mother,' David was saying, 'would have preferred me to fight for Franco instead of the republic.'

'I suppose so.'

'Of the two, that is. Actually she would rather I wasn't fighting at all. She thinks it unnecessary and not too good for business.'

'And dangerous?'

'And dangerous,' David agreed. 'So, you see, I wasn't being fair to her.' He started to talk about Alice again. He said that he had nothing to offer her.

'You've got your factory,' I said.

David looked hurt and said that Alice had never minded about money. 'What's the good of talking about it though. We don't even know where she is. What's happened to that beastly play?'

'It's going on,' I said, 'with the understudy.'

I was wondering whether, if David had come back from Spain earlier, anything would have been changed, for David would have protected Alice's world.

Or if he had asked her to marry him long ago when they were both quite young, would things then have turned out differently?

It was easy to imagine their life as it might have been together. David working at the factory and coming home in the evenings to hang around the house and be helpful and domesticated. For David was such a nice simple young man. Cassius' inconsequence and Felix's bad tempers were unthinkable in connection with David.

With Alice married to David, would things have turned out differently? Perhaps not, for even with David Alice might not have felt herself completely secure, and it was security that she had sought so desperately.

Late that evening Alice was found. She had completely lost her memory.

After David left, I had gone miserably to bed and was lying in the dark trying not to think and knowing that I should not sleep. Then the telephone rang. I had a wild idea that when I lifted the receiver I should hear Alice's voice. But it was Sonia's, controlled and at the same time overexcited. 'And she remembers nothing at all. She didn't even recognise Mummy.' There were tears in Sonia's voice.

'Have you seen her?'

'No, no one is allowed to see her except Mummy. She brought her straight here from the police station. The doctor has been, and Mummy says that I am not to tell anyone, not even you, where we are. But of course that's ridiculous,' and Sonia told me the name of the London nursing-home from which she was speaking. 'I think they are going to move her to a place in the country tomorrow. The doctor is trying to arrange it.'

'But can't you see her,' I said.

'I've tried, but the doctor says she must be kept quiet. Anyhow she's asleep now. Mummy is in a most frightful state and *terrified* of the papers. Isn't it typical of a doctor to say, "Keep the patient quiet," and then let Mummy loose on her?'

I remembered how Mrs. Norton had irritated Alice on the first night of *Eugénie*, and thought that Sonia was probably right.

'The unlucky thing *was*,' Sonia said, 'that Mummy was alone when she got the police message and went off by herself to identify Alice.'

I asked if there was anything I could do. There wasn't anything, of course. Sonia said that she was determined to see Alice the next day and she promised to let me know if there was any news.

A statement was issued to the Press. Alice had been found wandering on the Embankment. She was suffering from a breakdown caused by overwork. She was being cared for by her family. It was hoped that with rest and treatment her recovery would be speedily achieved.

And then, there was silence. Neither Alice's friends nor the Press were to know anything further. Alice was being cared for by her family. She was in a nursing-home. The doctors were agreed that she must see no one.

It was several weeks before I saw Alice again. When I was at last allowed to visit her she was in a nursing-home near Goring-on-Thames. David and I went down there together on the afternoon of a beautiful late spring day. We spoke to each other very little during the drive.

'They say that she's quite happy.' I turned to reassure David for the last time as we drove in at the gates. To myself I thanked God that the gates stood open. Had they been locked I do not think that I could have borne it.

We drew up at the house, a red-brick Edwardian atrocity. It seemed enormous but had obviously been a private house. We got out of the car and rang the bell. The door was answered by a portress in a green uniform.

'Mrs. Skeffington?' we said.

The portress looked doubtful. We followed her into the panelled hall. Inside it was almost dark.

'I will go and tell Dr. Lewis.' The portress started to move away from us.

'We have permission,' we said.

'I will tell Dr. Lewis.' The portress disappeared through an oak door.

We were left alone in the hall. Outside there was bright sunlight. In here it was almost dark and the light filtered through ugly stained glass.

A woman came down the staircase, crossed the hall and disappeared through the same door as the portress. The woman did not look at us and did not speak. She wore a plain blue dress. We did not know whether she was a nurse or a patient.

The portress came back and said that Dr. Lewis would see us. We followed her through the door and through a lot of passages. Except in the hall the place was light and there was a great deal of white paint. As we passed windows we could see people sitting in the garden. The portress came to a door where she stopped and knocked. A voice called to come in. It was a pleasant voice, deep and confident.

The portress introduced us into a small light room. A man got up from a desk.

The portress withdrew.

Dr. Lewis smiled. We sat down. Dr. Lewis talked a little about the weather and about our drive.

'How is she?' David asked the question eagerly; he had interrupted Dr. Lewis in the middle of a sentence.

'Well.' Dr. Lewis placed his fingers together. He had nice hands. Behind his glasses his eyes looked kind. 'Mrs. Skeffington is happy. You will not notice any difference in her physical appearance, and she is perfectly calm and perfectly rational.'

'But how is she?' David repeated.

'There has been no return of the memory—so far.'

'We can see her?' I asked.

'Of course.' Dr. Lewis got up. 'But you do know that she won't recognise you?'

We got up too and followed Dr. Lewis down the endless corridors and up flights of stairs. It seemed that we walked for ever as in a nightmare. Later we were to know that in losing her memory Alice had found the only peace possible for her. Now we had no such comfort and I prayed that she would recover.

Later one could be glad for what had happened. For had not Alice always been frightened of life? She was afraid that her world within the world would be swept away, that the liner would cease to float, and underneath there would be the bursting lungs and the living terror. As she walked along the streets towards the theatre, she must have felt that she couldn't go on any farther. Her fears had crowded round her and then suddenly she had felt that she was falling and mercifully the past was swept away.

The ultimate terror for which she had waited had happened and she was at peace. That which she had feared all her life had come to pass, and with it had come, not the expected horror, but peace.

That Alice who had suffered failures should have reached this crisis at the moment of success seemed at first strange, but gradually I came to understand that just *because* of those repeated failures she could not allow herself to realise that success had come. For by now she was attuned only to failure. The result was the all-obliterating wave which swept away memories of the past.

Across the years I could hear Mrs. Bryant's voice speaking on the telephone. 'How should I know where she is, I don't go around asking my friends who they sleep with.' Alice had never told me where she had spent that night, but when I came to think about it, I was certain it had not been with Felix. For Alice had told me that she had not lived with Felix until they went away together to Blythe.—Then Alice herself on the telephone asking me to spell Honoria's name—for she had *forgotten* the name. That time she had lost the memory of a single night and from then on she had lived with the knowledge and the added terror that strange things could happen to her.

Now that horror too was past. There were no memories to disturb the peace which she had found. Now at last she was free to build her world undisturbed by reality.

Later she did build that world. She had the lace curtains just as she had once imagined them. She had her picture of the deserted garden. The picture in which time stood still and which held an enchantment which could never be touched by the world. She had her books and she had the clock which had stood on the mantelpiece in the last scene of *Eugénie*, and above all she had peace, for when everything is swept away it isn't frightening, after all.

Had I only known that when I followed Dr. Lewis down the endless corridors of the nursing-home!

Dr. Lewis stopped at a door and knocked. A voice said to come in. It was Alice's and I felt that my knees trembled. I looked at David. The sweat stood on his forehead.

Dr. Lewis opened the door.

Alice sat on a chintz-covered sofa in a bright and pleasant room. She was dressed in black and the sunlight fell on the top of her head. She was looking towards the door and she was smiling.

For a moment no one spoke. Then Dr. Lewis introduced us to Alice as if we were strangers. She still smiled and I went over to her.

'I used to know you,' I said, 'a long time ago.'

THE END

FURROWED MIDDLEBROW

CPSIA information can be obtained
at www.ICGtesting.com
Printed in the USA
BVHW071457311218
536776BV00010B/549/P